MINETTA

Forever in my heart

MARY ELLEN JACKSON

E&MJ

This is a work of fiction. Names, characters, places, events, and organizations are entirely the products of the author's imagination or are used fictitiously. Any similarity to real persons, living or dead, is coincidental and not intended by the author.

Printed in the United States of America

For my family

MINETTA

Chapter 1

Minetta Mary Morgan woke to the steady buzzing of the white alarm clock on her nightstand. Her head under the bed covers, she reached out and silenced the miniature device. A few minutes ticked by, and Minetta slowly poked her head up, surveying the silver ceiling. She let her gaze roam about the room. They painted the walls pale blue as a backdrop for the bright shades of multi-floral patterns in bed linen and drapes. The sunlight reflected off the padded cushions on the window seat and danced over the white desk and cabinet in the corner. Above the writing-table were several photographs of her family and devoted friends tacked on the bulletin board. Minetta sat up in bed and reached for her white cellphone, checking to see if she had any messages. Throwing off the covers, she made her bed and headed for the bathroom. She glimpsed herself in the mirror, her summer tan highlighting her dark brown eyes and thick black curls. She gathered her mane and secured it snugly under a bathing cap. Stepping beneath the spurting water, she tried to visualize her outfit for the first time as a high school senior.

A few minutes later, when she turned the shower off, Minetta heard rummaging in her room.

"Hey Mimi, hurry up and get dress. We don't want to be late on the first day."

"Good morning to you too, bestie," replied Minetta as she entered the bedroom clad in a white body towel and head turban.

Kimberly Van Owens was one of Minetta's lifelong best friends, as well as her next-door neighbor. Kimberly was sitting in the window seat, clad in a soft pink tracksuit. Her head of luscious russet red curls gathered into a high ponytail and secured with a floral barrette. Her hair formed a curtain over her pale, freckled face as she looked at her pink cellphone.

"Help me decide what to wear, bestie," said Minetta, disappearing into her walk-in closet.

"Wear something pretty."

A few minutes later, Minetta emerged from the closet wearing a blue striped silk shirt worn loose over denim pants and white slip-on loafers.

"Excellent," said Kimberly, smiling and nodding approvingly. "Hey bestie, do you like my outfit?" she asked, looking down at herself.

"Sure, what's not to like? You're wearing your favorite color."

Minetta sat down at her makeup counter. Staring at her reflection in the mirror, she applied mascara to her lashes.

"Have we heard from Tabs yet?" she asked.

A soft voice from the doorway startled them. "Did someone call my name?"

"Tabs!" yelled Kimberly, laughing, and rising from the window seat. Minetta, right behind Kimberly, hugged Tabitha around the neck.

"You're living to a hundred, as Mrs. B would say," said Minetta, happy to see her friend.

Tabitha Marie Brown, affectionately dubbed "Tabs," was the third member of the girl's trio. Quiet and scholarly, she was the voice of reason when her friends' shenanigans threaten to become out of control. Tabitha and her younger twin brothers, Henry, and Edward, lived next door to Kimberly.

Tabitha's brown eyes matched her curly hair braided in one long plait and interwoven with colorful ribbon. Her clothing style was a mixture of bohemian prints and Victorian-era suede and ruffles. Tabitha never wore makeup but loved bright lip gloss. Tabitha was a member of the National Honor Society since middle school and was an accomplished gymnast.

She sat cross-legged on a floor pillow near Kimberly who had returned to the window seat.

"Ladies, I still can't believe we are seniors in high school," said Tabitha. She folded her red print maxi dress around her legs.

"Tell me about it!" remarked Kimberly.

"How was Monterrey, Tabs?" asked Minetta, returning to her makeup counter.

"Two weeks of glorious fun in the sun. You can't beat that." Tabitha searched in her red satchel for her lip gloss. "How was your time in Florida?"

"It was okay," replied Minetta.

"When did your family return from Palm Beach?" Tabitha asked.

"Saturday afternoon. I helped Matt pack his stuff for college, and we talked a moment. He left for school yesterday. Not much happened after that."

"I know the feeling," stated Kimberly.

"How was Charleston, Kim?" asked Minetta, fastening her signature gold hoops in her ears. She gathered her dark hair into a high bun.

"It was okay, but I'm sick of going down to South Carolina every year. The cousins come from all over, and it's more like a family reunion than a summer vacation." She sighed, audibly. "I wish we could spend time somewhere else."

"Do something different is what you're saying?" mused Tabitha.

"Isn't that where your family's from?" asked Minetta.

"My mother's side is from Charleston. We usually travel there every winter for the holidays, too," answered Kimberly. She opened her makeup bag and fished out her gloss, applying a peachy-pink stain to her lips with her pinky finger.

Minetta secured her hair with clips. "When did you return?"

"Late Saturday night, and I pulled one of Tabs numbers," said Kimberly, a grin pasted on her face. "I slept in and spent the day in my room. I wanted to be ready for this week."

Tabitha smiled. "The trip home was exhausting. I unpacked and did the same thing, Kim. I figured I'd see everyone today, so I didn't bother calling anyone."

"You're right, Tabs. Eddie's cellphone is turned off, and it was still that way this morning."

"Same with Ray."

Minetta glanced at the clock on her nightstand. "Come on, we need to get a move on."

The girls gathered their belongings. Minetta looked around her bedroom, making certain it was neat before closing the door. They descended the backstairs leading to the open kitchen. The Morgan's housekeeper, Beatrice, was standing at the stove stirring soft eggs in a skillet.

Beatrice Maxine Clemons was a recent widow when James and Marilyn hired her after the birth of their son, Matthew. Beatrice and her late husband were from Jamaica and had no children. She had become an indispensable member of the Morgan household.

"Good morning, ladies," said Beatrice in her soft Jamaican lilt.

She handed Kimberly a plate with scrambled eggs, pork sausage links, grits, and wheat toast. Beatrice poured Minetta a cup of black coffee and in Tabitha and Kimberly's cups, hot kettle water for their green tea. She waited with her head bowed as Minetta prayed a blessing over the food.

"Thank you, Mrs. B.," said the girls in unison at the prayer's conclusion.

"You're welcome, babies. Is there anything else you want while I'm here?" she asked.

Minetta said, "No, everything's great. Thank you."

"You're welcome." Beatrice turned on her heel. She located her handbag under the cabinet shelf of the island, along with two enormous, colorful shopping totes. Pulling on an embroidered cardigan, she fished her car keys out of her handbag.

"Don't forget to put your dishes in the dishwasher. Have a good day at school. Mimi, your mother is by the front door with her camera."

The girls giggled and Beatrice smiled.

"Bye, Mrs. B.," said Minetta.

Kimberly glanced at her watch. "Hey, it's time to go."

"Help me clean up," said Minetta. Rising, she took Tabitha's empty teacup with her to the sink. Tabitha wiped the table. The girls rinsed breakfast dishes and stacked them in the dishwasher. Grabbing book bags, they made their way down the hall that led from the kitchen to the front of the house. Minetta spied her mother standing in the foyer, looking into the back of a camera. Minetta's mother had begun taking first day of school pictures with her two children beginning when Matthew, Minetta's older brother, entered daycare. By the time Minetta followed three years later, the process had become a family tradition.

Marilyn Johnston Morgan was a diminutive woman standing a few inches above five feet four and weighing a mere one hundred twenty pounds soaking wet. The deep black intensity of her hair had slowly evolved to a thick screen of dark and silvery-striped curls magnified by her brown eyes.

In her youth, Marilyn had won numerous beauty pageants in high school which lasted throughout college. She earned a library science degree and worked as a librarian in Oak Hill Heights Elementary School. Two years later she married her college sweetheart, James Morgan, the young pastor of Cedar Valley Church.

"Mom, what are you doing?" Minetta asked.

"Seeing if the batteries are working," mumbled Marilyn.

She looked up and smiled, aiming the camera. "Are you girls ready?"

Kimberly sighed happily. "Yes and yes!"

"Hurry and take our picture. We don't want to be late!" said Minetta.

"Alright, girls." Marilyn lifted the camera to her face. "Ready… one, two, three."

The girls hugged each other around their waists and flashed toothy grins at the camera. Marilyn laid the instrument on the hall table and opened the front door.

"Ok, you three. Out with you."

"Bye mom, I love you." Minetta hugged her mother before joining her friends in the driveway.

"Bye, baby. I love you too. All of you have a nice day." Marilyn closed the front door.

Tabitha looked at Minetta's car. "This car reminds me of your birthday party last summer."

Minetta grinned. "Yeah, such a grand birthday celebration."

"Well, the birthday gift made the celebration!" exclaimed Kimberly, referring to the four-door white sedan Minetta was driving.

The girls laughed as Minetta whizzed down the driveway.

Chapter 2

Cedar Valley High School was within a two-mile driving distance of the girls' Oak Hill Heights community. The preparatory school, distinguished for its superior academic curriculum, award-winning athletic programs, and legendary marching band, was three buildings attached by enclosed crosswalks. The main hall housed the administrative offices and the dramatic arts center; the east wing was home to the sports department, gymnasium, auditorium, and the double-level cafeteria. The west side included the nurses' station, science and math labs, library, and classrooms. The parking lot extended across the front of the school building with faculty assigned numbered slots. Seniors received priority parking followed by juniors and sophomores, with remaining spots issued to first-year students on a first-come, first-served basis. Posted signs alerted visitors to open slots.

Minetta pulled her car into a vacant spot in the senior section of the school lot. The girls stood on the sidewalk looking at the building, each filled with a vague sense of euphoria. As the friends walked along the curved path leading into the edifice, they heard what sounded like soft wolf whistles behind them.

Turning, they saw Philip Jones and Eddie Stamps walking from the opposite direction. Both young men were in dark gray and ivory varsity jackets with C.V.H.S. in black script embroidered on the front. As they neared the girls, Minetta could see the side of Philip's red sport utility vehicle and beside it, in sharp contrast, Eddie's bright orange sports coupe parked four cars away from hers. She guessed the boys were waiting for them to arrive.

Minetta smiled as she watched Philip approach. Tall with a perpetual tan from being outdoors, Philip played three sports: basketball, baseball, and football and excelled in the latter. He coached Little League in the spring with his father. The youngest son of corporate attorneys, Philip's wardrobe consisted mainly of buttoned-down shirts and chino slacks. He rarely wore sneakers unless required in a sports-related program, preferring moccasins and loafers as daily wear.

Walking beside him was the second member of the male trio, Eddie Stamps. Eddie's most striking physical feature was his light hazel eyes and thick curly brown hair he had been wearing in a pompadour since the start of high school. An avid surfer, Eddie played football, basketball and excelled as a track and field star. Eddie was the flamboyant dresser among his friends, preferring the brightest colors he could find.

Eddie bowed low to the ground as they neared the girls, making them giggle and Philip smirk.

"Good morning, lovely ladies," said Eddie.

"Hi, guys! Ready for our last year?" asked Kimberly.

"Oh yeah!" Philip replied, "how was your summer, ladies?"

"Could not have been better," said Kimberly, smiling at Eddie. "I tried to text you over the weekend."

She had to look up as Eddie had grown significantly in height during the summer and was now taller than she was.

"I know, sweetie. I saw your texts this morning," Eddie replied. "I forgot I had my cellphone in my car. I meant to call you yesterday, but the folks had company."

Kimberly smiled. "I understand."

Eddie reached for her hand. They stood happily, gazing at each other. Philip looked down at Minetta and Tabitha.

"Did anything exciting happen to you two over the summer break?"

"Absolutely nothing," said Minetta. She gazed up at him. He had grown taller and broader across the shoulders. She smiled at him.

"Hey, guys."

They all turned at the smooth baritone voice of Raymond Mason in his varsity jacket walking along the path. Minetta saw his sleek black sedan parked on the other side of Eddie's orange coupe. Tabitha, a smile making the dimples in her cheeks prominent, walked to Raymond, and they locked hands.

Raymond was an extremely handsome young man. His mother's Native American heritage was clear in his rich tawny brown complexion and high cheekbones. His striking sapphire blue eyes he received from his English father and were his most arresting feature. Raymond enjoyed surfing, playing soccer, and football. He was the reigning national swim champion in his division.

"Hey guy, good to see you!" said Eddie.

Everyone in the group hugged each other. The couples paired off.

"Philip how was your family's vacation in Hawaii this year?" asked Kimberly.

Philip shrugged his shoulders. "Same as every other year." He looked around Minetta to wave at another student-athlete walking past them into the building. "A boring two weeks."

"It's only boring because the girls aren't there!" replied Eddie, grinning with his arm around Kimberly's shoulders.

Philip looked over at Eddie. "You might have a point, my friend."

"What about you, Ray? You mean you and Eddie found no mischief to do all summer?" Kimberly asked, laughing.

"Perfecting our surfing and staying in shape was our only mischief," replied Raymond, looking at Tabitha.

The young men devoted half of their summers to sports camps with all three young men's families vacationing in Hawaii together the latter half.

"Hey guys, what's everyone's plans for the weekend?" asked Eddie.

"I intend to sleep late," replied Minetta, grinning. Kimberly smirked.

"Why do you ask, Eddie?"

"I want to throw a back-to-school pool party this weekend," said Eddie.

Philip waved him off. "Nah, man. My dad's on me to finish my college applications. This weekend is off."

"Agreed." Raymond said. "I want to get a head start on any school assignments."

"I know what we can do," Tabitha spoke up in her gentle tone. "Why don't we meet at The Soda Shoppe after school today and catch up?"

"That's a great idea, Tabs," said Philip. "I need to look for a resource book in the library across the street before we meet up."

"Resource book?" asked Minetta, wrinkling her nose.

"Photography," replied Philip. "Your mom is holding some resource materials for me. I'll pick them up on my way to the Soda Shoppe."

Philip loved photography and videography. He was in his third year on the school paper as a photographer.

"Whoa!" exclaimed Eddie, followed by a low wolf whistle.

He was looking past the girls' shoulders. Everyone moved around to see what had caught his attention. As Minetta turned, she made out the figure of a tall girl with long honey-blonde hair. As she walked past them the scent of citrus fragrance hung in the air. She dressed entirely in blue denim that looked like somebody had poured it on her slim curves. Her walk was smooth and graceful, but it was her face that drew the most attention. She had large, bright blue eyes with long lashes, arched brows, a pert nose, rosy cheeks, and full pink lips. Her skin glistened with a translucent hue in the morning light. Philip, Eddie, and Raymond turned to watch her walk toward the building, as did every other male on the campus.

"Whew!" said another, shaking his head and smiling at the girl's retreating form. "That's fire!"

"Now, *that* is a beautiful girl," said his buddy as they walked past Minetta.

There were wolf whistles and hoots from male admirers. The young woman looked neither right nor left, but held her head high as she made her way toward the main entrance. As she neared the doors, several males crashed into each other in their haste to open them for her. Another student collided with Eddie, fell into Raymond, and bumped Philip as he rushed by the group to enter the building. The girls watched the chaos with puzzled expressions. When the commotion died down, Philip, Eddie, and Raymond shared a quiet laugh among themselves, oblivious to their girlfriends standing behind them.

"What was that all about?" asked Kimberly, her olive-green eyes flashing.

Eddie glanced at Philip and Raymond for help. "What?"

Kimberly stood with hands on hips. "You guys were staring like you never saw a girl before."

In a gentle voice, Tabitha scolded Raymond. "She is stunning, Ray. But was it necessary to ogle her like that?"

Raymond, in his smooth baritone, clasped her hand to his chest. "I'm sorry for that bit of disrespect toward you. I apologize most profusely, my love. But trust me, although my eyes betrayed me, my heart never will."

Tabitha's smile lit up the dimples in her pretty face. Kimberly shot Raymond a disgusted look, and Minetta rolled her eyes heavenward. Eddie turned his head to cover his laughter. Philip's face broke out in a huge grin. Tabitha and Raymond walked away.

"Thank you, Sir Ray Lancelot!" Philip yelled behind them. "Leave your comrades in the lurch."

Eddie smirked. "Lucky guy," he turned to face his girlfriend. "Come on, Kim, you know you're my gorgeous girl. Stop with the drama."

Kimberly folded her arms. "It's not drama, Eddie. Your behavior was disrespectful. Tabs can forgive Ray all she wants, but you guys were disrespectful to us."

"Disrespectful?" he repeated. "We only looked at a new girl. Is that a crime now?"

"Yes, when you have a pretty girl standing right next to you," she protested.

"I only looked, Kim. She's cute, but she can't take the place of you."

Kimberly rolled her eyes and walked away, with Eddie following her. Philip sighed. He looked down at Minetta, who was giving him a glaring stare.

"Before you say anything, Eddie's right. We were just looking. It's just what guys do. I didn't mean any harm by it."

Minetta smiled. "Just looking? Then you won't mind the next time I stop dead in my tracks, and just stare at a football player passing by. You'll know I mean no harm by it."

Philip gazed up at the sky and sighed. "I'm going to class. I'll talk to you later."

He turned and walked ahead of Minetta into the main building. She slowed her steps, trailing behind him. She watched as Philip crossed paths with two other student-athletes, Andrew Wyatt, and Ben Richards, both in their varsity jackets.

Andrew Wyatt was a formidable athlete; his size alone intimidated his opponents. Andrew was the reigning wrestling champion in the regional high school division and played football and baseball. He wore his hair bleached to a white-blonde tint and cut in a basic crew style. When not involved in sports-related activities, both ears held diamond studs, which he often changed out to elaborate colored ear disks.

Walking beside him and no less formidable was Benjamin Richards. Ben, as he was known, was nationally and regionally ranked as one of the greatest wide receivers in high school football history. He had earned All American status the previous year as a junior. His other sports endeavors were wrestling and baseball. Ben was also known for his high I.Q. and ability to understand complex mathematical equations, most notably, physics.

The oldest son of a prominent cardiothoracic surgeon, Ben's handsome looks and chiseled physique, made him popular among females. He wore his thick hair in braids that reached mid-back, but when actively involved in a sport, he tied them to keep the hair out of the way. His accessory of choice were usually colorful bandanas he wore around his forehead.

Minetta watched the athletes walk up the hall together, enmeshed in conversation. As tall and broad as Philip was, he appeared small compared to Andrew and Ben. She sighed to herself as she headed in the opposite direction. She saw Kimberly at the end of the corridor.

"Hey Kim, it looks like we're going the same way."

"My homeroom teacher is Mrs. Blakely," said Kimberly. "What about you?"

"Same."

They linked arms. Kimberly said, "What a glorious year this will be."

"I hope so," sighed Minetta.

Chapter 3

After homeroom was over, the morning was a blur for Minetta as she adjusted to her new class roster. She was walking fast and nearly running when she collided with another student coming from the opposite direction.

Scrambling to her feet, Minetta gushed out, “I’m sorry. I shouldn’t be running in the hall.”

“That’s okay. I wasn’t watching where I was going either,” replied the girl, rearranging her book bag on her shoulder. Minetta stared, speechless. It was the new girl from earlier in the morning.

“Hi, my name is Amber Paige,” said the girl.

“Hi Amber, my name is Minetta Morgan. I don’t believe I’ve seen you in school before. Are you a new student?”

Amber shifted her book bag on her shoulder. “Yes. I moved here from New York over the summer.”

“Are you a senior?” asked Minetta.

“Yes,” she replied, her attention on the phone buzzing in her hand. She typed a text message.

Minetta could not stop staring at her. The girl was taller and more athletic up close, and her hair was thick with natural body waves reaching mid-back. She was a pure beauty. Minetta found her tongue.

“I was going to meet up with my friends in the cafeteria. Do you want to join us?”

Looking up, Amber smiled. “No thanks. I need to find a quiet place to talk. Can you help me out?”

“Sure. We have a two-level cafeteria. The first level is on the ground floor, and is where the juniors and seniors usually hang out. You can sit and talk privately there. The second level is where the first year and sophomores hang out."

Amber looked around. "Am I going in the right direction?"

"No, it's this way," said Minetta.

The walk to the cafeteria was silent. Amber typed on her phone, oblivious to the admiring stares she received from students and teachers passing by.

"Here we are," said Minetta. She pointed to her right, "That ramp leads to the second level. But you'll want to stay on this level. There's the private area over there."

"Oh, this is nice," Amber smiled. "Thanks a lot for your help. It was nice meeting you."

She hurriedly walked in the opposite direction, found a table for one, and sat down. Minetta watched her for a second before joining her friends for lunch.

"Hey guys. Why are you over here?" She pointed to their usual table in the middle of the room, which was more prominent and larger.

"The guys aren't joining us today," said Kimberly.

Minetta sat down. "You'll never guess who I had the pleasure of meeting just now."

Kimberly leaned forward. "Movie actor or rock star?"

Minetta rolled her eyes. "No, Kim. It was the new girl. I just bumped into her on the way here."

Tabitha smiled. "What's her name?"

"Amber Paige," replied Minetta. "She's a senior."

"What did you guys talk about?" asked Kimberly.

"She wanted to find a quiet place to talk on the phone with her friend."

Tabitha frowned slightly. "I wonder if it's a boyfriend."

"If it's a boy, he must be a model because she's drop-dead gorgeous. I can only imagine how he looks."

Minetta studied the lunch crowd. "I wonder why she transferred here instead of being with him wherever he is."

"Did she say where she's from?"

"Yeah," responded Minetta. "New York."

"New York! There's your answer, bestie."

“He’s probably still in New York.”

“Wow! Can you imagine? I wonder if she’s an actress or something. You know, looking for a quiet year as a high school senior.”

“Yeah, like the child actors you read about who disappear for a year or more to finish their education,” said Tabitha. Her eyes widen with excitement at the reality of a celebrity attending the school. “It must be hard to be in the spotlight all the time.”

“Truly,” agreed Kimberly, nodding her head emphatically. “They have no privacy.”

“Do you suppose the paparazzi will follow her here?” asked Tabitha.

Kimberly looked at Tabitha with a wide-eyed stare. Her mouth formed an O. “Oh, my goodness! Can you imagine? We’ll be on television and our school, too.”

“Wouldn’t that be terrific?” Tabitha was speechless with awe. Her voice came out in a squeak. “A television series about our school?”

Kimberly looked up at the sky. “I wonder who would play me? There are few true redheaded actresses. Do you suppose they would hire me?”

“Excuse me, ladies,” interjected Minetta. “She did not say she was an actress, model, or anything like that. Only that she moved here from New York.”

“I wonder if one or both of her parents are from Cedar Valley,” continued Kimberly.

“Good point, Kim. Why would big city people move to our quaint little town? We’re not even on the map.”

“Ouch!” said Kimberly. “Thanks for the word description, Tabs.”

Minetta rolled her eyes, annoyed with her friends, and changed the subject.

“We have cheer this afternoon before we meet at The Soda Shoppe.”

Every year since middle school, Minetta, Kimberly, and Tabitha signed up for cheerleader tryouts. Once they became a member of the varsity teams, they attended cheer camp during the summers. Cheerleading was a year-round activity for these teenagers.

Tabitha, chewing absently on a celery stick, looked around the courtyard. “I almost forgot there’s a student council meeting directly after school today. Are you signing up this year, Kim?"

"We have cheer after school."

"I heard you, Mimi," remarked Tabitha. "There's something new this year with student council, Kim. We can take part in social media if we cannot make meetings. I will meet you in cheer once I've signed in. Do you want me to sign you up for the council and put you on the social media list, Kim?"

"That's a great idea. I was interested in joining since I was in student government last year. I'll save you a seat at cheer. Plus, we get our new uniforms today."

"Ok, no problem." Tabitha munched on a carrot. "I'll see you guys later."

Minetta asked, "are you guys getting food?"

Pointing to her tray, Tabitha said, "this is mine until we meet up later."

Minetta and Kimberly looked at their friend's platter. Tabitha had a water bottle and a bowl of celery sticks, baby carrots, apple slices, and another bowl piled with broccoli bunches, cauliflower, red pepper strips, and tortilla chips, with a vegetable dip on the side.

She smiled sheepishly. "This will fill me up nicely until later."

Kimberly smiled. "Okay, Tabs, but I'm starving now. Let's go find food, Mimi."

It was late afternoon, and Minetta was rushing. After a stop at her locker to retrieve her book bag, she hastened to the athletic facility. Once inside, she looked around. On the left side of the gymnasium, several assistant coaches sat among football players sprawled across the bleachers. She saw Jed Sloan, the quarterback coach, in discussion with Philip. Raymond saw her and waved. She saw Eddie, Ben, Andrew, and other athletes huddled with two coaches.

To her right was the cheer group. The team comprised three varsity squads of ten first-year students, nine to twelve sophomores and juniors, and twelve to twenty-four juniors and seniors. All but a dozen of the girls were from the Heights. The admission policy held any student could audition for a spot on the team. The financial obligations associated with varsity cheerleading proved cost-prohibitive to most working parents. Kimberly, seated next to Tabitha, called out to her from her position on the front row.

"Hey, Mimi! Over here."

"What's going on?" Minetta sat between Kimberly and Tabitha.

"The coach said she would be here in a minute," said Kimberly, her eyes glued to the athletes across the room.

Tabitha was scanning a textbook and had changed into a dark red track suit. Minetta waved at the other cheerleaders seated in the bleachers, who were excitedly talking and laughing together. She noticed Sam, Mike, and Theo had grown taller. They were the males on the squad. She reached in her tote for the attendance roster, looking around at the team.

Minetta looked at the roster of names and was happy to see two new names. Lizzie Mason, the younger sister of Raymond, and Kelly Van Owens, Kim's younger sister had made the junior varsity squad. Looking at the names, she smiled to herself. The new girls were hard workers and held previous background training in cheer or dance programs. She passed the attendance book to Kimberly and stood on the first bleacher facing the cheerleaders. The noise level died down.

"Hello, everyone. To our new people, my name is Mimi Morgan and I'm the cheer captain. My co-captain is Kim Van Owens. We are your leaders and trainers. Coach Sarah Blakely, whom you met at spring tryouts, oversees the program. If you have questions I can't answer, I bring them to her."

She stepped down, and Kimberly climbed up on the bleacher.

"Hi, everyone. I am the co-captain, Kim. I know we will have an exceptional year in cheer if summer camp was any sign. For the freshman group, learn as much as you can so you can be ready for tryouts next spring. The same thing applies to the members of the junior varsity team. Just because you're on the team this year, does not mean you will automatically be on the team next year. Tryouts are every spring for all of us."

Kimberly stepped down and stood beside Minetta, who was looking at the roster of names again.

"To the varsity team, it's good to see you all. Now I need everyone on the floor practicing stunts, jumps, or doing some stretching. Let's move! Let's go!"

The squad was on the floor ten minutes when loud cheers and hand claps from the football team across the room greeted the appearance of head coach Don Blakely, director of the athletic department. Walking beside him and smiling, his wife Sarah, who taught English Literature and coached the cheer squad and dance team. As Sarah walked toward the cheerleaders, Minetta had them return to the bleachers.

"Well, hello, squad! Ready for another exceptional year?" said Sarah as she approached the group.

"Hi coach," said Tabitha. "It's good to see you."

Sarah smiled. She was of medium height, with long white-blonde hair, deep blue eyes, and had been a high school and college cheerleader majoring in dance education. In her first year as coach, she brought the cheer and dance teams to the nationals, and they came away as champions. Sarah put her tote on a low bleacher, surveyed the cheerleaders, and pulled out folders. Minetta handed her the attendance roster.

"Thanks, Mimi. It's good to see you all," Sarah said. "You all know the drill. Have your parents read these guidelines, sign, and return these applications to me."

A frown appeared on Minetta's face. "I thought we had signed these forms after tryouts, coach?"

"You did," responded Sarah. "The principal thought we should change the applications to reflect changes voted in at the last PTA meeting."

They lost the rest of what the coach stated in the general uproar that ensued when a tall girl with honey-blonde hair walked by the football team on her way to the cheerleaders seated in the bleachers.

Chapter 4

Kimberly nudged Minetta hard on her side, directing her attention to the bleachers where members of the football team huddled around the coach. They were looking at the new girl, including Philip, seated in the middle of his teammates. Minetta watched as his eyes followed the girl to the bleachers, and when he noticed her staring at him, he turned away.

Patiently, the coach waited until the new girl had passed through the center of the room before trying to grab his athletes' attention. With his assistants, the coach ushered his players out a side door that led to the football field.

"Hi, Amber!" Sarah hugged the student and moved her closer to the group. Minetta gave the coach and new girl leveled looks.

Sarah gushed excitedly. "This young lady is Amber Paige. She is a two-time state competitive varsity cheerleader. She joins our varsity cheer squad this year, and it thrills us to have her!"

Amber smiled nervously, looking about shyly as she hesitantly half-waved. The cheerleaders gazed at the new girl with interest.

"Amber, these cheerleaders make up the varsity squad. Mimi Morgan is the captain, and Kim Van Owens is the co-captain."

Amber smiled at Minetta. "We met earlier in the hallway. Hiya doing?"

Minetta managed a pleasant expression. *Hiya doing?* The coach gave instructions for the upcoming cheer rehearsals. Minetta squirmed with impatience. She kept her eyes on her notebook, filing away handouts. She wanted to be out of that gym. As soon as the coach stopped talking, Minetta gathered her book bag.

"Are we done here?" She asked Sarah.

"Yes, I think so," said Sarah. "Rehearsals begin this Friday. Spirit week is in a few weeks. Please check your new calendars, everyone."

The coach consulted her scheduling journal. "Hey, hey," she yelled.

She stood on a bleacher for all to see her. "Please make sure your applications signed and returned to me as soon as possible. Uniforms are here, so sign for them today, please. The assistant coaches are in the locker room. Your new jackets have also arrived. Theo, Mike, and Sam, I have your uniforms, so please see me. Questions, let Mimi or Kim know sooner rather than later. See you all Friday."

Sarah turned to Amber. "Before you leave, Amber, I need your measurements to order a jacket and uniform for you."

Tabitha and Kimberly walked over to Amber and hugged her. One assistant came onto the gymnasium floor to collect the cheerleaders. Minetta ran ahead to the locker room. She signed for her items and moved through the crowd until she was in the parking lot. She fast walked to her car, opening it automatically with her hand remote. She threw the gray shopping bag containing her uniform and jacket in the trunk. Amber sped by in a black convertible two-seater with a deep gray interior. Minetta breathed deeply and closed her eyes.

"Hey Mimi, wait up!" yelled Kimberly behind her. "Are you okay?"

"I'm fine," Minetta responded tersely. "Are you guys still going to the Soda Shoppe?"

"Yes," said Tabitha, who was walking alongside Kimberly.

"Did you get to sign us up for student council?" Kimberly asked Tabitha.

"Yes," responded Tabitha. "It only took a minute. The sign-up sheet was taped to thc door."

Kimberly smiled. "Thanks, Tabs."

Minetta opened the trunk. The girls tossed in their belongings. Usually, Tabitha sat in the front seat to allow Kimberly room to stretch out her legs in the back. Today she sat in the backseat reading the text messages silently coming in on her cellphone. As they drove away from the school toward the Town Square, Minetta played a music tape. Kimberly sang and waved at fellow students with her pink sneaker feet resting out the side window. Tabitha remained silent in the backseat, bent over her cellphone. Minetta quietly reflected on Philip's attraction to the new girl.

Minetta pulled into a parking space in front of the Soda Shoppe as Raymond's black sedan eased in an adjoining slot next to hers. Minetta looked around the parking lot and spied Philip's red SUV and two cars down Eddie's bright orange sports coupe. As the girls stepped out of Minetta's car, Raymond walked to Tabitha, took her hand, and steered her toward the other side of his car. Eddie was standing by the door and opened it for Minetta and Kimberly to enter. Minetta looked over at Tabitha and Raymond. They were talking with their heads close together.

Eddie called out to them. "Hey guys, we're in the back booths."

Raymond waved Eddie away. With a shrug of his shoulders, Eddie followed the girls into the shop. The Soda Shoppe was a favorite spot for the town's local teenagers. On a corner, it was larger inside than it looked from the outside. No matter the number of renovations, the shop kept the novelty of the store's architecture. The black-and-white checkered floor, spacious red leather booths, and workable jukebox were original to the shop. Added innovations were the ceiling fans and fluorescent lights.

"Hey guys," said Philip. He stood up to allow Minetta to slide in beside him. He scanned around the room. "Where's Tabs and Ray?" he asked.

"The lovebirds are outside." Eddie picked up a menu and looked at it with Kimberly.

"How was your first day?" Philip asked Minetta, smiling.

"It was the first day," she said. "How was yours?"

Philip gave her a steady look before responding. "I'm glad this is my last year in this school. Are you writing for the school paper again?"

"Yes, I am. I enjoyed it last year, so this year should be better."

"True."

"Hey guys, sorry about that," said Raymond as he and Tabitha joined them.

Eddie moved closer to Kimberly, and Tabitha sat beside him with Raymond next to her. Philip handed out menus. Minetta looked at the crimson face of Tabitha. What had they been talking about that would make Tabitha blush? She glanced over at Raymond. His blue eyes were slits in his face as he stared back at her. She averted her eyes.

"What are we eating?" asked Eddie.

"The same thing we always eat, darling boy," said Kimberly in a husky stage voice, and they all laughed. The server appeared and took their orders for cheeseburgers, French fries, and milkshakes. Looking around, Philip drummed lightly on the table.

"Okay, gang. Time for roll call. I'll go first. I'm the team captain this year on the varsity football squad. I'm pretty pumped about that. I made the lead photographer for the school paper this year, and I was elected president of the student council."

Eddie performed a drum roll, and everybody laughed.

"Who's heading the photography section this year? I heard Mr. Benson retired."

"He did," said Philip. "Mr. Christian, my homeroom teacher, is also in charge of the photography club. He caught me as soon as I walked into his classroom this morning."

Philip nodded to Minetta. She said, "I earn a spot-on varsity cheer again as well as kept my captain status. This is my third year in the English Literature club, and I was elected president. I'm writing for the school paper again, and I signed up for the yearbook committee."

"What will your column be about this year?" asked Tabitha. "Same stuff as last year?"

"No. Last year I wrote about what I was assigned. This year I have a byline where I'll write about all the social activities we have at school."

"Oh, that's great, Mimi," said Kimberly.

"Yeah, you get to write about the social life of a senior's year from a first-person perspective," said Philip.

"Keepsakes for us and information for future students," said Tabitha.

"Plus, all the questions everyone always asks about cheerleading," stated Kimberly, and Minetta grinned.

"No sports?" asked Raymond.

Minetta gave him an exasperated look. "Hilarious, Raymond, but I'm still on the swim and diving team."

Everyone laughed, and Raymond smiled. Kimberly leaned forward.

"My turn. I returned as co-captain in cheer. This year, they gave me the role of head interior designer for our stage plays since Melva graduated last year. I'll remain on the student council if they hold their meetings on social media, as they mentioned last year."

"It's going to happen, Kim. We're sending out passcodes next week. I saw you and Tabs names on the sign-up sheet. Welcome aboard," said Philip.

"The sign-up sheet was your idea?" asked Tabitha.

Philip grinned. "I knew I wouldn't be there in time, so I wrote out a sign-up sheet. Seems like we're going to have more members than we've ever had now that we can hold meetings on social media."

"Great looking out, Philip," Kimberly responded.

Eddie looked around. "My turn? Sports involvement is still football, basketball, track and field. I'm back with the Performing Arts Center, where I returned as the set engineer for the stage plays. I also joined the physics lab at the request of Ben. He and I had physics last term, and he was my partner in class. The guy is a physics genius."

Philip agreed. "He's always been able to figure out mathematical formulas. Absolutely amazing. It's your turn, Tabs."

Tabitha was next. "Congratulations, Philip, as the new student council president. I know you will do a great job." She stopped to smile at him before proceeding. "I continued in my third year with student council, still in cheer and gymnastics. I might return to the swim team, but I don't think I'll compete this year. I was elected president of the Dead Poets Society." She stopped and her dimples appeared. "There's something else I'm very thrilled about. I became the head wardrobe designer for our stage plays."

Everyone around the table clapped. "Alright, Tabs!" said Kimberly.

"That's great, Tabitha," replied Minetta.

Philip looked at Raymond. "Still on the football squad, swim, and soccer teams and I returned to the physics lab."

The food arrived, and after the server left, the teens held each other's hands and Philip blessed their meal. Minetta sliced her cheeseburger in half and placed one half on Philip's plate, along with the fries.

Minetta said, "I think I am going to enjoy being president of the yearbook committee."

"Why?" asked Philip as he placed his condiments on his cheeseburger.

"Hmm… we determine the yearbook concept. This year the school is graduating the largest body of seniors ever."

"Really? I didn't know that" said Eddie.

"Yes, and that means our yearbooks will be thicker. It will be interesting to see how the yearbook develops. What pictures they will select beyond the students in class or sitting around on campus. What extracurricular photos chosen and placed during the designing phase."

"That is interesting," murmured Philip.

"You think the cost of the yearbook will increase?" asked Raymond.

"Why would it increase? We should have surplus given how hard the sports departments and the parent-teacher association have worked during fundraising efforts the last two years."

"You mean, how successful the associations were," stated Tabitha.

Eddie grinned. "That's exactly right."

Kimberly nudged Tabitha. "That reminds me, why were you coming out of Erickson's lab this morning, Tabs?"

Tabitha smiled. "I wanted to join the gardening club this year."

"Oh really? You thinking about becoming a gardener now, Tabs?" asked Eddie, smearing mayonnaise and ketchup on his cheeseburger.

Watching him rub the condiments on his food, Tabitha replied, "I want to learn how to care for real plants. But the gardening group meets on Saturday mornings, and I'm wondering whether I want to give up my weekends just yet."

Philip turned to Raymond. "I almost forgot, man. The coach wanted to know if you were still going to student-coach this year."

"No," said Raymond emphatically. "I told him no at the end of last season. I am concentrating on my grade point average this year."

Eddie gave him an incredulous look. "Man, besides Ben, you already have the highest-grade point average in the senior class. You both are shoo-ins for valedictorians this year."

Raymond did not respond and appeared focused on his food. If he resented the question, he did not show it by his demeanor. In all the years the group had been together, no one could recall him ever raising his voice. Instead, he was fiercely competitive. In the world of high school sports, nationally recognized in track and field, and swim competitions.

His position as a running back on the football team showcased his physical ability and toughness which equally matched his skills on the Cedar Valley soccer team as a goalkeeper. Raymond's handsome looks caught the attention of females, but it was his fierceness in sports that earned him respect among his coaches and team members.

Eddie, without warning, shouted. "Hey, guys! Over here."

He waved his arms wildly. Minetta looked toward Eddie's outburst and nearly choked on her milkshake. Coming in a beeline toward them were Amber Paige, Andrew Wyatt, and Ben Richards.

Chapter 5

Amber had changed into a black sports bra and matching high-waisted leggings. She was wearing her varsity jacket and had pulled her honey blonde hair into a low messy bun. Philip, Raymond, and Eddie stood, although there was little to no room in the booth. Minetta watched as Philip placed his hands on Amber's shoulders and guided her to where he once sat next to her. Raymond crossed the aisle, pulled three chairs from a neighboring table, and pushed it towards Andrew, another to Ben, and the last one to Philip. The young men aligned themselves at the table, with Philip next to Amber and Andrew next to Philip. Ben sat on the right side of Andrew, next to Raymond and Tabitha. Eddie and Kimberly were across from Minetta. Amber shrugged out of her jacket.

Kimberly nodded toward Amber. "Hey girl, I love the outfit."

Amber smiled. "Thanks. I was just leaving the fitness studio when I saw everyone's parked cars outside." She pointed to Andrew and Ben. "These two told me about this place as the group's hangout spot. So here I am."

"Hi Amber, it's good to see you again," said Tabitha. "How did you get a varsity jacket so quick?"

Amber grinned. "Someone quit the team, so I inherited her jacket and uniform. Thank goodness it all fits."

Kimberly smiled. "Lucky you! Now you can practice with us."

"Yes, and I'm looking forward to it."

Tabitha remarked. "We are in a lot of classes together, Amber. Have you received your class roster yet?"

"Yes, I did. Dr. Hennessy is our homeroom adviser and teacher for Advanced Calculus classes, correct?"

"Yes, we also have Advanced Physics with Ben, Philip, and Raymond. Dr. Kilbourne teaches that class. It was a mix-up on our class schedules."

"Okay," said Amber. She corrected her schedule card.

"You in the Advanced Honors Program?" asked Minetta.

"Yes," Ben interjected in his mellow bass. "And she's solid in calculus and physics. I'm impressed."

Amber smiled at Ben's remarks giving him a megawatt grin that highlighted her dimples and bright blue eyes. Ben, a bright blue bandana tied around his forehead, returned her smile as he removed his varsity jacket. The white knit jersey he wore emphasized his muscled neck, shoulders, and biceps.

Minetta tried not to stare at him. She noticed around his neckline was a long silver chain attached to a medallion engraved with a crescent and a 5-point star. It matched the ring on his right pinkie finger. Besides the large black watch, these were the pieces of jewelry he wore consistently.

Kimberly's elbow in her rib cage startled her out of her reverie, causing her to miss the way Ben and Amber smiled at each other before each looked away.

"Glad you guys are here," said Eddie, handing out menus. "Hey Andy, did old man Sloan keep you after we left?"

Andrew groaned. He took off his dark sunglasses, revealing pale blue eyes.

"Man, yeah, he did. I had to do push-ups and run around the track like I was a first-year nerd. I hate him, man!"

Raymond gazed at him quietly. "If you had not been goofing off when he was talking, he wouldn't have done that. As senior staff coach, respect him."

Andrew looked at Raymond but remained silent. He wore his varsity jacket over a faded gray school pullover and denim jeans. Andrew was packed solid with muscles and formidable skill, making him one of the best defensive tackles in Cedar Valley High football history. But, for all his fierceness, he loved to party as hard as he worked. He had developed bad habits as an athlete he kept well hidden from the coaches, but that he, Raymond, and Philip knew about.

The server appeared to take the newcomers' orders, and her presence broke some of the tension. Amber and Ben settled on cheeseburgers, French fries, and vanilla shakes. Andrew put in a double order of everything with the addition of pie.

Minetta turned to Amber. “Did you say you were leaving the fitness studio? Are you training at Cedar Motions Fitness Studio?”

“I was thinking about it. Why do you ask?” Amber’s smile was dazzling.

“It’s where we work out,” replied Kimberly.

Amber smiled. “Oh really? I didn’t see anyone I knew when I registered. What days do you guys go?”

“We go on Thursday nights,” said Tabitha.

“Oh, great! It’s an immense place,” replied Amber. “Three different size studios with lockers and showers on each floor.”

Eddie grinned. “Once my dad heard the vision, he expanded the space upward to house those three floors.”

Amber looked puzzled. “Your dad? What does he do?”

“Stamps & Associates are architects, city planners, and engineers.”

“Oh, fascinating.” said Amber. “What does your mom do?”

“Nothing much,” replied Eddie, not looking at Amber.

Kimberly sighed and smiled. “Eddie’s mom is the chef and owner of La Dolce Vita Restaurant in the Town Square.”

Amber looked at him, and Eddie grinned. Amber smiled and shook her head. Kimberly leaned forward in front of Eddie.

“My dad is a surgeon, and my mom is a physical therapist. She’s the co-owner of the fitness studio.”

Amber smiled at Kimberly. “Does your mother have hair and eyes like yours?”

Kimberly blushed. “Yeah, most everyone says we look like twins. Mom is often at the fitness studio during the day except on Thursdays when she’s there all day. I’ll introduce you to her.”

“Thanks, I’d like that. If you look like your mother, then it’s a wonderful compliment. I’ll bet your mother’s gorgeous.”

“Thanks,” mumbled Kimberly, looking embarrassed.

Amber leaned across Minetta. “Is the girl with the light red curls I saw you with at school your sister?”

Kimberly nodded. “Yeah, Kelly is sixteen. She has our dad’s coloring.”

“Wow! A beautiful family of redheads,” said Amber.

Eddie put an arm around Kimberly’s shoulder. “You don’t have to tell me twice. My girl *is* gorgeous.”

Andrew side-eyed Eddie and smirked, but said nothing. The server brought their food.

"By the way, I signed up for Thursday nights, too. So glad I will have someone in there I know," said Amber.

Raymond, his eyes on his food offered a suggestion. "FYI, Amber, a few athletes go early on Friday afternoons because of early dismissals for seniors. The studio isn't crowded, and sometimes the coaches and trainers are there too. The school pays for us, so remember to bring your school ID if you decide to go."

Ben and Amber glanced at Raymond, but neither uttered a word.

"Ben, I already know your parents are both surgeons and yours, Phil, are attorneys," said Amber. "What about you, Raymond? What do your folks do?"

Raymond, who spied the startled expression on Minetta's face, tried not to smile as he turned his attention to Amber. "Both are doctors at the medical center."

"Nice. What about you, Tabitha?"

Tabitha was looking at Raymond. "Ray is modest. His dad is the chief of surgery at the hospital. My parents are both college professors at Upper Medford Valley University."

Amber turned to Minetta. "What do your parents do?"

Minetta had been listening to the conversation and going over in her memory Amber's comments about Philip. She toyed with a paper napkin, her mind in a state of confusion.

"My dad is a church pastor, but he also teaches at the university where Tabs parents work. My mom is a librarian."

Before Amber could speak again, Raymond cut in. "Why don't we talk about something else besides our parents?"

"We just finished roll call. You guys want to take part?" asked Philip.

Amber looked confused. "What is roll call?"

"I'll start so you get the idea of how we do this," said Andrew. "By the way, my dad is a postal inspector, and mom is a school principal. For roll call, my sports are football, wrestling, and baseball. I joined the Performing Arts Center where I'll be helping design sets with Eddie."

Everyone nodded approvingly. "Glad to have you, big guy!" was Eddie's response.

"For me, sports remain football, wrestling, and baseball," said Ben. "I was also elected president of the physics lab, and I rejoined the science and math club."

Philip said, "that's great, man!"

"Thank you. This year I took on mentoring some junior class men in the physics lab. It's a tough discipline for some of them to master."

Minetta passed her energy bar to Ben. He gave her a bag of Hershey chocolates. Minetta's grin was wide and made Ben smile broadly. Amber smirked and cast a sideways glance at Minetta.

Eddie turned to Amber. "Your next, Amber."

"Well, other than the cheer squad, that's it for now."

"That's cool. Take your time," said Eddie. "This school has a lot of programs, and combined with the heavy academic load, it can kill you."

Smiling, Tabitha agreed. "You'll have company Amber because we are cheerleaders, too."

Kimberly looked around at Eddie. "No worries, Amber. Take your time and pick the extra stuff you love doing. This is our last year, so make it good."

Amber smiled. "I love cheering and I ran track and field at my old high school."

Tabitha joined in. "Why not try out for the school plays? They should put the audition schedule up soon. I think you might like it. This year they are trying to do more Broadway-type shows."

Amber smiled. "I'll look into it. Thank you."

They were all quiet as they dug into their food. Kimberly gave Eddie her pickles and tomatoes, and Tabitha was content to give Raymond most of her French fries. Minetta noticed Amber divided up her French fries between Ben and Philip. Andrew ate everything on his plate and looked around at their empty dishes.

"What's your favorite school subject, Phil?" asked Amber.

"I would have to say history," he replied. "What's yours?"

Amber smiled. "Photography. I love capturing images."

"Really? Why don't you sign up for photography? I'm the lead photographer this year, and I could use an assistant."

"I'll see," she said.

Ben stood up. “Hey, guys, I’ve got to go. This evening was fun, but it’s getting late. I have an assignment to turn in for tomorrow.”

He pushed his chair away from the table and returned it to its original post. He shrugged into his jacket and picked up the dinner tab to pay at the register.

“I have the tab,” said Raymond, pulling the bill out of his hand before he could respond.

Startled, Ben smiled. “Well, uh… thanks, man. My treat next time.”

He and Raymond hugged. Ben shook Eddie and Andrew’s hands.

“Hey, Ben. Let me talk to you a minute,” said Philip, rising from his seat.

They walked away from the table, speaking in low sentences. Minetta stared as their backs were to the group. The conversation ended and Ben and Philip shook hands and hugged. Ben hoisted his book bag on his shoulders, and waved goodbye to the girls. He strolled through the room toward the exit, his attention on the black phone in his hand. He was seemingly oblivious to the admiring female glances he received as he exited the shop.

“Well, I should head home myself,” said Amber, collecting her book bag and looking at her phone.

“Okay, glad you came over,” said Tabitha, reaching out and touching the back of Amber’s hand. They smiled at each other.

“Thanks, I’m glad I came over too.” Amber stood up, as did Andrew, Eddie, and Philip.

“I’ll walk you out,” said Eddie. “It’s gotten dark.”

“Wow, what a gentleman.” Amber looked at Kimberly. “He’s a keeper.”

“Yes, I know,” said Kimberly, smiling..

Andrew looked at Amber. “Hey, I’m leaving too. You can walk out with me.”

“I’ll walk her out,” Philip interjected curtly. Turning to Amber, he said, “I want to ask you something.”

Eddie shrugged and sat down. Andrew looked from Philip to Amber, picked up his book bag, and walked out. Philip watched him leave. Amber pulled on her varsity jacket, her attention on her phone.

“You ready?” he asked her.

Amber nodded. “Bye,” she said to the group.

Tabitha and Kimberly both smiled at her.

"See you tomorrow Amber," said Kimberly and waved.

Minetta watched as Philip walked with Amber toward the exit out of the building, engrossed in conversation. What could he possibly be asking the new girl? No one else was paying attention to Amber and Philip. She glanced around the table. Kim and Tabitha were in a discussion, Eddie was going through his wallet, and Raymond, peering at her with an impenetrable gaze. His sapphire stare glowed in the semi-darkness of the booth. She looked down at her hands resting in her lap and sighed.

Philip returned, and everyone prepared to leave. The boys followed Minetta's car out of the parking lot, Eddie and Raymond veering off as Philip trailed her car. They both honked as they sped past Minetta and the girls. Minetta drove home looking at the road and the traffic, and occasionally glancing in the rearview mirror at Philip behind her. She turned on the car stereo, and Kimberly stretched out on the back seat, was content to sing along with the music. Her alto voice blended smoothly with the vocalist. Tabitha sat in the front seat and looked out the window. Minetta pulled up to Tabitha's house, which was two homes away from hers. Tabitha's mother came to the door and waved at them. A flood of overhead lights enveloped her petite silhouette.

"Your mom's home," observed Minetta.

Tabitha retrieved her belongings. "Mom's teaching online classes this year so that she can be home with us more."

Kimberly opened the back door and hopped out with Tabitha. "Night, Mimi, see you tomorrow."

"Night, besties."

Minetta pulled into her driveway. Philip honked as he drove past. She watched his vehicle until the taillights disappeared. Minetta eased in the house and walked down the hall to the kitchen. She saw the pantry closet door open, suggesting Beatrice might be in there. Minetta hurriedly climbed the backstairs to the second floor.

In her bedroom, she eased the door shut. She wanted no company. Her mother would expect a full report of the day, and she was in no mood right now to answer questions. She tossed her book bag and the gray tote containing her cheer uniform on the window seat. She laid down on her bed bed and looked up at the ceiling, needing to process today's events in her mind's eye.

She was slightly dizzy, as if she were in a wind tunnel. Who was this new girl, and why was Philip behaving weird? In a few minutes, exhausted and weary from her thoughts, Minetta fell asleep.

Chapter 6

A week later, Minetta was sitting in the middle of her bed with her tablet on her lap. She was staring at her computer screen as her fingers punched in rapid staccato on the keys. A soft knock on her bedroom door, and a moment later, Tabitha and Kimberly entered. They fell across the queen size bed, and wafts of floral-scented cologne filled their noses. Kimberly played with the fringes on the blue chenille spread folded across the bottom of the bed while Tabitha fidgeted with the colorful bangles on her wrist. Minetta stopped typing and looked at them. After exchanging a glance with Kimberly, Tabitha related what Raymond had told her a week earlier outside the Soda Shoppe.

She concluded with, "I don't know if any of it is true, but I know Ray would not lie or exaggerate the facts. If he says Philip and Amber know each other, then I believe him."

Minetta was silent as she stared at the ceiling, her expression devoid of any signs of emotion. She looked over at Kimberly sprawled across the foot of her bed.

Kimberly shrugged. "I believe Ray too. I mean, if they met in Hawaii, what's the big deal? Why can't Philip tell you he knows Amber? It makes me wonder if they were ever an item."

"Something is going on between them," said Tabitha slowly. "Why pretend you don't know each other?"

"Yeah, especially when he broke his neck to walk her out of the Soda Shoppe the other night," replied Kimberly.

Tabitha looked wistful. "He likes her. That's for sure…"

Her voice trailed off as she caught the flash of annoyance on Kimberly's face. Still regarding Tabitha, Kimberly attempted to rectify what Minetta had heard.

“Well, look at our guy, Ray, for example. The first chance he got, he let Tabs know what was up.”

“Hmm,” said Minetta. She closed her tablet and placed it beside her on the bed. She looked at her friends.

“I don’t know about that. Why didn’t Ray tell you about Amber before now, Tabs? And Kim, what about Eddie? Just think of the number of summers Philip has been going to Hawaii. You can’t tell me those guys don’t talk about what they’ve done on their summer trips. I believe Ray and Eddie knew about Amber way before she showed up in Cedar Valley. It makes me wonder if Ray and Eddie are keeping Philip’s dirty little secrets.”

Tabitha shook her head vigorously. “Wait a minute, Mimi. Ray is not obligated to give you reports about who Philip is seeing. You guys aren’t a couple.”

Kimberly’s olive-green eyes flashed. “Tabs is right. We don’t need spy reports on our boyfriends on their time away from us.”

“Every summer, my family goes to our beach home in Monterrey,” continued Tabitha, hardly catching her breath. “My cousins and I see and talk to lots of kids on the beach. It’s all just harmless summer fun. I am not interested in those guys, nor do I go out with them. So, what would be the point of bringing them up to Ray when I come home? I am sure Ray is doing the same thing in Hawaii.”

Kimberly jumped in. “It’s called socializing, Mimi. I know Eddie well. He always sends me a postcard from the car shows he attends the two weeks he’s in Hawaii. I’m sure he’s not hanging with Philip twenty-four seven because we all know Philip is not into car shows.”

“What does Philip do when he’s in Hawaii? Has he ever told you?” asked Tabitha.

Minetta stared at Tabitha. “No. We never talk about our vacations.”

“Why not?” asked Kimberly with a slight frown. “Eddie and I usually talk about our vacations, especially if we’re into something new.”

“Raymond and I do as well. Sometimes we send each other postcards,” said Tabitha.

The girls were quiet for some time. Tabitha, irritated with Minetta, moved from the bed to sit in the window seat with her arms crossed.

"Well, I think one of Philip's summer crushes has come home to roost," said Kimberly, eyeing Tabitha. "I think he owes you an explanation, Mimi. Not Ray or Eddie but Philip."

Minetta's phone buzzed. It was Philip. She ignored it.

"You make good points, bestie, and I am sorry about what I said regarding Ray. I guess I don't understand what's going on with Philip this year. I had always thought we had an unspoken agreement, but I guess I was wrong. I don't know."

"What do you mean by an unspoken agreement?" inquired Tabitha.

"Last year, when Andrew asked me to the junior prom, I said no because I was waiting for Philip to ask me. It wasn't until a week before prom that I found out that Philip would not be in town. He never told me, and I saw him nearly every day."

Kimberly sat up. "That was sweet of Andrew to take you still."

"Well, he had no choice," said Minetta. "Everyone else was already coupled up. Besides, that was different. He's more like a big brother, at least, to me."

Kimberly leaned forward. "And we all knew Andrew was getting over his girlfriend Debbie's family moving to Japan."

"Exactly," responded Minetta. "Andrew and Debbie had been part of our group as a couple, and now he was alone."

Quietly, Tabitha stated, "I don't know why you said you and Philip have an unspoken agreement. That doesn't seem to be the case. Philip did not tell you he would be away during the prom when that's all we talked about in school and at our hangout. He was sitting there with us and talking about it, too."

Kimberly looked over at Tabitha in the window seat. "You know, that's a good point, Tabs. He knew he wouldn't be attending."

"If he hadn't asked you yet, why didn't you say something to him? You would have missed out if Andrew hadn't asked you."

Silence ensued as Minetta stared at Tabitha, who was now meeting her gaze. Kimberly coughed lightly. Minetta's phone buzzed again. The caller was Philip. She showed the number to the girls. Kimberly made the "call me" sign with her hand as she and Tabitha exited the room. Minetta waved back in response.

"Hi, Philip, what's up?" Minetta's voice was calm.

"Hey, are you busy?" asked Philip, in a low soft tone.

"Yes, I was. What is it?"

"Ok." Pause. "Look, Mimi, I am sorry if I hurt your feelings. I wasn't trying to."

"I know that Philip. I am sorry too."

Philip's voice perked up. "It surprised me to see Amber in Cedar Valley. I'm used to seeing her during summers in Hawaii."

"During summers? How long have you known her?" asked Minetta.

"I met her a few summers ago on vacation."

Minetta digested this information. "So, you've known her for a long time?"

"Well, I've seen her for a while if that makes sense," replied Philip, adding, "at least, every summer."

"And you never thought to tell me you knew this girl before now?"

"Tell you what? Amber is just one of the hundreds of girls whose families come to Hawaii for the summer, and I mean hundreds."

"I don't care about the hundreds of girls, Philip. What I care about is you acting like you have something to hide. You could have told me all this when we met up at the Soda Shoppe last week," rasped out Minetta.

"Told you all what? Are you serious?" Philip exclaimed. "Have you told me about every guy you met on your summer vacations?" His voice was smooth but had grown slightly deeper.

"Don't be ridiculous," she responded testily. "We go to our beach home every year, and there are millions of people around, especially guys!"

"Bingo! That's my point," he said. "Besides, we haven't been talking in-depth about what we do on summer breaks before, have we?"

"Doesn't matter," she responded. "When you saw Amber that first day, you stood on the sidewalk gawking like a pigeon after crumbs and never once mentioned you knew her."

"You sound insane," said Philip, clearly angry. "I didn't tell you about her because I wasn't thinking about her like that."

Minetta's voice rose. "Oh, of course not! You've only seen her every summer for years!"

Philip shouted back. "What are you talking about, Mimi? I do not know this girl personally. I never even knew her name. You think it's okay to give me the third degree over nothing?"

"Over nothing?"

"You heard me correctly, nothing."

Minetta caught herself and calmed down. She remembered that her friends' relationships differed from what she and Philip had. They were silent for a few moments.

In a calmer tone, he said, "look, I called to apologize about my behavior at school the first day, not to get you worked up. Are we good?"

Minetta sighed. "Yes, we're good."

"Great. Listen, Mimi, I need a favor." His voice had returned to its smooth, balanced tone. "Would you invite Amber to our monthly Bible studies at the church?"

The heat rose in her neck again. "Why? Can't she walk into a church on her own?"

Philip let out a sigh. "Her family just moved back to Cedar Valley. She doesn't know anyone besides our group. I thought it would be a good way for her to meet other people."

Minetta chewed on her top lip. "Why don't you invite her then?"

He said, "you're the pastor's daughter. That's why I am asking you to do this."

"Really?" said Minetta curtly. "I thought when you walked off with her at the shop; you would have asked her about her church affiliations and offered to bring her!"

Philip lowered his voice slightly. "Mimi, she has a boyfriend, okay? Besides, I don't want to have another one of these crazy conversations with you."

Minetta's mood instantly brightened. "Amber has a boyfriend. Does he vacation in Hawaii, too? What's his name? Where does he live? Have you met him? What school does he attend? Is he a model?"

Minetta positioned herself on her bed to listen carefully to Philip's answers in response to her questions, but none came. There was a momentary pause.

"Instead of being standoffish with the girl, why not become her friend? I'm sure she would love to talk about her boyfriend with you. Isn't that what girls do? Share everything in their personal lives with each other? Now, back to my question. Will you invite her to our Friday night Bible studies? It will go over much easier coming from you."

Defeated, she replied, "I will talk to her when I get a chance. She might want to join our youth missions group too."

"Let's take it one step at a time," said Philip. "We don't want to scare her away."

"Ok, one step at a time." She looked at her bedside clock. "Hey Philip, I've got to go. I have to get ready for school tomorrow."

"Same here," he said. "Thanks, Mimi. I knew I could count on you. See you at school tomorrow."

"Okay, Philip. See you tomorrow," she said. He hung up.

Minetta sat still, looking at her cellphone. *I knew I could count on you.* She laid back on her bed pillows and stared thoughtfully at the ceiling. After a minute, she called Kimberly and Tabitha to tell them about her conversation with Philip.

Chapter 7

It was a rainy Wednesday afternoon and Minetta was in the Performing Arts Center watching the auditions for the upcoming winter play, a French-inspired musical. The drama teacher, Elsa Coates, auditioned Amber for the lead after the student selected for the role suffered a broken leg. Minetta sat through two hours of Amber singing show tunes as Ben played the piano. She watched as Amber and company rehearsed an intricate dance ensemble choreographed by senior choreographers, Claire, and Mike. Elsa settled on Jake Holgren as the leading man. Jake and Amber ran over complex lines of a practice script written in French, with Elsa declaring Jake and Amber's French pronunciations and accents were faultless. At the conclusion of the audition thunderous applause broke out from the assembled cast and the faculty and students observing from the sidelines.

Minetta could still hear the ecstatic accolades and her friends raving nonstop about Amber's audition and talents as an actress, dancer, and singer. Minetta closed her locker for the day, contemplating whether she wanted to drive to the Soda Shoppe or head home. She had a massive headache. Kimberly and Amber walked up behind her. She noticed they were both in their varsity jackets.

"Hey Minetta," they said in unison and giggled.

"Hey, what are you guys doing?" Minetta asked, eyeing them quietly.

Kimberly was all smiles. "We know it's raining badly. We were trying to decide if we wanted to go to our favorite spot today."

"Yeah," said Amber. "The rain is kind of a downer."

Minetta looked at Amber. "We have Bible studies this coming Friday at church. Do you want to come?"

"I guess," she hunched her shoulders. "I was speaking to Phil about the youth group at my old church in New York. He said you guys were pretty cool."

"We are more than pretty cool," said Kimberly, grinning. "Tabs and I usually ride with Mimi. We can pick you up."

Minetta looked at Kimberly and over at Amber, forcing herself to smile. "Philip told me he had spoken to you about joining our Bible studies group."

Amber returned the smile. "I think Phil is just the sweetest guy."

Minetta turned back to her locker and reopened it. Over her shoulder, she said, "I'm not going to the hangout. I'm tired. It's been a long day. I think I'm going home. You want a ride home, Kim?"

Kimberly, caught off-guard, frowned. "Yeah, I guess it has been a long day with the rain and all."

Minetta rooted around in her locker. After an uncomfortable pause, Kimberly turned to Amber and smiled.

"Guess we'll see you tomorrow."

Amber looked at Kimberly, and at Minetta's back, and sighed.

"Okay, see you tomorrow, guys."

Kimberly watched Amber until she disappeared around the corner at the end of the hall. She turned to Minetta.

"That was awkward. What was that all about?"

Minetta slammed the locker door. "Phil? Did you hear her? Why can't she call him Philip as we all do? She has to call him Phil like she's so special."

"What are you talking about?" asked Kimberly, wistfully looking down the now-empty hall.

"Little miss perfect. Like she knows Philip better than I do," she fumed.

Kimberly stared at her. "I don't think that's the case, Mimi. She's a splendid girl, very personable and easy to talk to and…"

"And I'm not? You don't even know her. Where is this coming from?"

"I didn't mean it that way, Mimi."

"How about you try and remember how long we've been friends, Kim. Way longer than just arrived in town in her senior year, princess!"

Kimberly looked down the hall again. She said softly, "I don't know what's going on with you, Mimi. What's your problem with this girl? I've never known you to dislike someone like this."

"There's no problem with me, Kim. I'm just not falling down in love with her like all of you are."

She turned and walked ahead of Kimberly out of the building into the pouring rain. The umbrella she had taken out of her locker stayed firmly closed as she marched through the downpour to her car. Kimberly slowed her pace and followed her best friend with a thoughtful look on her face.

The Cedar Valley High Cougars played against the South High Bengals. Minetta and the cheerleaders watched the game from the sidelines, ready to encourage and uplift their team with chants and songs. Minetta adjusted her sleeveless dark gray cheer shell with its contrasting ivory and red stripes, and matching cheer skirt with its ivory-colored hemline at halftime. She grabbed her red pom-poms and ran onto the field amid enthusiastic shouts and yells from the crowd.

She looked around at her squad. There were three rows of ten cheerleaders in each row. On either side of her lining the front row were Kimberly, Tabitha, and Amber. They finished their routine with all the cheerleaders on the field. Minetta was the flyer and typically concluded with double flying leaps. Minetta's triple-back flip was always a crowd-pleaser, and she did not disappoint. She executed the stunt in mid-air, caught by Theo, tossed to Sam, and with Kimberly and Mike as the base landed firmly anchored. The crowd exploded with loud applause in the bleachers, and Minetta saw Philip, standing with his helmet under his arm, clapping. She smiled as brightly as she could.

On the bench, Kimberly whispered, "Philip never took his eyes off you."

"Really? I thought he would be in the back," replied Minetta, slightly out of breath with excitement.

"I'm sure his coach is reprimanding him," whispered Tabitha.

Minetta, imagining Philip risking discipline for her, was beyond thrilled. Cedar Valley High Cougars won against the South High Bengals, fourteen to seven.

On the way to Cedar Valley Church for the youth Bible studies class, Minetta was thrilled to discover that Amber lived in Maple Glen Heights, the same gated community as Andrew. The next time they were all together, she would mention it, alerting him to Amber's availability.

Minetta leaned out the car window to hit the buttons on the keypad entrance using the code Amber gave her. The double wrought-iron gates swung inward, revealing sizeable red maple trees forming massive columns along the winding road. She found Amber's home and drove up the path and onto a circular cobbled driveway. There were two dove gray cars identical to the black convertible of Amber's. A three-car garage and a fountain gushed water out of a stone urn suspended in the air to the far right of the courtyard.

The house sat atop an inclined hill overlooking the valley below. It was a massive structure. The style was a unique blending of contemporary and modern architecture resplendent with sharp angles, jutted stonework, and floor-to-ceiling glass pane windows. The girls sat in the circular driveway, staring at the house looming before them. They expected to see Amber appear through the heavy wrought iron-laden double front doors. Instead, they watched as Amber came into view from the side of the home, walking over to Minetta's car.

"Hi, ladies." Amber sat in the back seat with Tabitha.

As she drove, Minetta listened to the conversation between her friends and Amber.

"Do you have any brothers or sisters?" asked Tabitha.

"No. I'm an only child."

"Was that your parents' cars?" Kimberly inquired. "They're gorgeous."

"Thank you, and yes, but they're not home from their trip yet."

"What do your parents do?"

"My dad's an investment banker, and mom sells real estate."

"Nice."

"How long have you been cheering?"

"I started cheering two years ago at my old high school in New York. I needed something to do. It gets spooky being in a big house all by yourself."

"How long have you been dancing?"

"I've been dancing since I was four years old. I love to dance."

Tabitha smiled. "I love dancing too."

Kimberly turned at an angle to look at Amber in the back, seated directly behind Minetta.

"The coach said you won championships. Were they in dancing or cheering?"

"Both," said Amber. "A few years ago, my mom started entering me in beauty pageants. I have a few trophies from that as well."

"That's so cool, Amber. I'd love to see your trophies if you don't mind."

"Thanks, Tabitha. I don't mind. Maybe we could have a sleepover."

"A sleepover would be nice," agreed Kimberly. "We have them all the time. Did you decide on any clubs at school yet?"

"I joined the photography club and the Performing Arts Center. I never thought that I would be the lead in a school play. It's just the most awesome thing I've ever done."

All Minetta heard was photography club which was one of Philip's after-school activities. She gripped the steering wheel and tried not to glare at Amber in the rear-view mirror.

"Do you have other siblings, Kim, besides your younger sister?" asked Amber, leaning forward.

"No. There's just Kelly, and she's enough! She's sixteen and a junior. It's kind of nice, though, because we can talk about boys, clothes, hair, and makeup. When we were younger, we hung out together all the time. Not so much now. She has her crowd."

The girls laughed except for Minetta. Amber shifted herself to peer around at Minetta.

"What about you, Mimi? Do you have any siblings?"

Minetta gave her a steady look in the rear-view mirror. She kept her voice level.

"Please don't call me Mimi. Only people who are my friends call me that." She heard Tabitha's shocked gasp. "To answer your question, I have one older brother."

"I'm sorry." Amber stopped smiling, sat back, and looked out her side window. Kimberly looked at Minetta and sighed.

Tabitha touched Amber's arm. "You can call me Tabs, Amber."

Kimberly looked around. "And everyone calls me Kim."

Tabitha smiled at Amber. "I have younger brothers who are twins, Henry, and Edward. They just turned fourteen and are in the ninth grade."

"What? Oh, wow!" said Amber, brightening immediately. "That's great, Tabs. Tell me, how is being an older sister to not one but two younger brothers feel?"

"It has its good days and its bad days. My brothers can be cute one minute and annoying the next."

"I'll bet. I always wished I had siblings. It didn't matter if they were younger or older. It gets very lonely sometimes, especially when my parents are away."

Tabitha reached out and touched Amber's arm, and they smiled at each other. Minetta pulled into the church parking lot. She lamented the fact she had not mentioned Hawaii. Andrew's blue two-door sport pickup truck eased into a space alongside Minetta's car. He honked his horn and rolled down his window.

"Hey, Mimi," he said. "Wait up. I need to ask you about next week's book report for English Lit class."

Kimberly said, "Hurry, dear boy, we don't want to be late for our Bible studies class tonight."

As the group walked across the lot into the church, Minetta was unaware that Amber and Tabitha had exchanged cellphone numbers in the backseat of her car.

Chapter 8

The school year was picking up as Minetta, Tabitha, and Kimberly gathered with other students in the hall to read the bulletin board packed with upcoming announcements. Colorful flyers listed sports schedules, game nights, parent-teacher conferences, social events, the homecoming dance, and other news. The teens headed to the school cafeteria and their favorite seating.

A few minutes later, Eddie, Amber, and Raymond appeared with lunch trays in hand. Eddie slid in next to Kimberly, who moved her book bag from the bench for him. Tabitha put her belongings underneath the table for Raymond. Amber plopped down next to Minetta, who reluctantly pushed her book bag away.

"Hey, ladies," said Eddie.

"Why are you guys late?" asked Kimberly.

"We had an election in the physics lab club." said Eddie, opening cartons on his lunch tray. "Guess who's the vice-president for the last term in school?"

Kimberly leaned her head to the side and smiled. "Is it you, dear boy?"

Eddie laughed. "No ma'am, it's Ray, and Ben is the president."

"I'm the secretary," said Amber.

Minetta looked sideways at her. "You're the secretary? I didn't know you were interested in science."

Raymond grinned at Amber. "Yeah, Amber volunteered when no one else spoke up. It appeared Ben, or I was going to have to fill both slots."

Kimberly gave Eddie the extra meat she had on her sandwich, and he stacked it with his.

"Amber was certainly a lifesaver in that situation. Thanks for looking out."

Kimberly smiled. “Yeah, that was nice of you, girl.”

Tabitha gave Raymond her sandwich, and he reciprocated with an apple. Amber looked above Tabitha’s head.

“Hi Phil. There’s space beside me. Be careful. We don’t want to push poor Minetta onto the floor.”

Philip sat next to Amber. Varsity cheerleaders Sallie, Annette, Jewel, and Vanessa cleared spots immediately for Andrew and Ben at the table. Amber gave Philip the extra meat on her sandwich. After placing the ham slice carefully on his bread, he took a bite and chewed.

Ben, a bright orange bandana tied around his forehead, looked across the table. “Who’s this year’s lead photographer? I need some great football pics, guys.”

Philip said, “I’ve got you covered, Ben. I’m the lead photographer for the school paper this year. Amber’s my assistant.”

“Did you show Mr. Christian your portfolio, Amber?” asked Tabitha.

“Yes,” she said.

Philip gave Amber an orange for the extra meat. Ben reached across Philip and gave Amber a health-food bar. She smiled at him.

“Congrats,” said Ben, smiling back at Amber.

“Thank you,” she replied, her dimples deepening.

They smiled warmly at each other for several minutes. Philip cleared his throat and took a drink of water.

“That portfolio is why Mr. Christian made her my assistant. Those pictures are awe-inspiring,” Philip said.

“Was that portfolio Amber’s?” asked Raymond, looking at Tabitha.

“Yeah,” responded Eddie. “Great pics, huh?”

Kimberly smiled. “Stunning work.”

“Those photos are magnificent, Amber. You should consider photography seriously. You have talent,” said Raymond.

“Additionally, an eye for color and symmetry,” added Ben. “I enjoyed the sunset ones in the back of the album.”

Tabitha crooned. “Oh, me too, Ben.”

Minetta chewed in silence. Everyone had seen Amber’s photographs but her. When and where had all this activity occurred?

“I hear you’re a superb dancer as well, Amber,” said Andrew. “Did you try out for the winter play?”

"Yes, I did. I had to audition for the stage play because it was re-written to include a dance ensemble. The modern style form is one of my favorite genres besides hip hop and ballet."

"No one knew how talented she was until she auditioned," Tabitha remarked. "Ladies and gentlemen, we have a young lady sitting in our midst who can act, sing, and dance. Give it up for Miss Amber Paige."

"She's a triple threat," said Eddie and made a drum roll sound on the table.

Everyone laughed but Minetta. She kept pushing food into her mouth.

"What play are they doing?" asked Andrew.

"It's the musical, *Gigi*, adapted from the French novella by Colette," replied Amber. "It's one of my favorite movies because it stars actress Leslie Caron, whom I adore."

"Who is playing Gaston?" asked Minetta.

"Gaston is being played by Jake Holgren," said Amber.

"He did a great job during his audition."

"Yes he did."

"Who won the role of Honore Lachaille?" asked Minetta.

"I didn't know you knew so much about the theater, Mimi," remarked Philip, with surprise.

"I've seen this movie a dozen times. I could play the role of *Gigi* myself if I wanted."

Amber looked at Minetta. "Joshua Wyatt is playing the role of Honore."

The surrounding conversation continued to flow freely, but to Minetta, all she heard were the voices in her own head. She was thunderstruck by Philip's statement. How could Philip forget how much she loved musicals? She sighed and tried to smile at a joke Eddie told.

"Hey, bestie, stop daydreaming. We have practice today after school for this Friday's away game," said Kimberly.

"Oh, yeah!" Eddie, using a plastic fork and knife as drum sticks, beat a tune on the table.

"Everybody ready for the football game this Friday night?"

Andrew spoke up. "You know we are. We're gonna squash Central High."

"That's who you're playing against?" asked Tabitha. "What happened to Oak High?"

"Rumor has it sports officials put them on suspension for this season," answered Eddie. "I don't know why though."

"Hope it's not something serious like drugs," said Ben.

"I would hope the officials would sanction them a lot heavier than a one-year suspension," remarked Raymond.

"Not if there was suspicion and not proof," stated Philip.

Everyone quietly digested the comments. The Oak High Sentinels football team had always been one of their fiercest competitors.

"Well, they have themselves to blame if they were doing something unscrupulous," stated Andrew.

"Enough of that," said Ben. He looked at the cheerleaders. "Let's cheer on our football team this Friday."

"That's the spirit!" yelled Kimberly.

Immediately the varsity cheerleaders performed a victory song to the delight of the students and staff in the lunch hall.

Eddie turned to Ben. "Hey, is it true you won't be at the game this Friday?"

"Yeah," sighed Ben. "My dad is presenting a new medical technique in cardiothoracic surgery. We've been planning this trip since he accepted the invitation to speak at this conference a year ago."

"Coach Don excused him. He's bringing in Jerry off the bench to substitute for Ben in the wide receiver position," said Philip.

"Well, man, I guess I'll have to hold down the fort until you return," said Eddie, rubbing his hands together.

Eddie played the defensive end tackle position. Andrew looked over at Eddie and smirked.

"Don't worry about Friday's game. You're learning your dad's job firsthand, in a specialty you're considering," said Philip.

"Exactly. Your dad repairs and builds hearts. Whew!" responded Eddie. "That's an amazing skill set."

"Your dad creates buildings and towns. That's pretty amazing too," replied Ben.

"Don't underestimate your skills, my brother," Raymond's smooth baritone intercepted. "I've seen you in the dissection part of our science labs. Dr. Collins is always impressed with your skills in slicing open the cadavers we…."

"Hey! Hey!" yelled Andrew, cutting off Raymond. "Stop it, man! I just finished eating here."

The teens at the tables around them burst out laughing. Andrew looked pale and sweaty, like he was about to vomit up his lunch. Some of his teammates slapped him on the back. Another student-athlete, Dave, who played the tight end position, asked Ben if he would return in time for their game against some other rival before homecoming.

"This is a one-night conference," replied Ben as he rose from his seat. "I fully intend to play out the rest of the season."

The other football players whooped, and Ben grinned.

"That's great to hear because the girls' volleyball games are coming up. We need you guys cheering for them the way we cheer for you all."

"Yeah, my parents won't be at my first game due to a mix-up in scheduling. It will be my first away game without their support," said Amber.

"I'll be here for that game. And you'll always have my support," said Ben. They smiled at each other before Ben looked at Andrew. "Come on, Andy, I'm going to the gym. I can use a sparring partner."

"Aw, man. This should be epic," Eddie said to Philip.

Ben put his finger to his lips and nodded his head toward Kimberly. She was staring at them wide-eyed. Philip and Ben were talking in a low voice. Minetta looked at them and caught Raymond watching her. Darn! Why was he always watching her?

"We'll see you guys in school tomorrow," said Kimberly. "I'll be too tired after cheer practice to do anything but eat and sleep."

Tabitha smiled at Kimberly. Looking at Raymond, she said, "I'll text you when I get home." Raymond smiled.

"See you later, babe," Eddie said to Kimberly, kissing her on the cheek and grabbing his book bag before she could detain him.

Ben waved goodbye to the girls and smiled at Amber. All the males left the cafeteria trailing Ben and Andrew, the latter clutching his stomach. Philip walked out of the cafeteria without a backward glance at Minetta. She exhaled.

In the first away game of the season, Cedar Valley High Cougars football game against rival Central High Stallions was a competitive mashup. Both teams produced three unanimous national championships. The school newspaper profiled the students' school spirit and the student-athletes' determination to win victories for their respective institutions, highlighting the acuity of Philip as quarterback.

Another article detailed the winning athletes' healthy food choices and exercise regimen before and during the height of sports season. Amber took photographs throughout the course of the night when she was not cheering. She caught stunning angles of Philip as quarterback and a few more of Eddie when he made an unexpected touchdown. Minetta had to admit Amber had talent, but she did not have to like it.

In addition, Amber's videography of the Cedar Valley Marching Band's free style performance during halftime earned a four-minute segment on the local news. Closeups of Mark Richards, playing the tenor saxophone, and Joshua Wyatt, blowing the trumpet, were the source for cheerful conversations among their peers, family, and school staff.

The varsity cheerleaders' performance on rival turf was spectacular, and the team received high praise.

The Cedar Valley High Cougars fought for every point they earned, walking away with the winning score, twenty-four to six.

Cedar Valley Cougars hey hey (clap),
We coming right at you hey hey (clap)
Don't be shy and don't be scared (clap)
Cougars about to make your day (clap)(clap)(clap)

Chapter 9

On honeymoon with his new wife Allison in Paris, Dennis Stamps designed the family home from blueprints of early mid-century modern-style residences. The two-story house sat on a limestone foundation that sloped and curved around the building's base, with sliding glass twelve-foot walls connecting the interior rooms and varying exterior patios and balconies overlooking the valley. The state-of-the-art kitchen was a surprise wedding present for his new wife, enjoying success as a sous chef in a five-star restaurant.

As their only child, Eddie had an entire suite to himself on the back of the second floor, with an outdoor patio overlooking the pool grounds below. A glass-encased dormer allowed walk-in space as a playroom, but which later converted to an indoor sauna room.

When Minetta and her parents arrived, the Stamps housekeeper led Minetta to the expansive family room and her parents to an enclosed courtyard. Minetta looked about and sat on one of the plush velvet sofas to wait for her friends. She inspected the room with pleasure. Minetta had always enjoyed being in this space.

Alone, she bowed her head and recited a silent prayer of repentance. She had wanted to refuse to attend this dinner. But could devise no plausible excuse to give her family or friends for not being present at her lifelong friend's eighteenth birthday party. Smoothing down her hair, she looked down at the cranberry-colored lace dress she had bought for the occasion.

She sighed. Tonight's dinner was going to be a long one. A few minutes later, Tabitha and her brothers arrived. The twins, disgruntled because they had lost the battle to wear their favorite footwear from their plentiful collections of sneakers, plopped down on the sofa. Tabitha wore an orange suede dress with a slit at the knee and wide angel sleeves. The girls hugged and sat together on the sofa.

"You look beautiful in that color Tabs," said Minetta.

Tabitha gave her a shy smile. "Thank you, Mimi. Your dress is gorgeous as well."

Eddie entered the room from another doorway. True to his penchant for colors, Eddie wore a royal blue velvet tunic over matching loose-fitting slacks. A silver crucifix hung from his neck. His pompadour was curled high and tapered at his sideburns.

"Hello everybody," he said. "Ed and Henry, come with me. I polished the pool cues just for you."

The twins' jumped up from their chairs.

"Ladies, make yourselves comfortable. I'll be right back." The boys followed Eddie.

The doorbell rang, and a second later, Philip and Raymond entered the room.

"Hey ladies," said Philip as he approached them. He wore a light beige gabardine suit.

"Hi guys," said Minetta. Tabitha smiled.

"Where's our host?" asked Raymond with a smile at Tabitha.

Raymond wore a black textured high-collared suit. His sapphire eyes cast blue slivers of light over his high brown cheekbones.

Tabitha replied, "Eddie brought the twins to the game room." "Hello Ray, you look nice," said Minetta.

"Thank you, Mimi," said Raymond, looking at Tabitha. "You look lovely, Tabs."

"Thank you, Ray," said Tabitha, blushing. "You look handsome yourself."

"Thank you," said Raymond, reaching for her hand.

Philip sighed with exaggeration. "Come on, Mimi, let's leave these two in bedazzlement with each other."

Minetta giggled. Neither one looked in their direction or appeared to have heard Philip's remark. Raymond and Tabitha found a chaise to look out the picture window onto the valley below. Philip led Minetta across the expansive room to a set of velvet-lined chairs.

"They not only make a great-looking couple, but they're also in tune with each other," remarked Philip, watching Raymond and Tabitha.

Minetta remained quiet. Philip turned and spied the appetizer table.

"Ah, food and drink. Want something to drink?"

"That would be nice."

"Be right back."

Minetta sat where she could view the entrance. She was looking at her manicured nails when she glimpsed Amber's parents being ushered to the courtyard, followed by a glimpse of Kimberly's parents with Kelly in tow. Amber entered the room in a cream-colored silk dress with a ballerina neckline that emphasized her curves and gave her a luminous glow. Her blonde waves cascaded over one eye, giving her a glamorous look. Kimberly followed in a pink chiffon dress that flowed over her figure, stopping in a ruffled flounce at the hemline. She pulled her red hair in a half-up-half-down style that hung down her back in tight curls.

Minetta stood up, and the girls hugged.

"You look great, ladies," said Minetta.

"Thanks," said Kimberly, "You look great, too, Mimi."

"Thanks," said Minetta.

Amber looked around the room. "Anyone else here?"

Minetta said, "Tabs and Ray are over there in the corner. Philip went to get drinks."

Turning to Kimberly, she said, "I thought Kelly was going to stay in here with us."

Kimberly laughed. "Believe me; she is not interested in us. Where's our host?"

At that moment Eddie entered the room from the kitchen and walked over to Kimberly. He smiled at Minetta and Amber. Taking Kimberly's hand, they walked towards where Raymond and Tabitha were sitting. They stood talking with Eddie's hand resting lightly on Kimberly's back.

Philip entered the room carrying a napkin-covered glass in each hand. He handed Minetta the glass filled with ice cubes and red liquid.

"Hey, those drinks look good," she said.

"I thought you might go for the bright colored one." He looked at Amber, a big smile spreading across his face. Minetta turned away.

"Hi Amber. You look great."

"Thank you, Phil. Did you just get here?"

"A few minutes ago. Let me get you something to drink. Any preference?"

"I'll have what you're having. Looks yummy."

Philip handed her his glass. "Here, I'll get another."

"Thank you, Phil."

Amber walked over to the chairs where Minetta was sitting. Philip was still smiling as his eyes wandered over Amber's retreating figure. As Amber sat beside her, Philip realized Minetta's presence and saw her stern glare. He turned and fled the room.

"Seems like this is going to be nice," said Amber, looking about the room. She took a sip of her drink.

"Yes, Eddie's mom used to be a chef. She now owns La Dolce Vita Restaurant in Town Square."

"This house is amazing. His dad builds houses, right?"

"Yes. The Stamps family designed most of Cedar Valley Township."

"Impressive," she said. She looked at Minetta and looked at her dress from the high collar to the hem. She smiled. "You have a delicate figure. You should have worn the belt with that dress."

Minetta frowned. "What makes you think it had a belt?"

"Your right; it wasn't a belt. It was a wide sash. Either way, it would have shown off that great waistline." She took a sip of her drink. "The gorgeous Ray's father is the chief of surgery at the hospital, isn't he? Lots of doctors in this town."

"What's the point of these senseless questions? You know what everyone's parents do for a living."

Amber laughed. "Calm down. Just trying to make conversation."

Philip returned without a drink. He sat across from them in an armchair, looking worried. The housekeeper led Andrew and Ben's parents to the courtyard. Eddie and Kimberly went to the games room with Mark and Joshua.

"Ben and Andrew just arrived with members of your cheer squad," said Philip, as he watched the group depart the family room.

"Andrew asked about you, Mimi."

Andrew and Ben walked into the room and toward them. Philip stood up and shook hands with both young men. Andrew was wearing a deep blue unstructured suit that made him look enormous and more ungainly than usual. His white-blonde crew cut had grown higher, and he had tapered the sides close to his head. A diamond earring dangled in one ear.

"Hey man, hiya doing?" Andrew said to Philip before shaking hands. He looked at Minetta. "Hi, Mimi, you look pretty."

Minetta smiled. "Thanks, Andrew."

"Hi Andy," said Amber. "Hi, Ben."

The young men gazed with admiration at Amber. Ben, standing beside Andrew, looked as if he had stepped out of a gentleman's top fashion magazine. He was wearing a dark red plaid blazer and loose-fitting tailored slacks. His braids flowed unrestrained and loose about his shoulders, cascading down his back. Amber gazed at Ben, who was staring at her. He smiled, and she blushed.

Ben turned to Philip. "Where is everybody?"

"Everyone must be in the games room. I think Eddie was setting up for a game of cards or a game of pool. Take your pick. You know Eddie."

The girls stared at Ben. Minetta had never paid much attention to him. Although she had grown up with him, and he had always been in several of her Advanced Placement Honors classes at school.

"I'll go check out the games room," said Ben. He looked over at Amber. "Would you accompany me?"

"I would love to," Amber said.

Smiling, she handed Philip her glass in passing. Minetta watched them walk away. Ben's hand rested on the small of Amber's back as they departed the room. The gesture seemed familiar to Minetta, but she could not think why. Philip sat down, and Andrew cleared his throat.

"Want to come with me to the games room," he asked Minetta. "The housekeeper said they were waiting for more guests to arrive."

Minetta smiled at Andrew. "Sure, why not?"

She linked her arm through his as they walked away. Tossing her hair back, she laughed at one of Andrew's lame jokes, but she never looked back. She was fuming. Philip, infatuated with Amber, never noticed, or remarked on her new outfit. She had bought this new dress especially for this dinner. Hey Amber, you look great! It hurt her watching Philip devour Amber with his eyes.

She noticed the other guys were friendly enough toward her, but they remembered they had girlfriends. Whenever this girl was around, Philip treated her like a third wheel that was smothering him. She believed Amber enjoyed making her uncomfortable, and she found her actions as intolerable as Philip's.

The Stamps dinner guests dined in the formal dining room and mingled outside on the tree-lined terrace overlooking the valley. As the evening skies darkened, the Stamps turned on the courtyard lights, and dance music piped in. The parents left the young people in the courtyard. Minetta ignored Philip for the rest of the dinner, enjoying the nightfall with her friends. Much later, amid a sparkling light display by the in-ground pool, his parents returned with Eddie's birthday cake. The servers had given each guest a glass filled with champagne.

Dennis Stamps walked to the center of the courtyard with his wife, Allison. Eddie was a walking replica of his father only taller. Dennis raised his champagne glass. "May I have everyone's attention, please. To our son, Eddie. It's been a joy raising you. Your natural inquisitiveness and thirst for living while remaining alive for another day has brought great joy to us," said Dennis to much laughter from the assembled guests.

"Friends, please join me in welcoming our only child into adulthood. Happy birthday, son!"

To proclamations of "happy birthday, Eddie," Allison hugged her son, her eyes misting up. Dennis and Eddie hugged in a bear hug. Allison pulled Kimberly to her and hugged her as well. Dennis kissed Kimberly's cheek.

Eddie said, "this has been a great birthday with all my friends here. Of course, no celebration would be complete without my best friend, my beautiful girlfriend, Kimberly, by my side. Thank you for coming babe."

"Aw," said Lisa Van Owens, her long red curls waved over her shoulders. Her husband, Robert, smiled and waved his glass at Eddie while putting an arm around his wife's waist.

"Is that it, Dennis?" asked Charles Mason, his deep blue eyes merry with laughter. Raymond's mother, Elizabeth, standing regal beside her husband smiled.

"A young man turns eighteen and there's only champagne?" joined in Thomas Brown.

Julianne, standing next to her sons, Henry, and Edward, said to Allison, "I know there's a surprise birthday cake."

"I doubt if there's just a cake, Julianne," said Bob Paige with his wife Marcie and daughter Amber on each side of him.

"Just when I was trying to watch my waistline," groaned James Morgan. All the adults laughed.

Eric Richards, standing between his wife Michelle and their sons, Ben, and Mark, stated, "I'm sure we can put you on a healthy nutrition plan after this party, Jim."

"Just make sure I know about the plan, Eric, so I can keep him on it," said Marilyn. Everyone laughed again.

Harold and Joyce Wyatt standing next to James and Marilyn were laughing at the faces Eddie was making as he looked around the patio. Dennis and Allison beckoned to the servers who brought out a rolling table on which sat a three-layered chocolate cake decorated in multi-colored icing and topped with the number eighteen in a bright orange candle. Eddie's face broke out into a huge grin. Holding Kimberly's hand, he walked near to the cake. His mother lit the candle. Eddie closed his eyes and blew out the candle to applause.

"Hey Eddie, what did you wish for?" asked Andrew.

"Ah! It's not what he wished for, but what he did not wish for," replied Allison.

Dennis said, "Eddie, we know you love your car. Since you'll be attending college in a few months, your mother and I thought you needed an upgrade."

Allison, leaned around her husband and handed Eddie a set of car keys.

The applause was deafening. The entire party followed Eddie and Kimberly around to the front of the house. In the driveway sat a deeper orange four-door sport utility vehicle. Eddie grabbed Kimberly in a bear hug and, then he hugged his parents. The teens gathered around Eddie's new vehicle.

"What a nice set of wheels," said Ben, examining the interior.

"It will never get lost on a parking lot," exclaimed Raymond.

"Dad, we're going for a spin," said an exuberant Eddie.

"Okay, son. Be careful, please. I know you're excited, but watch your speed," said Dennis.

"I will, Dad. I promise. Come on, babe."

Eddie climbed in the car with Kimberly. The young people began pairing up to follow Eddie in their vehicles.

Allison turned to their guests. "I think it's safe to say the young people will be out here awhile."

"At least," said Joyce.

"Come on ladies, and help me get the dessert set up. I also have sorbet to go with the cake," said Allison as she made her way to the back patio.

"Mmm...I love sorbet," said Michelle.

"Remember that little Italian ice cream shop that was around the corner from the school?" said Stacy.

"The mom and pop shop?" asked Allison.

"Which one?" asked Joyce. "I remember there being two."

"I think you're talking about the bistro," replied Michelle.

Marilyn agreed. "Exactly. The mom-and-pop shop sold water ices, ice cream, and hotdogs."

"I remember it," said Julianne, her long brown hair engulfing her petite frame.

"Well, that shop is where they sold sorbet," said Marilyn.

Stacy laughed. "We almost got caught one night sneaking in past curfew with our water ices. Remember that?"

A few of the ladies laughed recalling that experience as they followed Allison back to the patio. The men stood in the driveway talking among themselves and watching the teens as they formed car groups.

Andrew looked at Minetta. "You want to ride with me?"

"No thanks, Andrew."

Minetta saw Amber walking towards Philip's vehicle. She turned and followed her mother. She did not care to see anything else.

Chapter 10

Cedar Valley Church's youth center located directly behind the main sanctuary in an adjoining building housing classrooms, a nurse's station, a chapel, and a fellowship hall with an attached kitchen. The monthly youth Bible studies group met monthly. Minetta's father, Reverend Doctor James Morgan, as he was formally known, had pastored Cedar Valley Church before her birth. Most of the people she saw in the worship center were the same ones with whom she had grown up.

Raymond entered the room along with several other young people.

"Hey, ladies."

"Hi Ray," said Kimberly.

Raymond looked at Tabitha and smiled. "You want to sit down?"

"Yes. I want to show you this article I've been reading." As she walked across the room, Tabitha turned to Amber, "you can sit with us."

"That's okay," said Amber. "You go ahead." She smiled.

Tabitha joined Raymond, who was holding the back of a chair for her. Amber kept staring at them.

She whispered to Kimberly, "wow! He is truly gorgeous! He could be a model."

Kimberly looked over at them. "So is Tabs. They make a great-looking couple."

"Are they a couple?"

"Not officially. We can all actively date once we graduate high school or turn eighteen, whichever comes first."

Kimberly walked around Amber to follow Minetta to empty seats in the middle of the room. Amber followed, sitting next to Minetta, who pulled out her workbook and lesson plan. Philip and Eddie, along with a group of

Cedar Valley High athletes, walked in. Eddie immediately sat in the seat next to Kimberly, who had put her book bag there. Philip sat behind Minetta and Amber, although Minetta had saved a seat for him beside her.

During the break, Minetta returned to find Philip seated between her and Amber.

"Oh, I asked Phil to join us instead of sitting behind us. I hope you don't mind," said Amber in a soft voice.

"Not at all. I was saving a seat for him, but he sat behind us."

"Oh, you should have said something. This arrangement is better, though. I get to talk to both of you."

Minetta said nothing. Amber smiled at him. At the end of class, the teens gathered in the fellowship hall for refreshments before going home.

"Where were you?" asked Philip when he spotted Minetta walking into the classroom.

"I was in the kitchen. I was looking for a cup of yogurt," Minetta stammered. "Seems the staff forgot to put it out tonight."

"Mimi, I already have your yogurt. You didn't think I would let them forget your favorite treat, did you?"

He handed her the container with a plastic spoon wrapped in a paper napkin. They walked to the table where their friends were sitting. Seated next to Raymond was Amber typing on her gold-colored phone. She looked up as Philip and Minetta sat down.

"Phil tells me you guys have known each other since your diaper days."

"Our diaper days? Then, yes, we have known each other all our lives," responded Minetta.

Philip smiled as he tipped his water bottle to his lips. Amber kept her gaze on Minetta, who was busy opening her yogurt cup.

"That goes for the group. We've grown up together," Kimberly inserted.

Amber spoke in a soft murmur. "It must be nice. Having a group of friends, you've known all your life."

Philip's phone buzzed; he read the text and put the instrument in his pocket. Amber looked down in her hand at her phone which was silently buzzing. After typing a message, she pulled car keys out of her tote.

"Hey guys, it was fun being in class together. But, I've got to head home now," she said.

Kimberly looked around. "Wait a minute. How are you getting home? You came with us."

Amber smiled nervously. "My car is here."

"Your car is here?" repeated Minetta.

"Did you call an Uber?"

"No," said Amber as she gathered her belongings. "Our housekeeper brought it. I need to stop somewhere before going home."

She stood up. Philip stood as well. "I'll walk you out."

Amber put a hand on Philip's chest, restraining him. "No, stay with your friends. I'm fine."

Philip gently removed her hand. "I understand that, but I'm still walking you out."

The firmness in his voice caused her to relent. As they walked out of the room, Minetta followed them outside. She stood in the doorway behind the screen, watching Philip walk across the parking lot with Amber. They were nearly the same height. They were too far away for her to hear their words. She watched as Amber unlocked her car door. Philip leaned on the car window ledge and whatever he said caused Amber to look up at him and laugh. Amber's golden hair glowed in the shadows of the moonlit night. Minetta continued to watch as Philip regaled Amber with conversation that caused her to render soft peals of laughter into the night air. As she watched them, pangs of jealousy ignited in Minetta's heart and simmered.

Philip straightened and Amber sped by him in her convertible, honking the horn. He smiled and waved after the retreating car. He was walking back across the lot when a pickup truck came speeding out of the dark. Philip jumped to the side as the vehicle sped by. The momentum caused him to stumble and fall. Minetta's eyes grew large, and she cried out when she saw Philip crumble to the ground. Pushing the screen door open, she rushed to his side.

"Are you okay?" asked Minetta, stooping to help him to his feet.

"Yeah, Mimi, I'm fine." He dusted himself off. "Did you get the license plate number?"

"No, I didn't see him until he was on you."

"Well, I think it was a guy, but the lights blinded me."

He looked around as two men approached. Deacon Eldridge was a retired police detective and the head of church security.

"Are you okay, Philip?" asked Deacon Hall, a family practitioner at Cedar Valley Medical Center. "How's your wrist?"

"Yes. I jumped out of the way so as not to get hit."

"Good thinking and good reflexes, son," replied Eldridge. "You never want to play hero with your life."

Another man walked up. Deacon Gray, hearing the commotion, joined the group.

"What's going on out here?"

"It seems someone was speeding in the parking lot," replied Eldridge.

Philip was embarrassed and slightly irritated. "Who speeds through a church parking lot, anyway?"

"Good question," replied Hall, examining Philip's wrist for injury.

"Were you able to get his tag number?" asked Gray.

"No, he went by too fast," said Philip.

"Why were you both outside?" Gray asked, looking from Philip to Minetta.

"I was walking someone to her car. The truck came out after she pulled off," replied Philip.

"How much after?" asked Eldridge, curtly. "Did the truck follow the young lady?"

"No," said Philip. "It turned left. Amber turned right."

"Is she the new girl?" inquired Gray.

"Yes," said Minetta. "I brought her tonight."

"What's her name?" Gray asked, taking out a notepad.

"Amber Paige."

"Bob and Marcie Paige's daughter?" asked Hall.

"Yes."

Gray walked back toward the building. "Okay. Let me call her parents as a precaution."

Eldridge took charge. "Okay, you two kids, get back inside. We'll take over from here. You have a few minutes until we close for the night."

The deacon punched numbers on his cellphone. He walked away from them with the instrument to his ear. Minetta could have sworn it was her father's voice she overheard speaking with Eldridge. A chill enveloped her, and she trembled slightly.

"Mimi are you okay?" asked Hall. He looked at Minetta with concern on his face.

"Yes, it just happened so fast, Deacon Hall," she stammered. In a shaky voice, she said, "Philip almost got hit."

"You're shaking a bit. You want to call your parents?"

"No, I'm okay," she said.

Eldridge walked back toward them. He looked with concern at Minetta before transferring his gaze to Philip.

"Take her inside, Philip, and send the guys out here. I want to talk to only the guys, you included. Okay?"

Philip nodded. He looked down at Minetta and placed an arm around her shoulders. She folded her arms across her chest. They looked at each other wordlessly and returned inside to their friends.

Later, Philip drove behind Minetta on the way home. He waited as she parked in her driveway and exited with Kimberly and Tabitha. Philip beeped his horn once as the girls each entered their homes.

Chapter 11

The annual alumni-sponsored football game was always the highlight of Cedar Valley High's Alumni Week. The cheerleading squad was a part of the scheduled activities. In her role as team captain, Minetta led the school's cheerleading squad in a practice session. As she took to the field in a series of brisk leaps, she noticed the confused look on the faces of the other cheerleaders.

Kimberly whispered, "Mimi, we're doing Amber's choreography from last Thursday's practice."

"Oh? Sorry," she mumbled. In mid-step, Minetta effortlessly switched her routine, and the others joined in.

After cheer practice, Minetta weaved her way through the crowded hallways to the athletic department and the private offices of the lead coaching staff. There were two students in the outer vestibule, but Minetta paid little notice of them. She was intent on finding Coach Sarah. She burst into the office, banging the door hard against the wall.

Startled, the coach seated behind her desk looked up at Minetta.

"Good afternoon Minetta. Are you okay?"

Minetta's voice was tense. "Since when is a team captain's choreography switched without her input or knowledge?"

"I don't know what you mean, Minetta, but you know we switch choreography all the time."

"I know that coach. I've been in cheer since middle school."

"So, what's the problem?" asked Sarah. "You know the choreography, as evidenced by your outstanding performance today."

"Of course, I know the choreography. I was there during rehearsals."

"Then I don't understand what you're upset about," said Sarah, keeping her voice level.

"What I am upset about is that we didn't agree to perform this choreography today."

The coach continued to look up at Minetta. She beckoned to a chair by her desk.

"Sit down, Minetta, so that we can discuss your concerns, and please close the door."

Minetta glared down at the coach. "Give me a break. If you cared to discuss my concerns, we would have had this talk before now."

"We voted on this change at tryouts and it's what we've been practicing for pep rallies and spirit week. These new routines have become our standard routines, replacing the old ones."

"Standard routines? Who decided that coach?"

"I decided it, Minetta, and I've said it at every practice. As team captain, I gave you the choreography for your book, and to learn with your team. You had no questions, concerns, or complaints then."

"Because I didn't know we were replacing our regular routines!"

Sarah, keeping her tone leveled, folded her hands, and patiently explained.

"It's in the packet you brought home a few weeks ago. We decided last year to implement some fresh changes to our routines. You agreed, so I don't know what has changed. But we can go back to some of the old routines this year if that makes you more comfortable. But as team captain, I expect you to tell the girls we are returning to some of our old routines and explain why."

Minetta glared down at Sarah. "Oh no, you're not making me the villain here, coach."

"The villain? What are you talking about?" said Sarah, throwing up her hands. "You're the one upset over the new routines. The routines that you voted on and learned by heart."

"I just don't understand these drastic changes."

"I thought our dances and chants needed more vibrancy. We've been doing many of the same routines since I was on the squad. It was time for a change."

Flashbacks of previous cheer practices came to Minetta.

"You didn't think we needed more vibrancy until Amber joined the squad."

"That's where you're wrong. We're stuck in a rut, and I'm not ashamed to say that. Amber brought new life into our routines."

"That's fine, coach, but you should have waited until next summer's camp to introduce new choreography."

"Look, Mimi, you're a senior this year, and what you've accomplished as captain with varsity cheer has been great; however, I have to think ahead for the new squad next year. That means beginning this year making some changes with introducing new stuff. As team captain, you want to be in on the recent changes and help by leading them."

"I think your bias is showing, coach. I heard none of this awakening nonsense until Amber showed up."

"Amber and I have been talking. Her ideas have been innovative and on-point," said Sarah. "Much as your ideas were several years ago. I did the same thing then as I'm doing now. I introduced new choreography to the team, and that team captain did not cause a scene in my office."

"That's great, coach, but I should have approved all this. What you've done is gone behind my back, which is unethical. You know it, and so do I."

Sarah sighed. "Let's get something straight. I'm the coach. I make the final decisions based on what I believe will help our team thrive. We have an award-winning championship cheer squad that is the envy of every high school in this state."

"I know that" screamed Minetta. "I've been a part of this championship team since the ninth grade, remember?"

"Yes, I remember," shouted Sarah. "But do you remember bringing me ideas for the routines we had been doing then? When you introduced your ideas, those team captains cheered you on, encouraged you. Do you remember that?"

Minetta lowered her voice. "Whatever. All I know is you weren't thinking about changing our routines until Amber came along."

"That's not altogether true. Like a championship team, we have to bring new routines to our competitions."

"But you changed nothing until Amber arrived," fumed Minetta.

"That's because neither you nor Kim brought me any new routines. Amber sat in on one practice and immediately came up with some clever moves that the other cheerleaders loved, including you, at one point."

"I didn't say her moves weren't good," admitted Minetta. "I just don't see why we have to change our routines this year."

Sarah slowly stood up and placed both hands firmly on the top of her desk. With a stern face, she looked Minetta squarely in the eye.

"Here's a request for you, Mimi. We return to our former routines, and you tell the squad why or stay with the new stuff. Which is it?"

"Keep the new stuff. I'll be out of here soon enough."

She stormed out of the coach's office, grabbing the knob and pulling the door with her. The door slammed hard, making the glass pane rattle. She nearly collided with Ben and Raymond in the outer vestibule, not recognizing either in her passionate fury. Both young men watched Minetta storm down the hall, oblivious to the fact that Raymond and Ben had heard her tirade in its entirety.

Chapter 12

The homecoming game was in two weeks. Minetta was in the schoolyard, sweating heavily, and squinting against the late afternoon sun as she led the girls in one of the older cheer routines. The varsity cheerleaders had the moves memorized, but they needed to synchronize with the squad's newest members.

"Okay, ladies, let's get in formation." Minetta closed her notebook. She pointed to where she wanted Kimberly to stand.

"I need you over here, Kim, and you over there, Janie. Now, listen up, ladies. We will run through this last routine one time only. I need Sam, Vanessa, Amber, Tabitha, Lynn, Karen, Gloria, Susan, and Carole on the front line, and everyone else behind them. Tania in the middle in the second row, please."

Minetta was about to perform her infamous double back flip and land in a split. It was always a crowd-pleaser. She surveyed the lineup once more.

"Who's missing?"

"Sorry, Mimi." The voice belonged to Sallie, a senior on the varsity squad. "We were on the track field."

Minetta waited while Annette, Patricia, Linda, Veronica, and Jewel joined the lineup. These girls, like Kimberly and Amber, were considered the school's 'super-athletes' because they competed in two or more sports, and were national and regional champions.

"Alright," yelled Minetta. "Let's go."

As the girls moved in rhythm to the chant, Minetta prepared to do her triple back flip. She made two offbeat steps, realized she had a problem in mid-air, but could not make herself stop. The first back flip was clumsy and caused her to turn prematurely. Even as she was falling Claire, her spotter, was attempting to catch her. Minetta's descent was quick and hard. She landed on her ankle in an awkward position, but managed to twist herself to offset pressure on the ankle bone. The resounding pain instantly skyrocketed up her leg. With a bit of outcry, she rolled onto her side and let out a gasp of pain. Claire fell to her knees in tears and Mike, her boyfriend, put his arm around her shoulders.

"Mimi, you, okay?" she heard the anguish in Amber's voice through the sounds of her wretched sobs.

Minetta choked out, "my ankle," as she writhed in pain. She could hear her teammates' muffled sobs and saw Kimberly and Tabitha down on their knees beside her with tears in their eyes.

"Mimi, don't cry," Tabitha said, as tears rolled down her face.

Linda, Ellen, and Jewel ran to get the coach who had gone into the girls' locker room. Sam and Karen were trying to calm Minetta, who was on the verge of hysteria. All activity had stopped across the field as the girls' screams caught the football players' attention. Coach Don came running across the field with Philip, Raymond, Ben, and Eddie close behind.

Sarah, on her knees by a wailing Minetta, looked up with a worried expression. "Coach, could you help me get her to the locker room?"

Theo and Sam moved to help Minetta, but Philip sidestepped them, and picked Minetta up. He carried her inside, followed by Tabitha, Lizzie, Kelly, and the rest of the cheerleaders. The football players on the field cheered, howled, and clapped. Ben had walked over and was hugging a distraught Amber by the side of the bleachers. Eddie, stood a little way off, watching Ben and Amber before returning to his teammates.

Philip deposited Minetta on a bench inside the locker room and gently removed her arms from around his neck. The cheerleaders pushed him out of the way and gathered around a weeping Minetta. Sarah thanked Don and Philip for their help. Raymond, consoling a weepy Tabitha, walked out with the coach and Philip.

"Kim, please go down to the nurse's station and ask one of them to come here," said Sarah. "Where's Amber?"

"Here I am," said Amber, walking into the room. Her eyes were red.

"Please finish up with the cheerleaders and tell Tania she will be our flyer for next Saturday's game."

Amber said, "okay, coach."

Minetta was writhing in pain. The coach sent the rest of the cheerleaders outside, as some had broken down into tears. She allowed Tabitha to stay with Minetta, whose crying was inconsolable.

Claire, sobbing as hard as Minetta, said to Sarah, "I tried to catch her, coach. She just came down so fast."

"Mimi is pretty fast with those turns," said Mike. "I hope her ankle's not broken."

Claire started sobbing again. Sarah's eyes grew misty. "It's okay, Claire. Her ankle doesn't look broken to me. She will be fine. Accidents are a part of any sports activity. She'll be fine."

Kimberly returned with one of the on-duty nurses. After looking at the swollen ankle, the nurse instructed Sarah to send for an ambulance and placed a call to Minetta's parents.

James and Marilyn sat in the visitor's lounge at Cedar Valley Medical Center. They were holding each other with their eyes closed, deep in prayer. They had never had to visit the hospital for one of their children. Matthew, like his father, was involved in a multitude of sports but had never been injured. They worried about the extent of Minetta's injuries. A nurse in blue scrubs and a messy blonde ponytail approached them.

"Hello? Are you Minetta's parents?"

"Yes, we are," replied James.

"Your daughter is fine," she said. "Dr. Richards is our resident orthopedic surgeon. She would like to see you both before releasing your daughter. Please follow me."

"Can we see our daughter first?" asked Marilyn.

"Yes. Of course. I'm sorry. She's right this way."

She led them down a corridor into a room where they saw Minetta lying back on a hospital bed. Her foot and ankle bandaged up to mid-calf, she was still in her cheer outfit. Marilyn gave a little gasp and rushed to the bedside. Minetta opened her eyes.

"Hi, Mom. Don't cry. I'm okay," she said groggily.

The nurse said to James. "She's been given some pain medicine. She will be a little groggy, but she's fine."

James, watching Marilyn, smiled somberly. "Can we see the doctor now, please?"

He walked over to his wife and gently lifted her to her feet. "Come on, baby. Let's see the doctor, and then we can take her home."

He leaned over and softly kissed his daughter's forehead. Her eyes fluttered slightly. They followed the nurse down another corridor and stopped before a door bearing the inscription: Dr. Michelle Richards. She knocked twice, and they entered. A tall, elegant-looking woman in a white doctor's coat sat behind a large oak desk.

"Thank you, Joan," Michelle said to the nurse.

"Hello James, Marilyn. It's good to see you both again, although not under these circumstances."

She beckoned to two chairs. "Please sit down. I don't want to alarm you because Mimi's injury was minor. This is not a serious sprain, but with more weight, she could have broken it. The good news is that she's healthy, and the ankle should heal in about six weeks."

"Will she need medication?"

"No medication will be needed," replied Michelle. "If she complains about the pain, I'll give you a non-refillable pain prescription that you can give her. However, with elevation and ice packs to help the swelling go down, she should experience minimum pain."

"What about school?" asked James.

Michelle smiled. "I suggest a few days of staying off that ankle. Then she can return to school. We will give her crutches to help make it easier to get around."

Marilyn sighed. "Thank you so much, Michelle. We thought she had broken it."

Michelle laughed. "Then it's a good thing you weren't in here when she arrived on a stretcher. Such a drama queen. It makes me thankful I have two sons."

James joined Michelle in laughter. "Yes, that's our Mimi."

Marilyn sighed. "I'm only glad it wasn't worse. This year is Minetta's senior year. As it is, she won't make the homecoming dance."

Michelle frowned. "She can attend homecoming events. Her ankle will be better by then. At least enough that she can attend the dance."

James shook his head. “Our little diva will most likely be right at home. I would be surprised if she went.”

Michelle smiled wisely. “I’m not a betting woman, but if I were, I would bet you she’s going to make the dance. It’s a big deal as a senior.”

“That’s true. Remember when Allison sprang her ankle two days before my wedding?” said Marilyn.

“Do I ever. She cried all day and night but managed to look beautiful for the day.”

James looked from his wife to the doctor. “When was this? I don’t remember Allison in crutches.”

“That’s because she was wearing a long dress and spent most of the time sitting down,” replied Marilyn.

Michelle laughed. “How about when Bob showed up in crutches on his wedding day?”

James laughed. “Yeah, Marcie wasn’t too happy with him.”

“What woman would be?” asked Marilyn.

“Maybe its why I went into orthopedics. To keep my friends bones together.”

“Now you’re working on our children,” said James, laughing.

“Can we take Minetta home now?”

“Of course, Marilyn. I’ll sign her release papers now, and here’s a non-refillable pain prescription.”

“Thank you, Michelle. We must have you and Eric over for dinner sometimes. We miss hanging out with you guys.”

“I can’t believe Eric is a heart surgeon the way he used to play football,” exclaimed Marilyn.

Michelle countered. “Um, excuse me, but whose husband is a peace-loving pastor who also played football? I recall James was fierce on the field as a defensive end.”

James laughed. “Eric was a great quarterback, and we had some great times together. He took that concentration and intellect into the operating room. I’m proud of my friend.”

“So am I. It seems like yesterday we were standing at each other’s weddings. Returning home was a godsend for us.”

"Where does the time go? I'm so happy you guys are back home here," said Marilyn, smiling at her.

"It's good to be back, and so good seeing you both at Eddie's birthday dinner. It was also good to see Thomas and Julianne again as well."

"The old group back together, again," said James. "Those were good times."

"Yes, they were," agreed Michelle. "Speaking of which, Allison truly outdid herself for Liz and Charles anniversary dinner. That evening reminded me of all those weekends in the sorority house when she would cook for the House when the staff wasn't there. Remember that Marilyn?"

"Do I ever? I was always nervous someone would squeal on us, or something would happen."

"Yes, you were always a worrywart."

"How do you like the remodeled restaurant?" asked James.

Michelle's eyes lit up. "Beautiful atmosphere. That was the first thing Eric noticed being the son of a chef. I am sure Dennis had a hand in its formation."

James laughed. "Exactly right, Michelle."

"Eric and I love her restaurant."

"The meal she put together for Eddie's birthday party was scrumptious, as well," said Michelle.

"Wasn't that a fabulous meal? I loved the sorbet on the side with that delicious cake."

"Tell me about it. I always think to heck with diets when Allison is near a kitchen."

"Fabulous evening of food, friends, and fun times."

James rubbed his stomach. "Yes, it was."

The three long-time friends laughed warmly together.

Chapter 13

The homecoming game found Minetta sitting in the bleachers in her cheer uniform with her leg in a medical boot that covered her leg from ankle to mid-calf. Her crutches were leaning against a pole. James had insisted on half-carrying her to the stands. Marilyn made her promise not to move unless she was going to the bathroom. Minetta was almost certain her mother was watching her through binoculars. Matthew had come down to watch the game with a few of his fraternity brothers who had also attended Cedar Valley High. Minetta balanced the school-issued laptop on her thighs and typed notes to herself about the game. Although her ankle was still healing, much of the pain and swelling had subsided.

Cedar Valley High's football team was playing against the Northwest High Falcons. As Minetta watched Amber's cheer skills on the sidelines, her mood alternated between admiration for her rival and anger at herself for being careless. During a break in the game, she saw Amber taking photos of the football players, cheerleaders, and some teachers scattered with their families in the bleachers. Engrossed watching Amber, she did not notice when Philip came running to her from the locker room. Startled, she looked down at a white paper bag he was holding out to her.

"What's this?" She peered inside the bag at the heart-shaped box of chocolates and smiled.

"Something to cheer you up." Philip took off his helmet. Sweat covered his head.

"Thank you, Philip. This candy is so sweet."

"You look so pretty over here. I know you're in pain, but I'm glad you came to the game."

"I wouldn't miss it," she said. She smiled, and Philip returned her smile. She popped a chocolate in her mouth. "Besides, I have to write about the homecoming game for the newspaper."

"Yeah, Amber's already sent me lots of photos to include with your byline."

"Hey, Jones!"

Coach Sloan ran towards Philip, who grinned at Minetta before putting his helmet on and sprinting in the opposite direction, away from the approaching man. He waved as he disappeared down the runway to the athletes' locker room, followed by the coach. She giggled. Her mood had perked up considerably. The Cedar Valley High Cougars football team scored successfully against the Northwest High Falcons with a wide margin of twenty-one to seven.

The homecoming dance was turning out to be a tragic event for Minetta. Although she had bought a dark blue silk dress for the occasion, she was depressed as she sat at a table watching the other students dance and enjoy themselves. Philip could not attend the dance. He was home recuperating from a cold.

She was sitting because her ankle was still too sore if standing on for long periods. She had to lean on the crutches for support. She glanced down at them neatly stacked under the table. She was wearing one dark blue pump with the other in her closet at home. Her parents wrapped her foot and ankle in a shoe cast. She watched with crestfallen eyes the approaching figures of Tabitha and Raymond. Tabitha handed Minetta a gray tablet with the school's logo engraved on the front.

"Hey Mimi, I thought you might want the school tablet to type notes," said Tabitha. She was wearing a purple chiffon dress.

"Might take the edge off your boredom with having to sit at this table," remarked Raymond, clad in a blue serge suit.

"Philip would have taken pics if he were here," said Tabitha, smiling.

"Thanks. I guess I can write something while I am stuck in this chair," Minetta said crossly.

"The outline for your article about the dance would be appropriate, as you can't move anywhere," offered Raymond. The blue of his suit intensified the deepness of his sapphire eyes.

Minetta slightly sneered. "You two are just so helpful, aren't you?"

They laughed. Still grinning, Raymond stood up. "Come on, Tabs, let's get away from all this negativity." He led Tabitha to the dance floor.

"Traitors," called Minetta after them.

She adjusted the bottom of her dress and looked up to see Mark, Kelly, and Lizzie coming towards her, with Andrew and Joshua walking behind them.

"Hi Mimi," said Kelly, her red curls cascading in wild abandon over her deep green dress. She was the image of her older sister.

"Are you feeling any better? Did you get the box I sent you?"

Minetta smiled at Lizzie in her yellow taffeta dress. She resembled her brother, with her long dark hair framing her blue-gray eyes.

"Yes, I did," replied Minetta. "As always, I appreciate your kindness and thoughtfulness, Lizzie. I sent you a thank-you card in the mail."

"Oh, thank you, Mimi. That is so considerate."

Andrew was standing to the side with his hands in his pockets, looking at Minetta's crutches. He was wearing a black suit with a buttoned collar shirt. Mark, beside him, reminded Minetta of his handsome older brother. He sported braids like Ben but kept his shorter as he was on the wrestling team. Mark's best friend and wrestling peer was Joshua, Andrew's younger brother. Joshua was tall and built physically, like Mark. Joshua had thick, dishwater blonde hair and a well-trimmed beard. He wore his long hair in man buns most of the time except for now when it was loose and flowing to his shoulders.

Mark handed Minetta a bouquet of pink and lilac nosegays.

"Thank you, Mark."

Mark blushed. "You're welcome. Sorry about your accident."

"You feeling better?" asked Joshua, giving her a bunch of wildflowers.

"Thank you. My ankle is still sore but not as bad as it once was," Minetta said, holding onto her flowers. "You guys go have fun. You don't need to babysit me."

Kelly smiled. "We just wanted to check on you. Not just because you're the captain of our cheer squad but as a friend, too."

"You guys are so sweet. Thank you," said Minetta. "Now shoo! Go have fun."

"Feel better soon. Catch you later," said Andrew as he ushered the group towards the auditorium. Minetta smiled when she saw Mark move around Andrew to walk beside Kelly, and Joshua position himself beside Lizzie.

Kimberly and Eddie walked over from the opposite side of the room where they had gathered with other students from the track and field team. Kimberly, in a mustard yellow dress, balanced out Eddie's crème and purple striped suit. They sat down next to her.

"Are you okay, bestie?" asked Kimberly.

"I'm okay, bestie," said Minetta. "I guess I shouldn't have come since I can't stand for a good two minutes without being in pain."

"I know."

"Hey Mimi, why don't I get you something to eat," said Eddie, standing up. "You'll feel better."

Not waiting for a response, he headed for the banquet table in the adjoining room. Kimberly, cast a sad look after his departing form.

"Eddie feels bad that Philip couldn't be here."

"Yeah, but if you think about it, he would have been busy with Amber, anyway."

"Here comes Amber now."

"Hey Minetta," said Amber as she and Ben sat down at the table. "We not too long ago spoke to Tabitha and Ray. Ben came up with an idea that we think will help cheer you up."

Minetta cast a suspicious eye at Amber and remained mute. Amber wore a blue organza dress that brought out the blue in her eyes. Ben was in a blue striped suit with his braids held neatly at the nape of his neck.

Kimberly smirked. "By all means, tell the girl what it is. She's dying over here."

Amber laughed, and her foot accidentally touched Minetta's ankle, incurring stinging pain and causing her to grimace.

"I'm sorry. Are you okay?" asked Amber worriedly.

Minetta said tersely, "I'm fine. What do you want?"

Ben, ignoring her rudeness to Amber, said, "when I was out of town and couldn't make the relays, Phil video streamed the game to me."

Minetta looked at Ben with a quizzical stare. Amber and Kimberly grinned broadly. "What do you mean?"

"We thought you could video chat the dance highlights with Phil as if he were here," Ben informed her. "What do you say?"

Minetta smiled, forgetting her discomfort. "That's a great idea!"

"May I?" asked Amber, reaching for the laptop on the table. Minetta nodded. She watched as Amber typed in a code, and the screen opened.

"Here you go!" Amber returned the laptop to Minetta.

Eddie arrived with a covered plate of food and bottled water. He sat the food on the table. Minetta was gazing at the screen.

Eddie looked at the laptop. "What's she doing?"

Kimberly stood up. "She's video chatting with Philip."

"Cool!"

"Nothing like a technology intervention to help a situation," remarked Ben.

Amber said, "Don't worry about dance pics. I've taken loads since we arrived. I'll edit and send them to Phil for the school paper."

Minetta's eyes were glued to the screen on the laptop. "Thanks."

"Enjoy your video chat," Kimberly said.

The couples moved away to the dance floor. For the rest of the evening, Minetta happily engaged with a bedridden Philip through video chat.

Chapter 14

The following week the girls' volleyball team introduced new player, Amber Paige, to the lineup. There was a resounding round of applause from Cedar Valley High as the students welcomed the newcomer. The junior varsity team lead by Sallie cheered the girls' volleyball game. Minetta sat in the bleachers with Tabitha. She was getting around better with the orthopedic boot.

"What position is Amber playing?" asked Tabitha.

"I don't know," replied Minetta. She saw her parents enter the gymnasium and was happy they moved to the other side of the room.

"Hello, ladies. Who's winning?" Minetta recognized the deep baritone without looking around.

"This is only the first few minutes into the first half," said Tabitha, giggling.

Raymond sat beside Tabitha. Eddie sat next to Minetta.

"Where's Philip?" she asked.

Eddie pointed. Philip was on the sidelines taking pictures.

"What position is Amber playing?" Tabitha asked Raymond, who was following the game closely.

"She's playing the right-side hitter," he murmured.

Eddie appeared transfixed as well. "Now, I see why babe was so excited about Amber. She's awesome."

"She's also a good opposite hitter, too," said Raymond.

Minetta watched Philip on the sidelines with Amber at one point. They both had cameras and were laughing. As Minetta watched, it seemed as if they were sharing a candy bar. Minetta left the game early. Since Tabitha and Kimberly's boyfriends were in the stadium she felt no need to stay to the end, and watch Philip flirt and carry on with Amber.

The following week, school officials at Cedar Valley High celebrated their student-athletes' victories with a school-wide festival on the campus grounds. The Parent-Teacher Association and the local School Board sponsored the event.

Minetta was sitting high in the bleachers, absently watching the dance team practice choreography. Her orthopedic shoe had been removed.

"Hey Mimi, want some company?" yelled Kimberly.

Minetta smiled and waved her up. "Hey, Kim, what's going on?"

"Happiness! No homework, no surprise quizzes, nothing. Just a blissful day in the neighborhood. Why are you sitting up here? The gang is trying to decide whether we should take a vacation and go to the movies and later, we'll all go to Ben's house."

"Nah, count me out. You go. I'm heading home in a few minutes."

"What's the matter, bestie? You haven't been yourself in a while. Is it Amber?"

"Can I tell you the truth, Kim? It's not about Amber."

"What is it about, then? It seems like you don't like her a heck of a lot," responded Kimberly, in a matter-of-fact tone.

"I think I don't like her because of the way Philip is around her. He's blushing and grinning and walking her to her car."

Kimberly looked down at her lap. She made a steeple with her fingers.

"Mimi, don't take this the wrong way, but I think you just don't like Amber. Philip is that way with women and children. You know that. He walked me to my car the other night when it was late, and I was in school alone."

"That's different," argued Minetta.

"Different? How is it different? I'm a girl, too."

"You are my best friend. Philip knows you as a sister and, as Eddie's girlfriend. Amber is not a member of our group."

"Why can't she be a member of our group? She's a cheerleader, and in all of our advanced prep classes. She's also an athlete and a darn good one.

I don't see why she shouldn't be a member of our group. She's one of us."

"I think she's more of an athlete than a cheerleader."

"Is that so? Stop being a hypocrite. You certainly don't care how many male athletes have slowly joined our group."

Minetta looked away from Kimberly. "Don't forget, Philip has lied about knowing her."

"Okay, I hear what you're saying. But I think you're making a big deal out of nothing. We're all friends, and you're keeping yourself outside of the group for no reason."

"Whatever, Kim."

Kimberly was looking at a text message on her phone. "Hey bestie, come on with us. The marching band is performing later. Ben invited everyone over to his house for homemade hamburgers and shakes."

"Say hello to Ben for me. I'm going home, Kim."

Kimberly, still reading the text message, laughed. "The guys are going to grill us burgers, and we are making the shakes."

"Who are we?"

"The varsity football players and cheerleaders. Remember when Ben's parents gave him that awesome fifteenth birthday party, and we swam in the swimming pool that evening with all those fairy lights overhead? That's the night Eddie told me he only wanted me as his girlfriend."

"That's nice. I just want to sit here in peace and watch the sun going down. Then I'm going home."

Kimberly gave her a short, sideways glance and climbed down off the bleachers.

"Suit yourself."

A few minutes later, she walked past with Eddie. They both waved, and she returned their wave.

Youth Bible studies class was about to begin, and Andrew, Eddie, and Raymond, along with a few football players and cheerleaders, quietly entered the room and found seats in the back. Five minutes later, Philip and Amber came in and sat down.

During the break time, Eddie and Raymond joined Kimberly and

Tabitha. Philip sat next to Minetta, and Amber sat next to him with Andrew behind them.

"Hi, Mimi," said Philip.

Amber munched on a cupcake. "Who do you guys favor to win the Super Bowl?" she asked.

"Cowboys all day long," replied Andrew.

"You've gotta be kidding," said Philip. "The Giants for the win."

"Now look who's kidding," said Andrew.

"Gentlemen, please. You're both wrong. Eagles for the win!" said Amber and laughed.

The three spent break time discussing Super Bowl teams. Minetta ignored them and completed her religion workbook assignment. When the class dismissed for the evening, Amber walked over to the girls. She had tucked her workbook into her large tote, along with her Bible.

"Hi ladies!" said Amber, approaching the girls.

"Hi," said Minetta, not looking at her as she straightened her book bag.

"Hi Amber," said Tabitha, smiling.

"Why were you late?" asked Minetta sharply. Kimberly gave her friend the side-eye, but said nothing.

"I was here when you guys got here," stammered Amber, taken aback by Minetta's curtness. "You didn't see me because I was sitting in my car. I was talking to my boyfriend."

"Talking to your boyfriend?" Minetta repeated out loud with a nasty sneer. "You're always with one of our boyfriends."

Amber's face reddened, and her lips pursed together. "I don't know what that's supposed to mean, but I have a boyfriend. We're talking about getting married when we finish school."

"Finish school? You mean high school?" interrupted Minetta.

Kimberly's eyes widen. "You're getting married right out of high school?"

"I wouldn't do that if I were you," said Minetta, crossing her arms and sneering outright.

Kimberly lowered her voice. "No one gets married right out of high school these days, Amber. We are not in the 1950s."

Amber stared at Kimberly. "What? I didn't mean…"

"Why not go to college? Or even trade school?" continued Minetta.

"You're missing out on so much," said Kimberly with a worried look.

Amber gave them a skeptical look, but before she could reply, Tabitha's gentle voice said, "you guys must be so in love."

Amber turned her face in Tabitha's direction. She smiled. "Yes, we are."

She looked at Minetta and Kimberly with a pained expression in her eyes.

"You two are being judgmental without knowing all the facts. Hopefully, your transition into college with your boyfriends will be smooth sailing. I have a unique situation to think about."

Tabitha said, "whatever you and your boyfriend decide, we will support you as your friends."

"Just because he wants to get married right away doesn't mean you have to marry him," said Kimberly offhandedly.

"What are you talking about, Kim? And what's wrong with getting married?" Amber asked.

"You need to speak to a counselor about furthering your education," said Minetta. "You have a lot going for you."

"I can still go to college," replied Amber. "I don't see what the big deal is. Many people get married and attend college together."

Kimberly nodded her head knowingly. "Yeah," she agreed. "But they struggle."

Amber laughed. "Struggle? Struggle with what? You two don't know what you're talking about. Okay? Besides, this conversation has veered way off course."

"Guys, she's right. Stop it! What are you doing?" Tabitha attempted to intervene on Amber's behalf. "Please stop this runaway train now."

Minetta snickered. "What will your boyfriend do for a living?"

"That's none of your business," said Amber. "This entire conversation is none of your business. You don't know what you're talking about."

When she saw Amber stiffen, Minetta's mouth formed a cruel smile. "Seems like you might support him if you marry him, or maybe your parents will support you both." She laughed with scorn.

Amber spun around to Minetta, causing her to fall back a step. There were tears in Amber's eyes.

"Shut up!" she screamed. "You know nothing about my boyfriend, and you don't know what you're talking about. I thought you two would be different, especially you," she said, pointing to Minetta. "You're no better than anybody else. Why are you so judgmental about me? What have I ever done to you two? You both need to spend some quality time in your Bibles reading the Scriptures on how not to judge people."

As Amber headed toward the far side of the parking lot, she turned back to Kimberly.

"Hey Kim," she yelled. "Eddie is crazy about you. All he talks about is you. I hope you know you're a lucky girl."

"Wait," yelled Tabitha after her. "Please don't go, Amber."

Amber kept walking to her car. Opening her door, she yelled over to Minetta.

"By the way, Phil speaks highly of you, too, *Mimi*," she spat out her name. "Too bad he doesn't seem to know how mean-spirited you are."

The girls watched as Amber pulled out of the driveway in her black convertible and sped past them off the lot. They watched the lights on the back of her car until they faded into the distance.

"Well, that went well," Kimberly remarked in a shaky voice.

They piled in Minetta's car, and she turned on her car radio. Tabitha leaned forward and turned it off. Minetta glanced at Tabitha, who was looking at her with a sour expression on her face.

"She's right, you know. You guys were horrible to her for no reason," said Tabitha. "What right do any of us have to question someone else life choices, especially when we're not too sure about our own?"

"Hey Tabs, they were legitimate questions!" stated Kimberly in a belligerent but soft voice. She tossed her hair, folded her arms, and looked out of the side window.

Minetta, keeping her eyes on the road, joined in. "How many times have they drilled us on getting an education or a job skill before getting married?"

"Yeah," agreed Kimberly. "She seems in a rush, is all. We're just trying to help her out."

"Be quiet, Kim," said Tabitha in her gentle voice. "We are not the pastors, deacons, Sunday School teachers, or her parents. We aren't usually the ones that handle interviewing other youths about their life choices. Whatever happened to us spreading the good news about Jesus? I didn't hear either of you ask her if she enjoyed the Bible studies class tonight."

"She's always talking to her supposed boyfriend," mumbled Minetta.

"So?" countered Tabitha. "What's wrong with that?"

"Does she have an actual boyfriend?" snorted Kimberly, looking at Minetta.

It was a sore point that their parents had forbidden them to date until they were high school graduates or enrolled in college.

"Whether she has a boyfriend is none of our business. You guys attacked her for no reason," said Tabitha. "That's not right."

"Well, who gets married so fast?" insisted Kimberly.

Tabitha was persistent. "How about because they love each other? What about maybe he is in the military and about to be deployed? My dad never knew his parents because they died when he was young. But what if my mom's parents had forbidden them to marry? I would not be here or my little brothers."

The girls were silent, but Tabitha continued. "I know you're both jealous of Amber because Philip and Eddie, like most of the guys in town, walk around hypnotized when she's around."

Kimberly looked at the back of her friend's head and smirked. "Please, Tabs!" She rolled her eyes.

"Nobody's jealous of little miss perfect!" Minetta hissed between clenched teeth.

Tabitha turned in her seat to look at Minetta. "Oh yes, you are! But you'd better get yourselves together. She is not doing anything wrong. She is just trying to get along with us. Why can't you see that?"

Minetta parked in front of Tabitha's house and kept the engine running. Tabitha gathered her belongings.

"Ray thinks she's beautiful, and I think so, too. But it's not just her looks. She's also got a beautiful soul, and that's priceless."

Minetta pulled into Tabitha's driveway. "Your right, Tabs. We judged her based on our own bias. We can't preach the Good News if we're not living it."

Tabitha looked at Minetta and put her head down. She then glanced in the backseat at Kimberly before looking directly at Minetta again.

"Mimi, you need to be careful about what comes out of your mouth. And it would help if you changed your attitude toward this girl. You dislike her, and it shows. Oh, boy! Does it show! You need to get on your knees and pray to have the thorn removed from your eye and the jealous streak from your heart. You are a pastor's daughter and a youth leader at the church. Other kids are looking to you for guidance and leadership. Yet all I have seen you do is ignore this girl or speak nasty to her. You have no reason to be jealous of her. If you give her a chance, you just might find you like her."

Turning to Kimberly, Tabitha stated. "Kim, you, and Amber seemed to get along, so I don't think you have a real beef with her. You are just following Mimi. It is time you learned to stand on your own two feet. Friendships are about encouraging and uplifting each other. When friendships become toxic, we should examine our reasons for continuing them."

With that, Tabitha exited the car, opened the back door for Kimberly to move to the front seat, and then walked up the steps to her house. Although internally Minetta was fuming, she loved and respected her friend. Tabitha lived by certain principles and codes of conduct that were enviable. She had shown kindness and consideration to Amber, thus living by the commandment of love.

Minetta had to admit Tabitha had delivered powerful spiritual counseling on attitude change and done so in a calming, soothing manner. Never once did Tabitha raise her voice. She and Raymond were well-suited for each other. Minetta glanced over at Kimberly, who was looking out her side window at Tabitha's house.

Into the stillness, Minetta said, “Tabs is right. I don’t like Amber.”

“Well,” sighed Kimberly. “That makes one of us. Amber is a splendid girl. She’s loads of fun. I have to be honest, bestie. Tabs is right on all counts. I don’t know why you don’t like her, but you’re my bestie and always will be.”

With that pronouncement, Kimberly exited the car. Minetta sat in her driveway watching until Kimberly had closed her front door. She had acknowledged her true feelings about the girl. It was a relief to vent her emotions about Amber, but somehow it rang like a hollow victory. Tabitha would cool off, and without a doubt, Kimberly would always be a loyal friend. It was Philip she was uncertain about.

Chapter 15

Cedar Valley High's cheer squad was in the girls' locker room waiting to go out on the field to perform their cheer routines. Cedar Valley High's football team was playing against Meadow High Panthers. This was an away game and Minetta was glad her parents were in the audience. She was respectful toward Sarah, but that was the extent of it. A few more weeks and then the beginning of the holiday season.

Minetta inspected herself in her locker mirror and straightened her ivory and black mock neck pullover. She pulled her sleeves smoothly to the wrists. Pulling her hair in a high ponytail, she snapped the ivory ribbon hairpiece around her hair, securing it with hairpins on both sides.

"Hey, Mimi, are you ready?" Kimberly was standing behind her. Together, they joined the other cheerleaders gathered around Sarah.

"Okay, ladies. You're all looking beautiful. Do you have questions before you hit the bright lights?"

Kelly raised her hand. "This is my second season, but I'm nervous. That turf is wet, and I was sliding walking on it just now."

"What were you doing out there?" asked Monique.

"Never mind, Monique," said Sarah. "Sliding can happen on dry ground. You really shouldn't be sliding, though. Let me look at your shoes, Kelly."

As Kelly walked over to Sarah, Susan said, "stop thinking about Mark and concentrate on your steps. You'll be fine."

"I just saw him enter the stadium with Josh," said Wanda.

"Hmm... that Josh is a hunk, too," replied Janice.

"What is it about marching band men?" asked Wanda, grinning, and shaking her brown ponytail.

"I don't know," said Lisa, "but I'd sure like to find out!"

The cheerleaders began laughing. Meanwhile, Kimberly noticed Amber and Jewel were both on their phones in the corner. She caught Minetta's attention and pointed them out.

"Ladies," said Minetta. "Let's remember our choreography, okay? Plenty of time for conversation later. Amber and Jewel, could you please join us over here?"

Lizzie flexed her shoulders and arms. "When are we going out?"

Sarah walked over to Minetta. "Kelly's shoes are fine. She's just nervous. I talked to her. She'll be fine."

"Thanks, coach. Here's the attendance roster," said Minetta.

Tabitha raised her hand. "My parents are here tonight. Do we have to return to the school on the bus?"

"Hey ladies, can I have your attention, please? Tabitha just asked a question that our PTA Board voted on at their last meeting," said Minetta.

The cheer squad gathered around Minetta and Sarah.

Sarah smiled. "Everyone ready? I believe most of you have your parents here. You can go home with them provided you sign out. Is that clear? If you leave without observing the proper protocol, you will be suspended for the entire year."

"Kim and I will handle the sign-out sheets," added Minetta.

Debbie, a natural performer, stood with her hands on hips. "We got it."

"Alright, Minetta, take your squad out. Break a leg, girls!"

Minetta stood at the door. "Formation, ladies."

Kimberly and Tabitha lined up in single file behind Minetta. Vanessa, Lynn, Karen, Amber, Gloria, Carole, Linda, Veronica, Jewel, Sallie, Annette, Patricia, Theo, Barbara, Claire, Ashley, Kayla, and Simone followed them.

Cedar Valley High Cougars won the final game of the season against the Meadow High Panthers, twenty-one to zero.

For the Morgan and Johnston clan, celebrating the holidays together had become a joyful family tradition. The families took on alternating roles in hosting the holidays. For the Thanksgiving celebrations, James and Marilyn typically spent the weekend with his parents in his childhood home on the outskirts of Cedar Valley beyond the Heights.

James had grown up in the rural countryside in a spaciously renovated farmhouse. Gazing out the side window of her father's vehicle, Minetta took in the scenic beauty of the family's drive through the mountainous regions of the valley. Soon, her grandparents' home loomed into view. Someone correctly aligned the majestic splendor of the white home with black shutters and the red door with the robin's egg blue of the cloudless sky. Beneath the raised porch, the boxwood shrubs stood meticulously groomed, with the grass still lush. As breathtaking as it all looked now, Minetta sensed nothing could rival the beauty of the first snowfall and the crispness in the air the cold weather brought.

James said, "Ah, here we are."

He pulled into the circle driveway. Robert and Mary Morgan greeted them, waiting for them on the porch. Robert was a massive man of physical size and appearance. He was known as a peaceable and genial man of sound mind and character. Perfectly suitable to his former vocation as a university professor of religion and a church pastor. Robert's only child, son James, was the spitting image of his father in every way, shape, and form.

Robert's wife, Mary, was his college sweetheart. Her thick hair was dyed honey-blonde and cut into a shaggy pixie style with side-fringed bangs framing her face. She had been a great beauty in her day and was a stunner now in her later years.

"Hi, Dad, we made it," said James. A huge grin spread across Robert's cheery face. The father and son embraced.

James turned to his mother, and wrapped his arms around her. "Hi Mom."

"How are you, young lady?" asked Robert as Minetta stepped forward.

She hugged her grandfather. "I'm fine, Pop-Pop."

Her grandfather and father brought the luggage into the house as Mary and Marilyn hugged, speaking in low tones to each other.

"Alright, you two," said Robert. "Come on inside and don't start no mess either."

James laughed. "You know how they are, Dad. Always up to something."

Minetta laughed. Mary's gold-flecked brown eyes flashed, but the corners of her mouth played with a smile.

"Leave me alone, Robert."

Minetta hugged her grandmother and walked behind her mother and grandmother. Her grandmother Mary was slightly taller than her mother and broader in body size.

"James, would you mind going to the market and getting a few things? I was just about to leave when you drove up. If you are tired, I'll go myself."

James took the list from his mother's hand. "Stop it, Mom. You know I don't mind. My beautiful bride will accompany me."

Marilyn smiled. "Mimi, Matt should arrive soon. We'll be back shortly."

On his way upstairs Robert let his voice drift down to them. "Son, only get what's on that list. No roasted peanuts, lunch meats, sliced cheeses, pickles, crusty French bread, potato chips, or ice cream. No sir, just what's on that list."

"Okay, gotcha, Dad. I also won't be getting any candy bars."

Mary put her hands on her hips. "Very funny, you two. That's the payment I get for trying to help certain folks keep their blood sugar levels in check."

"Long as you know where the insurance policies are, you're good," said Marilyn. She and Mary chuckled. Robert remained mute, and James turned away.

James said, "Let's go, sweetheart. It gets dark up here early."

Sometime later, Minetta was in the living room kneeling on the window seat when she spotted her older brother's black jeep coming up the drive. She alerted her grandparents, who were in the kitchen, drinking coffee.

"Matt!" Minetta yelled as she flung herself into her brother's arms.

Matthew, laughing, hugged his younger sister. "Hey Mimi, you're looking pretty as usual."

"I missed you," she pouted.

"Yeah, I missed you too, sis," he said.

Matthew was as tall as his father and grandfather, with a broad chest and tight biceps and abs. Like his sister, he favored his mother's side of the family in physical looks with his black curly hair and dark eyes. The baseball cap backward on his head, he greeted his grandparents.

"Hey Pops," said Matthew as he embraced his grandfather.

"How's school, son?" asked his grandfather.

"Just fine, sir. I believe I'm making the dean's list again after finals post next month."

Robert slapped him on the back. Matthew was a mathematics major in his senior year. He was also a proud member of Omega Pi Fraternity, having joined the legacy of the Morgan men in following in his father and grandfather's steps. He lived in the Omega Pi House, which allowed him to realize how fortunate he was to be where he was currently in life Matthew had learned humility in college and was grateful for his life, strength, and health. He looked down at his beautiful grandmother and said a silent prayer of thanks for his family. His grandfather had taken his backpack out of the car, and Minetta had his laundry bag.

"Where's Mom and Dad?" he asked Mary.

Hugging her grandson around the waist, she smiled. "They went to the supermarket for a few necessities. They should be on their way back now. Would you like some coffee? I just made a fresh pot."

"That sounds great, Nana. You can tell me about your shenanigans with the women's ministry since we last visited."

Mary smiled up at her grandson, her gold-flecked brown eyes merry with laughter. "You rascal, last time you visited, you were supposed to help me with my tomato garden."

"Oops, sorry, Nana," said Matthew, feigning mock surprise.

They both laughed, as did Minetta and Robert, listening to them. Mary had been growing various tomato plants for a few years now, and Matthew had always helped her cultivate them.

"Can I see what you've been doing in my sorry absence?" asked Matthew.

"Yes, you can. The beefeater tomatoes have been doing well..." They went out through the kitchen door to the greenhouse Robert had built for her.

Later that afternoon, Minetta was seated on the window seat in the living room when a large black Lincoln Town car pulled up in the driveway.

Timothy and Elouise Johnston were Marilyn's parents. Timothy, a tall, distinguished-looking man with a close-shaven Van Dyke beard, and a slim build was a newly retired prosecutor turned law professor. His wife Elouise, carrying a bouquet of fresh-cut flowers for the dining table, was still a practicing Family Court judge. Elouise had dark silver-streaked hair that fell in graceful waves to her collarbone. Deep blue eyeshadow highlighted her dark brown eyes, and her lips glossed with red lipstick. A former beauty queen, Elouise always wore a full face of make-up, no matter if she was staying home or going out on the town.

Timothy handed Robert a bottle of confetti that was labeled as a bottle of imported whiskey. Both men grinned. It was a running gag from their fraternity days as neither man drank liquor. Robert had a collection of such bottles he proudly displayed on one sidewall in his den.

An early supper of homemade pizza eaten in the family room allowed the women enough time to prepare Thanksgiving dinner. In the kitchen, Minetta cut, sliced, and diced the onions, garlic, and celery. She was working with Elouise, clad entirely in blue. Her neck and wrists encased in double strands of blue and gold bracelets.

"How are you doing in school so far?" asked Elouise.

"I'm fine, Nana."

"I'm sure you are doing well, dear," replied her grandmother. "I meant, are you getting ready for your prom, class trip, and all that? Have you done any shopping yet for all the parties I know you'll want to attend?"

"Oh," said Minetta and smiled.

Her grandmother Elouise had on thin gloves and was dicing garlic on a chopping block. She could see her French-tipped manicured nails through the semi-transparent gloves.

"Not yet, Nana," said Minetta.

Elouise smiled. "I know you'll look beautiful."

"Oh yes, she will," said Mary, who was operating the dough machine.

Her yellow manicured nails glistened, matching the speckled blue and yellow print of her caftan. Yellow eyeshadow emphasized the specks of gold in her brown eyes reflected through the fringe of gold in her hair.

Marilyn, stirring sugar into the fresh cranberries and water she set on the stove, chimed in. "Well, Mimi looks like me. She looks beautiful in anything she wears."

Marilyn had tied her long dark hair into a low ponytail. A large blue apron covered her yellow jumpsuit with her name scrolled across the front in yellow script.

Mary looked over at her daughter-in-law, "She does, dear, yes she does." She looked at her sister-in-law. "Elouise, how did you get so lucky to have such a beautiful daughter for my son to pick out? I mean, it was love at first sight, is what I heard."

Elouise threw her head back and laughed. "Heaven blessed your son. That's all I can say. Keeping it humble, of course."

Both ladies laughed.

"You two are horrible," said Marilyn, smiling and shaking her head.

The kitchen door swung open. The women in the kitchen looked at the intruding menfolk.

"Hmm, something smells good in here," said James, walking into the kitchen, followed by Robert, Timothy, and Matthew.

"Get out, dear," said Marilyn, smiling up at him.

Matthew walked over to his mother and put his arm around her shoulder. "Mom, we're hungry. We need a snack."

Marilyn gazed up at her son. "It's a good thing we stopped at the deli counter. There's sliced ham, turkey, and pastrami in the fridge over there and some hoagie rolls in the pantry. We bought a block of cheese that you're going to have to slice yourself. The cheese slicer is under the counter there."

"Be quick about it," said Mary in a semi-stern voice as her husband Robert was putting condiments on the side table.

Timothy was slicing open the rolls, and James was pulling apart the deli packaging. Matthew layered the meats and cheese. The men took less than fifteen minutes to prepare their sandwiches. Elouise and Mary, standing side by side, surveyed the carnage left behind as the men, armed with their food, disappeared into the family room to watch football on television.

"Hmm," said Elouise with folded arms. "Why do we put ourselves through this every year?"

"Can't live with them and can't live without them," said Mary, shaking her head.

“We can try,” said Minetta, grinning. Both grandmothers looked at their granddaughter and over to Marilyn, who was busy mixing stuffing.

“Um, no baby, don’t say that” said Elouise, shaking her head.

“We were just kidding around,” said Mary. “It was a private joke between Lou and me.”

“Men and women were created to live and work together,” said Elouise. “That’s why when a man finds a wife, he finds a good thing.”

“We’re sorry if you took our joke the wrong way,” said Mary. “We were out of line, anyway.”

Minetta looked from one to the other. She said crossly, “I was kidding too. I am not ten years old.”

“Watch your mouth, Mimi,” said Marilyn, not looking up.

Contrite Minetta explained. “I just meant I know you all were playing around. I just wanted to say something funny, too. You sound like hypocrites trying to teach me about relationships, but you two are the ones making the disparaging remarks.”

“Okay, no more such talk,” said Marilyn, wiping her hands on her apron and addressing her mother- and mother-in-law. “It leads to confusion with our young people. Older women are to set the example for younger women. If we disparage the men in our families to our daughters and granddaughters, and then chastise them for doing the same thing, what messages are we sending?”

“Conflicting ones,” stated Mary, looking at Minetta.

“Come here, sweetie,” said Elouise to Minetta. She hugged her granddaughter tight. “I’m sorry. I love you very much, darling. Your mother is correct. There was nothing humorous about our behavior.”

Minetta hugged her grandmother back. “I love you too, Nana.” She looked at Mary. “Both of you.”

“Hey, what about me?” asked Marilyn with a playful pout. “Don’t forget I defended you against those two.”

Minetta walked over to her mother. “You know I love you, Mom. You are always going to be number one in my book.” They hugged.

“You are so spoiled, Marilyn,” said Elouise, shaking her head at her daughter and smiling.

"Give us grandmothers a break. You get her year-round. It just makes no sense to be so selfish. Don't know where you get it from."

Mary laughed. "All her daddy's fault, I'm sure."

"You got that right," said Elouise, grinning. "His princess for sure."

"Well, you know, that's how they get spoiled and out of control," said Mary, shaking her head in mock disbelief.

Marilyn rolled her eyes to the ceiling and looked at her daughter. "Here we go again. The smaller one is a judge in Family Court egging on the other lady. Such a corrupt judge even if she is pretty,"

Minetta giggled.

On Thanksgiving Day, Minetta helped prepare the dinner table as the men watched football in the den. Robert led the meal with prayer and praise for the blessings the Morgan and Johnston families received throughout the year.

Chapter 16

It had become a tradition among the three best friends to have a sleepover before they parted ways for the Christmas holidays. The girls alternated houses, and this year it was Tabitha's turn. Tabitha's bedroom was bohemian-inspired with bright, bold splashes of color in linens and furniture against off-white-washed walls. Her central color theme was a deep carnelian red interwoven throughout the bold prints in her window coverings and bed linens. A colorful tapestry hung over her bed. A gift from Raymond after his family visited Morocco several years earlier. The girls sat on the red shag-carpeted floor eating Christmas cookies they had baked earlier.

"What did Ray give you for Christmas Tabs?" asked Kim, clad in green plaid flannel pajamas and munching on a cookie in the shape of a reindeer.

"I am not opening my gift until Christmas," replied Tabitha, biting down on a cookie shaped like a Christmas tree. She was wearing red and green print flannel pajamas.

"Party pooper," said Kimberly. Tabitha laughed.

"Just because you opened yours doesn't mean I have to open mine," said Tabitha.

"What did Eddie give you?" asked Minetta, reaching for a star-shaped cookie, and pulling up the sleeve on her red print pajama shirt.

"This," said Kimberly and stuck out her wrist to display a silver charm bracelet laced with charms.

"Nice," said Tabitha.

"What are the charms?" asked Minetta.

"A heart, moon, my birthstone, a rose, tiara, his birthstone, ballerina, poodle, car, basketball, and track shoe," Kimberly smiled as she named each charm wistfully.

"Wow," said Tabitha. "He must have been collecting charms for a while."

Kimberly smiled shyly. "He told me his mother helped him select the charms, and yes, he started a while back. Isn't he sweet?" She blushed as she looked at her arm.

"What did Philip give you, Mimi?" asked Tabitha as she reached for a peppermint stick cookie.

Minetta took a bite of her star-shaped cookie and chewed carefully, not meeting her friends' eyes.

"I haven't seen Philip," she said.

There was a moment of awkward silence. Kimberly and Tabitha exchanged glances.

Kimberly said, "Maybe he just forgot. This year has been hectic for all of us."

"Philip has never forgotten to give me a gift."

Kimberly said, "I don't think he meant to forget you, Mimi."

"But he did forget me. He went away for the Christmas holidays and did not call me as he usually does. He always left my gift with Mrs. B. if I wasn't around, so there's no excuse."

Kimberly shook her head vigorously. "He'll either try to catch you tomorrow before you guys leave or give it to you after the holidays."

"Yes," said Tabitha. "You know Philip is always thinking."

"Yeah, I know Philip is always thinking, and that's why this is the first year since we've been exchanging gifts he's forgotten," replied Minetta. "He seemed to avoid me last week and this week in school. And we all know why. Little Miss Amber told him all about our little run-in, and he's taking her side."

Kimberly and Tabitha looked at each other again. Neither one wanted to rehash the incident with Amber in the church.

At last, Tabitha said, "Let's not go back there. It was an ugly night. I repented for my part in it."

"Your part?" Kimberly looked at Tabitha in confusion. "Tabs, you did nothing wrong. It was Mimi and me. We should have kept our big mouths shut. But you did nothing wrong."

Tabitha shook her head. "I should have done something or said something to help Amber. I should have done more to stop you two."

Kimberly looked at her friend with affection. "Tabs, you did all you could. It was up to us to stop ourselves. We had no right going in on Amber so hard."

Tabitha looked at Minetta. "I should have been praying for peace between all of you. I didn't pray as I should have."

Minetta looked at Tabitha. "Your right, Tabs. It was an ugly scene and all my fault. I am sorry I got you guys involved in all that."

"Don't just apologize to us, Mimi," said Tabitha. "You also need to find it in your heart to apologize to Amber fully. She didn't deserve what happened to her."

Kimberly reached for a Christmas tree-shaped cookie and sighed.

"Can we exchange our gifts now?"

Tabitha grinned. "Okay."

She handed both girls large white shopping bags with red poinsettia drawings on the front. Minetta pulled out a plush oversized yellow pillow and a blue floral-covered journal with Scripture readings on the bottom of each page.

Minetta hugged Tabitha. "Thank you, Tabs."

Kimberly had received a pink miniature beauty refrigerator. Her eyes immediately popped. She threw her arms around Tabitha and hugged her fiercely.

"Oh no, you didn't! I love it, Tabs. Thank you so much. I wanted one of these for so long."

"You are both welcomed," said Tabitha, hugging Kimberly back and smiling.

"Okay," said Kimberly. "Here's to you both."

She pushed a plain white gift box wrapped in a red and green bow toward Tabitha and an identical one towards Minetta.

Tabitha's gifts included a gold heart-shaped picture frame with a photo of her and Raymond, and a jewelry box encrusted with colorful gems on the lid that spelled her name.

"Oh, I love my gifts. Thank you, Kimberly," said Tabitha, hugging her friend.

Minetta had received a white silk blouse adorned with pearlized French cuffs from her favorite boutique and a string of opulent white pearls. She smiled. “This blouse will go great with that suit I bought last month. Thank you for the pearls, Kim. You know I love them.”

Minetta handed Tabitha and Kimberly red satin boxes with gifts wrapped with silver sparkled bows.

“Your turn, ladies.”

Tabitha’s box contained a limited edition copy of a book on the Christian Crusades. Minetta had neatly tucked a white lace-trimmed scarf with Tabitha’s initials engraved on one corner tucked between the book pages. Tabitha held the book in her arms.

“Thank you, Mimi, thank you.” Tabitha loved reading historical books.

Minetta broke off another piece of her star-shaped cookie.

“I had to enlist your mom to help me locate the publishing house so I could order it.”

Inside Kimberly’s box were a green striped sports bra, green velvet sweatpants, and matching green velvet jacket.

“Thank you, bestie. This outfit is gorgeous,” she said.

The girls hugged each other as they sat in a circle on the shag carpet.

“Hey, let’s make some eggnog,” suggested Tabitha.

“That sounds good,” said Minetta, wincing. Kimberly was nudging her hard in her ribs.

Kimberly said, “I’ll be down in a minute. I’m going to use the restroom.” She dashed into Tabitha’s bathroom.

“I might as well too,” said Minetta.

“Okay,” said Tabitha. “I’ll get mom’s cookbook.” She stopped in the doorway. “You can use the guest bathroom downstairs Mimi.”

“Thanks, Tabs, but since I’m up here, I’ll wait,” said Minetta.

“Okay, suit yourself. See you guys when you come downstairs,” she said. “I’m going to get the ingredients together.”

Kimberly opened the bathroom door a crack. “Is she gone?”

Minetta rolled her eyes. “And if she wasn’t? Why were you poking me in the ribs?”

Kimberly came out of the bathroom. “Just wanted to tell you that Amber gave Tabs a pearl bracelet for Christmas.”

“Really? How do you know it was a bracelet?” said Minetta, frowning slightly.

“I was standing right there when Amber gave Tabs the gift bag.”

“Standing right where? Where were you?” asked Minetta.

“In school. It was the day after that final exam we had in Hennessey’s class. We were standing by the lockers waiting for you when Amber came by, and they exchanged gifts.”

“I see,” said Minetta, staring off into space.

“Want to know what Tabs gave Amber?”

“No, I don’t,” said Minetta. “Let’s go downstairs. Tabs is our best friend. No matter what she does, Amber can’t take that away.”

Cedar Valley Town Square held a Christmas parade every year on Christmas Eve and was the highlight of the season for the town. Cedar Valley High’s Cheer Squad performed in the parade every year. This parade was Minetta’s third year in a row, taking part as a varsity cheerleader. She was as thrilled today as when in previous years selected. She looked across to the stands and saw her mother in her blue puff coat seated next to her father in his brown woolen coat and waved.

She grinned when she recognized her brother Matthew in his black jacket waving at her. She realized the girl with the dark blonde hair seated beside him she had seen before. She often was with him during church services, but Minetta had not met her yet. She was in a blue three-quarters coat with a yellow and blue stripe scarf around her neck.

The coach walked over to them. She wore a gray woolen pants coat with gray corduroy pants and black boots. Her white-blonde hair was loose and waving in the breeze. Minetta was watching the teleprompter and the band members in front of her. She looked around at the assembled cheerleaders. She was missing Linda, Veronica, Jewel, Sallie, Annette and Patricia, her senior varsity squad, and members of the girls’ super athlete group.

She asked Kimberly. “Where’s your fellow athletes?”

Kimberly looked at her and sighed. "I don't know."

"I hope they're not protesting because of our spat with Amber."

"What do you mean, our spat, Mimi? I'm getting a little tired of having your back and getting nothing in return."

Minetta looked at her friend, who was not looking at her. She saw the coach walking toward them.

"Everyone here?" asked Sarah.

"People are still coming off the stands, coach," replied Minetta.

"It's getting cold out here," complained Gloria.

"We should start any minute now," said Tabitha. She looked around. "Where's Amber?"

Minetta saw the teleprompter blinking. "I don't know, but get the girls in formation, Kim."

Sarah waved at the girls. "Break a leg! See you at the finish line."

At that moment, Amber walked up. She and Tabitha hugged. Amber walked to the other side of Kimberly without speaking, and they formed a straight line. Following Amber were the missing team members. They got into their places.

Minetta raised her hand and counted down to one. The band's horn section began playing, and everyone moved forward. Minetta led the cheer squad. Minetta kept her eyes in the stands as they performed their routine, looking for Philip in the crowd.

When the parade ended, Sarah met the team at the end of the route and congratulated the girls by giving out hugs. Minetta walked over to the coach and hugged her.

"Merry Christmas, coach, and happy new year," she said. "I'm sorry for my rotten disposition. I'll do better."

Sarah looked as if she wanted to cry. "Merry Christmas and happy new year to you too, Mimi."

Ben walked up with Philip, Andrew, and Raymond. Ben looked great in a dark gray double-breasted woolen coat over a gray turtleneck sweater and blue jeans. Andrew was in a brown suede parka with his cowboy hat.

"You looked great, Mimi. Merry Christmas and happy new year," said Ben, hugging her. She hugged him back. Boy, he smelled great!

"Thank you, Ben. Merry Christmas and happy new year to you too!"

"Merry Christmas, Mimi," said Andrew, kissing her on the cheek.

Philip, in a gray wool trench coat and white turtleneck, was beaming.

"Looking pretty, as always. Want my coat? Are you cold?"

She smiled. "I'm fine. All that movement keeps you warm, and I am wearing thermals under this outfit."

She thought he was going to hug her, but Philip walked around her to Kimberly and Tabitha. Raymond smiled and hugged her in a navy-blue pea coat with a matching turtleneck and slacks.

"Good show Mimi. Merry Christmas and happy new year."

"Thanks, Raymond, same to you."

She hugged Kimberly, "Merry Christmas, bestie. See you in the new year."

"Merry Christmas, bestie," said Kimberly. "Let me find my parents. I saw Eddie a minute ago with Kelly and Joshua."

They locked arms and walked through the crowd. Minetta spotted Philip, Eddie, and Amber standing by the concession stand next to the exit.

"Oh, there they are," exclaimed Kimberly.

"Okay, Kim. I'll see you after Christmas. I've got to find my parents," said Minetta.

"That's right," said Kimberly. "You're spending the holidays with your grandparents. Have a wonderful holiday, bestie."

Kimberly walked over to Eddie, Amber, and Philip. Minetta turned in the opposite direction. She found her parents en route, looking for her. Her mother had her winter coat.

"You looked great out there, sweetheart," said James. "Have you said all your goodbyes?"

"Yes, Dad. I'm ready to go," said Minetta. "Where's Matt?"

"He's meeting us up there," said James.

"Here, baby, put on your coat," said Marilyn. "Your team was fabulous out there. I am so proud of you."

"Okay, ladies, we have to get on the road soon."

Chapter 17

One hour later, James, Marilyn, and Minetta were standing in their driveway surveying the inside of the trunk of the eight-passenger black Suburban vehicle James drove. He securely wedged his duffel bag behind his wife and daughter's luggage. Minetta had brought down her three-piece set. The pastor arranged her suitcases alongside Marilyn's five-piece set with the matching makeup case and jewelry bag on top. He settled the suitcases to make room for their Christmas gifts. James wanted an early start to beat the holiday rush traffic.

James and Marilyn spent the Christmas holidays at the home of Marilyn's parents in Upper Medford Valley. It was a four-hour-drive one-way from Cedar Valley. They joined Marilyn's older brother, William "Bill" Johnston, his wife, Janet, and their children, Craig and Annie, and James' parents.

Turning to her daughter, Marilyn asked, "Did you call your grandparents?"

"Grandpapa said they might still be at the store when we get there."

"Oh, okay," said Marilyn. She was looking in the trunk. "James, will the gifts fit in there, or do we need to put them on the backseats?"

"Hmm… I believe my duffel bag is fine where it is. It's behind Mimi's luggage."

"Your duffel bag should fit on top of our luggage," said Marilyn, looking up at him.

"Yes, it should," he agreed. Studying the angles, he said, "However, I won't be able to see clearly out of the back view window if it slides. I want everything to be as flat as possible."

Minetta giggled. "We do this every year. How come we never remember how the suitcases go in the car?"

"Because every year, you both add something to the pile," said James, smiling.

"Oh my," said Marilyn, feigning mild shock.

James grinned. "Don't oh my me, Mrs. Morgan. You're the primary culprit, and now you've got your sidekick picking up your bad habits."

Marilyn and Minetta laughed. "Oh," said Marilyn. "Let me remember to put the door keys in my purse. Just in case."

James called out to Marilyn. "Have Mrs. B. come back with you." Marilyn waved her hand in response.

Turning to Minetta, he said, "sweetie, could you bring me the gifts?"

James rearranged the luggage to make room for the presents.

"Dad?"

"Yes, sweetie." He still needed to put in the Christmas gifts, which comprised overstuffed shopping bags.

"Are we picking up Matt along the way like we did last year?"

"No, sweetie. He's a junior now. He will be fine driving to your grandparents alone, as I stated earlier." The pastor chuckled to himself. "He might even prefer it."

Marilyn reappeared with several shopping bags, followed by Beatrice.

"Mimi, could you please bring those boxes out for me?" Her mother was breathing hard.

"Are you okay, baby?" asked James as he hurriedly relieved her of her burdens.

"I'm fine, James," she said. She handed him the bags as Minetta returned with the boxes.

Beatrice handed him a picnic basket. She always sent along fresh homemade jams she prepared herself. Beatrice was fond of Elouise Johnston as they were both natives of Jamaica. James arranged all the packages in the truck and slammed down the hood. Everyone gathered in a small circle.

James said, "With all hearts and minds on one accord, let's pray for a safe and enjoyable trip, and holiday season." They bowed their heads.

After the prayer, Marilyn and Minetta hugged Beatrice. She always tidied up the house before taking a cab to the airport. She would spend the winter holidays on her native island and return to Cedar Valley after the new year.

Marilyn asked James, "are we just about ready?"

"Yes, I just need you two to get in the truck," James said.

Both women grinned and fast-walked back into the house. James shook his head, smiled, and climbed onto the driver's seat to wait.

Later that afternoon, the Morgan family arrived at the Johnston's English-Tudor style home in Upper Medford Valley. The Colonial-style home set on an incline with a towering forest behind it. Timothy and Elouise greeted them in their driveway. Timothy came forward to shake his son-in-law's hand.

"Hey son, how are you doing? How was the trip?" asked Timothy, stooping to hug his daughter.

"It was great, sir," said James as he hugged Elouise, who was right behind Timothy.

"We only saw two accidents," said Minetta as she hugged her grandparents.

"You didn't snap pics of car wrecks or fallen deer again, did you?" asked Elouise, giving her granddaughter the side-eye. Timothy and James laughed.

Minetta grinned. "No, Nana, not this time."

Elouise looked at Marilyn. "You look tired. Come on, let's get you all settled, and you can rest some. I know how it is with long drives."

James said, "Go on, baby. I got this."

He gently guided Marilyn away from the truck and toward the front entrance, where her mother was waiting. He reached to his side and pulled Minetta along, too.

"Go on, ladies. Your luggage will be with you shortly."

Matthew pulled up alongside his father's truck as the women disappeared through the front door. James frowned slightly at the sight of his nephew, Craig, sitting in the passenger seat. Matthew was his usual perky self, sporting a thin mustache and scant beard. He was wearing an Omega Pi knit pullover and matching baseball cap with the brim turned backward. Around his neck was his fraternity lanyard.

Standing beside him, his cousin Craig was taller but inclined toward plumpness. His reddish-blonde braids were across his shoulder blades, and sunglasses with dark-toned lenses concealed the light gray eyes he inherited from his mother.

"Hey, Pops."

Matthew greeted his father with a grin, noticing James' face as he glanced at Craig. Timothy looked at his grandson but said nothing. The four men embraced and stacked the luggage outside of the vehicles on the ground. James, Matthew, and Craig each had a duffel bag. The eight suitcases belonged to the two women inside the house. The men looked at each other and shook their heads.

"Come on, let's clear this stuff before the others arrive," said Timothy.

"Yeah," said Craig. "We have way more suitcases arriving."

All the men laughed. Once the vehicles cleared, James drove his car around back to the garage, and Matthew moved his vehicle to the far side of the driveway. When James returned to the front of the house, he saw his parents had arrived. His father was talking to his father-in-law, Timothy. Robert turned around to greet his son.

"Tim tells me you recently got here. How are you doing, son?" Robert asked.

"Hi, Dad," said James. "Traffic wasn't bad. We got here about twenty minutes ago."

Mary embraced her son. "Good. I take it the ladies are upstairs already?"

Timothy said, "We completed the guest rooms, and we put you all in adjoining rooms."

Robert seemed pleased. "The renovations finished?"

"Finished about a week ago. Eager for you to see it," stated Timothy.

James asked, "the wall wasn't a problem after all?"

"No. It opened up more space than we knew we had. We could install a shared bathroom, complete with a sauna," said Timothy.

"The ladies will enjoy that," said Robert.

With Timothy leading the way, the group followed him inside the house, each carrying luggage. Timothy bypassed the wide front stairs leading to the bedrooms upstairs and walked down a hall, veering to the right and opening a door leading to an alcove with two separate entrances. Going to the left door, he knocked, and they entered a bedroom and sitting area decorated in muted pastel shades. Elouise, seated on a floral chaise, talking to her daughter and granddaughter, immediately rose and hugged everybody.

"What a beautiful room," exclaimed Mary.

"Your contractor did a great job," said Robert.

"The room next door is a replica of this one, said Timothy. "We thought you all might enjoy spending quality time together."

"I was just showing Marilyn the connecting bathroom." Elouise said to her sister-in-law, "come on, Mary, let me give you a guided tour. There's a sauna in here too."

Marilyn and Minetta followed the older women into the bathroom. The men watched them.

"Hey Dad, Uncle Bill and Aunt Janet's here," said Matthew as he brought in the last of the women's luggage.

"Everybody alright now?" asked Timothy as he headed toward the door.

"I'll help you, Tim. Let the ladies talk," said Robert, winking at his son and grandson.

James, Craig, and Matthew followed Timothy and Robert to the front of the house. Parked directly behind Matthew's vehicle were Bill and Janet Johnston's four-door black sedan. They were unloading as the men hit the bottom steps.

William "Bill" Johnston was a successful criminal defense attorney in private practice. He was of medium height and slim, with thick dark hair slightly grayer than his younger sister's hair. His wife, Janet, was a forensic scientist. She leaned toward plumpness and was always on a diet. Her reddish-brown shoulder-length hairstyle complemented her light gray eyes.

"Hey, son," yelled Timothy. "Glad you all made it safely. As you can see, the gang's all here."

Bill laughed. "Hi everybody. Glad to be done driving, that's for sure."

"Hey, Dad," said Craig. He and Bill hugged. They had a whispered exchange before Janet walked over from hugging her father-in-law.

"Hi, baby," she said to Craig. "How did you get here so fast? I thought your car was still in the shop?"

"It is. I got a ride with Matt," he said before hurrying off with a suitcase his cousin handed him. Janet looked puzzled.

"Mom, did you pack my pink case?" yelled Annie as she climbed out of the backseat with her cell phone in hand. Annie was medium height and slim with ash-blonde waist-length braided hair and light gray eyes.

Janet looked around at her. "Yes, it's in the trunk."

Timothy said, "you all are upstairs in your old room, Bill, same as always."

"Did you complete the final renovations, Dad?" asked Bill.

"Yes, shortly before Thanksgiving. You were away attending that symposium with Janet, and I forgot to tell you."

"I forgot to ask."

The men grinned and grabbed the luggage to take into the house. Minetta came outside. She and Janet ran toward each other and hugged. The first cousins were the same age, making their level of social interaction welcoming.

As he passed Janet with luggage, Timothy said, "Janet, the ladies are in the first-floor guest bedrooms downstairs. We finally got them finished."

Janet smiled as she lifted out a pink case and handed it to Annie. "That's great, Tim. I know it was a long and exhaustive process. Come on, girls, let's go inside."

"You look great, Mimi," said Annie to her cousin.

Minetta smiled. “Thanks, cousin. I love your hair like that and the color of it.”

“Thanks,” said Annie. “I didn’t think I would like it at first, but it’s grown on me.”

Minetta said, “let’s go upstairs to our room. I have so much to tell you.”

Annie grinned. “No, cousin. It is I who have so much to tell you!”

Giggling, they entered the house and ascended the stairs to the blue and yellow striped patterned bedroom they had been sharing on family visits since they were toddlers.

The grandchildren typically organized and prepared the Christmas Eve dinner and served it buffet style in the Johnston’s spacious family room.

“Mimi, where’s the cheese board?” asked Annie.

“Right there,” said Craig. He pointed to the board hanging on the wall behind Annie’s head.

“Oh, Nana moved it,” said Annie. She laid out several varieties of cheeses and crackers on a silver platter. On another tray, Annie placed an assortment of cut-up vegetables and salsa. On a third plate, she repeated with mixed fruit and dips.

“How is the hoagie coming along?” asked Craig.

Matthew and Minetta prepared a six-foot-long Italian-style hoagie roll and sliced it into six-inch portions.

“Looking great,” said Matthew, brandishing an olive. Craig smiled.

“I’m going to work on the sandwiches now,” said Minetta.

“Okay, sis,” said Matthew. He carried several bags of potato chips and pretzels to the family room.

The men typically ate the hoagies as the women preferred sandwiches. Minetta carefully cut the crusts off the bread slices before filling them with either tuna salad, egg salad, or ham salad, as her mother had taught her. The family gathered around the table, holding hands. They bowed their heads as Timothy prayed with gratitude that all had arrived safely and blessed the food. Two hours later, the entire family took part in the clean-up process, helping the time to pass swiftly. As they were all tired from their travels and the day’s general excitement, the house was quiet past midnight.

Chapter 18

The men who enjoyed showing off their culinary talents and decorating skills to their womenfolk always prepared Christmas morning brunch. Minetta and Annie put on season-inspired pajamas and joined their mothers in the spacious family room to play a game of spades. The grandmothers sat by the fireplace working on new crochet patterns.

"Ladies, we present Christmas morning brunch," said James.

The sliding doors rolled back, separating the breakfast nook from the family room, revealed the table laden with food and drinks.

"Yeah!" said Annie, "I'm starving."

"Tell me about it," Minetta said, gazing hungrily at the spread.

As everyone gathered around the feast, they held hands, and James gave the morning prayer.

Mary looked across the table at her granddaughter and asked, "Tell me, Mimi, how is your last year coming in school?"

"Just fine, Nana," she said.

"Have you applied to Medford yet?" she asked.

"Yes. I haven't heard anything yet," Minetta replied.

Mary said, "no? That's odd. When did you send in your application?"

"Mimi, did you also apply to Foxcraft?" interrupted Elouise.

"The Morgan family has always attended Medford," interjected Mary.

Elouise eyed Mary. "She's also a Johnston, or have you forgotten she has two sets of grandparents?"

"I did not forget she has two sets of grandparents," replied Mary.

Robert laughed nervously. "Surely, ladies, it's her decision."

Elouise sipped her water and hissed. "Why can't she attend my alma mater? It's just as good a university as Medford."

"I never stated or implied otherwise," said Mary.

Timothy said, "both schools are exceptional to gain a quality education."

"I want to go to Medford. I always have," said Minetta.

She picked up her glass of orange juice, and her hand shook slightly. Both grandmothers arguing about her choice of school made her sad. Marilyn noticed her daughter's hand twitching.

"Please, you two," implored Marilyn. "This is family time. Please don't argue."

"It's unnecessary to fuss like this," joined in Janet.

"As long as she gets admitted to a college, I'll be happy," said James and winked at Minetta.

"Yeah, I want her to come to Medford so I can monitor her," said Matthew, arching his brows devilishly. Minetta, Annie, and Craig laughed.

"I don't see why I can't speak to my grandbaby about her school choice. She is my grandchild as well, and I love her too," sniffed Mary.

"Mom, I'm sure she'll get in where she wants to attend," said James, hoping to appease his mother.

"How can you be so certain?" she asked him.

"Because Matt's admission letter didn't come until early summer. We didn't panic then, and we aren't panicking now," he said.

"Why can't she attend Foxcraft is all I'm asking," sniffed Elouise, refusing to let the matter rest. "Foxcraft has graduated some of the best scholars."

Timothy patted his wife's hand. "It's her decision Lou, let it rest."

James threw his napkin on the table dramatically.

"Seems to me I should be the one upset. I will have three tuitions to pay, and I'm sure Mimi's will be much higher than Matt's."

"What?" stated Mary, Elouise, and Janet, their faces each registering looks of puzzlement and confusion. Timothy looked amused, and Bill stared at him.

Marilyn said, "Three tuitions, James?"

"Furnishing Mimi's dorm room will be a tuition payment in itself."

Everyone at the table laughed.

"Dad! I can't believe you said that!" said Minetta, joining in the laughter.

Bill smiled at his niece. "I think Mimi will fine no matter what school she attends."

Annie spoke up. "No one asked me where I'm going."

Her brother, munching on blueberry pancakes, said, "that's because no one cares."

He and Matthew laughed. Timothy cleared his throat, and the laughter died down.

"Sorry, sis," said a chagrin Craig to his sibling.

Janet prompted her daughter. "Tell the family where you're going, Annie."

Annie cleared her throat. "They have accepted me in the Honors program at Foxcraft University."

"How wonderful," said Marilyn. "That's your alma mater, isn't it, Janet?"

"Yes," said Janet gushing. "I did not know Annie had applied. I am just speechless."

Marilyn turned to her nephew, Craig. "I know you'll be giving Annie some pointers on Foxcraft."

Matthew, Annie, and Minetta looked at Craig, who lowered his head to his plate. Silence ensued.

Quietly, Bill said, "Craig?"

Craig avoided looking at his mother. "I transferred to Medford this past Fall."

"You did what?" Janet's voice rose slightly.

"I transferred out. I'm now at Medford."

Janet turned to her husband. "Did you know about this?" she asked.

"Yes, we talked it over before he transferred."

"You talked it over before he transferred? And neither one of you thought to include me in these talks?" Janet's voice had risen slightly.

"Janet, calm down," said Bill. "I would rather have him in a school he wants to attend than one he hates."

"One he hates?" echoed Janet in a high-pitched tone. The words came tumbling out.

"Let me get this straight. He didn't hate it when he made us visit it three times to be certain it was the school he wanted to attend. He didn't hate it the last two years when he made the dean's list. He didn't hate it this year when we bought him a car that he totaled the first week before returning to the campus. And, he hasn't hated it the last three years. So, please tell me, when did all of this hate start?"

Janet was angry. Her face had reddened, and her voice scratched from trying to control her volume. She glared around the table. No one looked up. As the uncomfortable silence lengthened, Janet sniffed and threw her napkin on the table.

"That's fine. Craig changed his mind. That's okay. What's not okay is making a major decision without the courtesy of including me in the conversation. I guess I don't have the intelligence to understand why he suddenly hates a school in the middle of his fourth year. Furthermore, as he has two parents who have worked together to pay his bills, I'm rather puzzled why this decision was made without even considering making me aware in the matter."

Turning to Bill, she said, "You could have told me before we came here. I don't understand what all the secrecy is about."

Janet turned to her son. "And you! You could have told me before now. It seems I failed in teaching you common courtesy."

Throwing her napkin on the table, she said, "Excuse me," and walked out.

"Well, that went over nicely," Matthew said to Craig.

"Are we still exchanging gifts once brunch is over?" asked Minetta in a clear, loud voice.

Everyone at the table looked at her. Oblivious to the pained silence, she helped herself to a second cup of coffee. Then she noticed their stares.

"What?" she asked.

Immediately after brunch ended, Bill left to check on his wife. He returned with Janet, whose countenance remained quiet but withdrawn. She avoided looking at her son. The exchange of gifts occurred in the family room overlooking the lake outside. Janet's presents remained unopen and stockpiled in front of her. The rest of the family let her be. After everyone had opened their gifts, Janet excused herself and returned to her bedroom. Timothy had Minetta and Annie store Janet's unopened gifts in a hall closet. Matthew regaled his family with math riddles. His mother cut in periodically with foolish questions that made them all crack up with laughter.

The Christmas dinner featured Marilyn's specialty dish, a stuffed rack of lamb she prepared for these holiday affairs. Robert gave the blessing for food and family. Janet still visibly upset, but she and Bill appeared to have reconciled. They sat close together during the meal, and he would occasionally whisper in her ear, and she would smile. The conversation at dinner flowed smoothly from one topic to another. The family discussed the latest stage plays, recent movies, Oprah's reading list, celebrity gossip, and church humor. The family omitted in their languid dinner discussion any topic remotely connected to education.

After dinner clean-up, Janet and Bill retired to their bedroom, and the rest of the clan returned to the family room. They watched a timeless movie classic with Matthew and his mother mimicking the dialogue of most of the characters, and the rest of the family in hysterics. Later, everyone enjoyed a tray of Christmas cookies, fruitcakes, and finger sandwiches while playing a holiday-themed charades game. Minetta and Annie brought a tray of cookies and warm eggnog to Bill and Janet's room, but there was no response to their knock. They returned the food to the kitchen. Minetta had such a great time with her family she forgot about her troubles back home with Amber and Philip.

The day after Christmas, James and Marilyn were on the road heading back to Cedar Valley. Matthew volunteered to drive Minetta home as Craig was going home with his family. It thrilled Minetta to be in the presence of her older brother.

"This has been a good Christmas," said Minetta. Matthew, his eyes on the road, agreed. She glanced at her brother.

"Did you know Craig had not told Aunt Janet he transferred?"

"Yes, why?"

"I felt bad for Aunt Janet. She was so hurt."

"Didn't seem like you cared one way or the other."

Minetta was quiet. *What was wrong with Matthew?* She stole a glance at his face. He kept his eyes on the road.

"I don't want to talk about Craig. I want to talk to you. What's going on with you lately?"

She frowned. "What do you mean?"

He glanced at her. "Don't play stupid with me. I hear you're jealous of some girl that Phil likes. What's up with that?"

"Where did you hear that? I am not jealous of anyone."

"Look, Mimi, let me give you some advice about guys. If Phil likes you like that, he will tell you. The worst thing any girl can do is to chase a guy, let alone make enemies with another girl he may like."

Minetta was furious. "First place, Matt, I don't know where you're getting your information from, but I am not chasing anybody. Second place, Philip and I are friends and nothing more. Third place, the girl I'm supposed to be jealous of has a boyfriend already. It would be best if you were giving Philip all this advice. If he doesn't stop chasing her, her boyfriend will start chasing him."

Silence ensued as Matthew concentrated on his driving, and Minetta stewed in her thoughts. After a while, into the silence, Matthew spoke slowly and clearly.

"I will say this one time only. Right or wrong, you are my sister. If I hear Phil has hurt you, I'm kicking his ass."

Minetta looked over at her brother. She could tell by the way his eyes squinted at the road he was angry. She kept quiet. Matthew dropped her off at home without saying another word. He brought her suitcases inside and sat them by the bottom steps. She walked behind him to his car. He glanced at her as he opened the car door. He slammed the door shut, and pulled her to him in a bear hug. She hugged him back tightly. He released her, got in his vehicle, and sped down the driveway.

Minetta's gift from Philip was waiting for her when she opened her bedroom door. The pale blue box tied with white organza ribbon sat in the middle of her bed. Inside the box was a silver heart locket with her initials engraved on one side and his on the other. Within the necklace were pictures of them in first grade with the caption *forever in my heart*. Minetta shed happy tears for Philip's return to her. She sat on the side of her bed, contemplating the locket and remembering when they met in first grade.

She called Kimberly, "A merry late Christmas bestie," she said.

"Merry late Christmas to you, bestie," said Kimberly.

"Merry late Christmas, Mimi," yelled Tabitha.

"Hey! How come you guys didn't text me you were having a sleepover?"

"Because we're not. Tabs came over to show me her Christmas present from Ray," said Kimberly. "You want us to walk over?"

"Yes, I have something to show you guys too," she said.

A few minutes later, the girls stretched themselves across Minetta's bed, inspecting Tabitha's gift from Raymond. She turned her neck from side to side as the diamond earrings in her ears caught the light.

"Wow, Tabs, those are gorgeous," said Minetta. "Are they real or good fakes?"

Tabitha stopped smiling. "Does it matter?"

Kimberly looked at Minetta, slightly irritated. "They are not fakes. Mimi is trying to be funny and doing a poor job of it! They are beautiful Tabs."

"I am joking, Tabs. I doubt if Ray would give you anything cheap. He's too classy for that," said Minetta.

Kimberly smirked when Tabitha's dimpled smile returned. Minetta opened her bedside drawer and took out the pale blue box. Kimberly and Tabitha collectively gasped when she displayed the contents. They swooned further when she put the locket around her neck. Tabitha fastened the clasp.

"I knew it! I knew Philip had bought you a gift," Kimberly said.

"Oh, definitely," Tabitha happily agreed.

Kimberly stood up. "Let's go outside. I want to show you guys what Santa brought me."

They stood in the driveway of Minetta's house. "Okay, what?" said Minetta.

"Look over at my house in the driveway," said Kimberly. "What do you see?"

"Wait a minute. Is that a new car?" said Tabitha's mouth flew open as she pointed across the driveways.

Kimberly laughed merrily. "Yes, dear friends, it is my new car. It is my Christmas present from my adoring parents."

Tabitha laughed. "Oh, my goodness! I walked right by it and never noticed."

Kimberly smiled a smug grin. "How could you know, dear one? It looks like my mother's car, just a tad bit smaller, I think."

The girls ran over to Kimberly's driveway. The car was a four-door shiny black sedan with a solid white leather interior.

"It's beautiful, Kim," breathe Minetta.

"Looks like we were all blessed this Christmas," said Tabitha. The three friends hugged each other.

Cedar Valley Church held its Watch Night Service with the youth choir conducting worship services. The choir typically wore long black robes, with the musicians dressed in black and white. Minetta saw Tabitha had pulled her long brown hair back into a low ponytail, revealing the flashing diamond earrings Raymond had given her. Mrs. Horne checked their places on the choir stand.

"Alright, alright," she said. "Places everyone. Let's get into our places. Where are my sopranos?"

Amber arrived and sat next to Tabitha. She waved to Kimberly, who waved back. Andrew and other males appeared in their choir robes and sat in the bass section.

Mrs. Horne said, "will my musicians, please come up here. Everyone get into their places, please."

The musicians filed onto the platform. Minetta saw Philip dressed in a black wool suit nod towards the choir stands before taking his place at the piano. Eddie came next, wearing a loose-fitting black suit with a black shirt, and carrying his drum bag. He waved at his parents seated in the front row.

Raymond climbed up last with his saxophone case. Raymond wore a black striped wool suit. He looked over at the choir stand, smiled, and waved at Tabitha. All the girls giggled and waved back. The congregation was amused, and Mrs. Horne discretely looked down at her notes on the podium, trying to hide a smile. Signaling for attention, she cleared her throat. Amber stepped forward. She sang a Christmas song with the choir backing her.

The congregation stood up as James and Marilyn walked down the center aisle, climbed three steps, and entered the pulpit. James, clad in a black clerical robe embroidered at collar and cuffed in gold with three red velvet chevrons on the full sleeves, sat in the center chair. Marilyn, adorned in black velvet, sat at his right side. James, three assistant pastors clad in the same black clerical robe, sat to his immediate left. The remaining clergy followed the pastors in their robes and walked down the center aisle two by two. They parted to fill up the first row of seats on either side of the center aisle.

Clad in solid black were the deacons and deaconesses. The deacons sat behind the clergy, with the deaconesses seated behind them. The missionaries were sitting behind the group. Looking out into the congregation, Minetta spied her brother. He sat inconspicuously among the congregation with the blonde-haired woman. James nodded to Mrs. Horne, who signaled for the musicians to play and the youth choir to stand. Minetta and Kimberly held hands. This service would be their last official New Year's Eve service as high schoolers.

Chapter 19

Minetta stretched and reached for her buzzing alarm clock, turning it off. A new year had arrived, with one more day until school opened after winter break. She flung the bedcovers back and swung both legs to the floor. She was heading to the bathroom when she glimpsed her reflection in the bureau mirror and smiled. Her cellphone was buzzing on her nightstand when she came out. It was a text message from Kimberly: *Have the new catalog from La Femme Divine. Tabs and I will be over in fifteen minutes.*

Leave it to her best friend to be on the mailing list of one of the most exquisite and exclusive boutiques in Cedar Valley Township, even though her attire of choice was often leisurewear. Minetta opened her Bible app and read the morning devotional message along with the Scripture reference. She reached for the new blue floral journal she had received as a Christmas present from Tabitha. Minetta touched the silver locket at her neck and brightened up when images of Philip came into her mind's eye. She remembered her last conversation with Matthew, and the smile left her face. She knew her older brother well. He was usually pleasant with her, but he was direct in his approach and mannerisms when he was serious about something.

She pulled on an oversized blue cashmere sweater and denim leggings and went down the back stairs to the kitchen below. Her father was sitting at the breakfast table reading the newspaper app on his tablet and drinking coffee. His plate displayed the slight remains of a hearty meal. He looked up at Minetta. A smile appeared on his cheerful face. He put his tablet to the side. "Good morning, sweetheart!"

"Good morning, Dad," she said.

Minetta walked over to her father and hugged him. For as long as she could remember, they had never had cross words with each other. Her father found solutions to problems through prayer and meditation. He remained calm in whatever storm was raging.

She remembered a situation where her father picked up the telephone to receive news of a fatal accident occurring with one of the church members. Later, when Minetta asked her father what he was doing when he closed his eyes standing by the telephone, his reply had been "praying for miraculous healing."

She walked over to the counter and filled a coffee mug. Her mother had long ago adopted the habit of relaxing on Monday after spending the weekend in church. Besides her role as a librarian, the women's ministries within the church kept her busy, as well as her other charitable pursuits outside the church.

"Good morning, Mrs. B.," said Minetta to the woman coming into the kitchen from the backyard door.

Beatrice was an early riser. It was she who always turned on the coffee maker and prepared her father's breakfast. She smiled upon seeing Minetta. Beatrice regretted she had been useless in altering the meager eating habits of Marilyn or the fussy eating habits of Minetta.

"You want me to fix you a plate or perhaps an omelet?"

"No, thank you." Minetta smiled coyly.

Kimberly walked into the kitchen with her red curls gathered in a messy topknot and dressed in a strawberry pink suede tracksuit with matching sneakers, carrying her school tote bag. Tabitha followed in a long purple coat over a purple floral dress and carrying her knitting sack.

"Good morning, everyone. Hello Pastor James, Mrs. B," said Kimberly.

Tabitha, with her usual shyness, merely smiled. Kimberly smiled and sat down at the breakfast table opposite James. Beatrice brought her some orange juice. Her voracious appetite amused James. She never seemed to gain weight, and he attributed that fact to her highly active lifestyle. She was a solidly built girl. He nodded a thank you to Beatrice for bringing over the orange juice. Tabitha shook her head in response to a look from Beatrice.

"Good morning, young ladies. How are you today?" asked James, amused at how different these young ladies' personalities were.

"I'm good, Pastor," said Kimberly, taking a sip of orange juice. She had eaten at home but did not mind eating again if offered food. Beatrice sat down a plate with three large pancakes in front of her, and Kimberly poured maple syrup on them. Tabitha and Minetta screwed up their faces at the gooey concoction. Beatrice wagged her head at them in a no-no gesture.

"If there's nothing else you need, Pastor, I'll be bringing First Lady her breakfast," said Beatrice to James.

"No, there is nothing more from me. Thank you, Mrs. B. Girls, you want anything before Mrs. B. leaves?" he asked the girls.

"No." They responded in unison.

Beatrice climbed the back stairs, carrying a tray laden with coffee and pancakes to visit with Marilyn. James smiled at the retreating figure of Beatrice. His wife would drink the coffee and Beatrice would eat the food. He switched off his tablet.

"Well, girls, let's pray before I leave," he said.

All four bowed their heads, and James prayed for providential care and blessings for the day. The church was closed today, but he and a few of his senior clergy and deacons would be there until early afternoon praying for an abundance of blessings in the new year. After the prayer, he kissed his daughter on the cheek and waved goodbye to Kimberly and Tabitha before leaving out the side door leading to the garage.

Kimberly finished eating as Minetta sat with her arms crossed, watching her.

"Mimi, have you heard from Philip yet?" Kimberly asked between bites of pancake.

"No," replied Minetta. "We rarely speak every day. Why?"

She glanced warily at Kimberly, who had her eyes on her plate. She looked at Tabitha, who had pulled out her knitting yarn. Something was up. They were avoiding looking at her.

"I saw Philip and Amber yesterday in the mall," said Kimberly.

"So?" replied Minetta. She kept her arms crossed to keep from shaking.

"There does not appear to be a boyfriend." She looked straight at Minetta. "Every time I see them, there is never anyone else present."

"What do you mean by every time you see them? How many times have you seen them together?"

"They have been in the mall together over the Christmas holidays and leading up to the new year. I saw Amber eating dinner with Philip's family in La Dolce Vita Restaurant just last week. Just ask Eddie. My parents had taken us all out to eat, and that's how we saw Philip and Amber sitting together with Philip's family."

"Also," interjected Tabitha, swallowing as she kept her eyes on her knitting needles. "Ray and I were at the Fitness Center, and they were there together. She seemed to be showing him how to use a particular machine."

Kimberly brought her dishes to the sink and rinsed them before placing them in the dishwasher. Minetta was mute. She touched the locket around her neck. What was going on with Philip? He told her Amber had a boyfriend. Yet Kimberly had seen him all over town with Amber while she was away with her family. It hurt her.

"Eddie says Philip hasn't told him anything about his relationship with Amber either."

"Nor has he spoken to Ray," said Tabitha.

Kimberly finished with the dishwasher and walked back to the table. Minetta sat back in her chair and sighed. There was a lump in her heart. She stood up.

"Okay, besties. Let's go to my room and look at that catalog," Minetta said, heading for the stairs. "After we can play some video games."

"Wait a minute," Kimberly called after her. "You don't care if they might be dating or something?"

Minetta looked back at Kimberly and Tabitha from the stairs and smiled a sad smile of defeat.

"I care. I'm just not going to compete with Amber for Philip. I know Philip. If he were dating her, he would tell me. I don't know what's going on, but I don't think it's something I'm going to worry about."

Tabitha smiled. "Good for you, Mimi. They just seem like good friends to me. Who knows? All those summers in Hawaii probably… ouch!"

Kimberly pinched Tabitha on her arm. In the deepest part of her heart, Minetta was having difficulty believing what she said to her best friends. Nor could she explain the smothering sensation in her chest whenever she saw Amber and Philip together. If Minetta were honest with herself, she would have been able and willing to tell her two closest friends it was killing her inside, envisioning Philip liking another girl. She was confused about her feelings and more confused about Philip. She watched her friends gather their belongings and exhaled. Why did life have to be so darn complicated?

Cedar Valley High School's Performing Arts Center was conducting the last dress rehearsal for the winter play, an adaptation of the musical, *Gigi.* Minetta, seated midway in the auditorium, had a broad view of the stage. She had never seen it packed this full of students and teachers and saw a few parents as well. Minetta looked to the far right of the area. She saw Josh, Lizzie, Kelly, Eddie, and Kimberly sitting on the floor with several other students. The drama teacher, Elsa Coates, signaled to Mark in the Audio/Visual Control Room. There was a hush as Amber walked onto the stage dressed in a pink and white velvet gown. Ben played the piano. Amber opened her mouth and sung one tune from the third act. The room was quiet.

"Hey Mimi, really exciting, isn't it?" whispered Philip, seated to her right.

Minetta was there to write for the school paper, and Philip to take photographs. Kelly, followed by Lizzie and Josh, joined them.

Kelly gazed at the stage in awe. "I didn't know she could speak French, let alone sing in it."

"She's amazing, isn't she?" said Josh.

"Oh, and so beautiful," whispered Lizzie, her eyes glued to the stage.

"She's one talented girl, that's for sure," said Philip.

Minetta agreed. Amber's voice never warbled, and no matter what costume she wore, how dim the lighting, how drab the background, her beauty shone.

"Kim did a great job with the background scenery," said Lizzie.

"Let's not forget who designed the costumes they're wearing," offered Kelly. "Tabitha can make any item of clothing, it seems."

"Not to mention Eddie's work on the background scenery," said Josh.

"I knew Ben played the saxophone. I didn't know he played the piano, too," said Kelly.

"Yeah, he plays the piano, saxophone, and violin. I'm proud to be here, man," said Philip, his voice cracking. "There's so much talent on that stage."

Minetta glanced sideways at him. Oh, Brother! The song ended, and Amber received a standing ovation from her cast mates on the stage with her. Philip rushed down to take photographs, with Kelly, Josh, and Lizzie following. Minetta packed her laptop and left. Across the aisle, seated near the back, Raymond and Tabitha watched her exit the auditorium.

When Minetta and Kimberly walked into the Soda Shoppe, a guy wearing a party hat stood by the front door waving his water bottle in greeting. Their classmates from the play packed the place. The jukebox was playing a popular tune, and some teens were dancing.

"What's going on, Jake?" Kimberly asked the boy at the door.

"A pre-celebration party for the cast," Jake said as he reached behind her to get his girlfriend's attention, who walked in behind them.

"Ladies, our reserved seats are this way," shouted Eddie as he took hold of Kimberly's hand and weaved through the crowd.

"Ben and Amber are holding down the fort," said Philip taking Minetta's hand.

Minetta felt vaguely uneasy. Someone had placed orders for burgers, French fries, and milkshakes. In the next booth sat Josh, Lizzie, Kelly, and Mark. Minetta tried to control her breathing as the noise in the place was deafening in intensity, and she wondered when it had become customary to celebrate before a play rather than afterward.

Kimberly was exuberant. "That was an awesome last rehearsal, Amber."

"Thank you, Kim. I was so nervous. I kept thinking I would forget a line or fall or something idiotic like that."

"You were great," joined in Tabitha. "I didn't know you could sing in French."

Amber blushed. "I speak French, Spanish, and Italian."

"Where did you learn to speak so many languages?" Raymond asked.

"The different places we lived growing up. Ben has helped me perfect my French for the play."

Philip looked at Ben. "I didn't know you could speak French. Why didn't you join the French Club?"

Looking slightly embarrassed, Ben replied, "I learned French when I was younger, and my paternal grandparents lived with us. They're from Jamaica."

"That's pretty cool," said Eddie, salting his French fries.

"Ben, don't you also speak Spanish and Italian?" asked Philip. "I remember how good your Spanish was in our advanced language classes last year."

"Yes. I think foreign languages come easy for me to understand."

Ben was stockpiling pickle and tomato slices on his hamburger from Amber and Minetta's contributions.

"I wish I could say the same," moan Kimberly. "I can't wait to be done with French class."

Eddie laughed. "For someone who can read and write French pretty well, I don't know why you have so much difficulty with your pronunciations."

Kimberly playfully swatted Eddie. "Never mind making fun of me. How did you like my designs for the interior scenes?"

"They're perfect, Kim." Eddie's light eyes seem to glow as he discussed the design concepts related to the play. "The sofa for the boudoir scene looks great in that purple velvet fabric. The Paris street scene will need to be adjusted because we have specific measurements we have to work with."

Kimberly leaned in. "What about the dance hall scene? I'm supposed to use a heavy dark curtain as a backdrop. Will you be building up the back part?"

"Yes, and no. Ben, I'm going to need your help in looking at the elevation piece. I can't seem to get the math together there. Something's missing."

"Anytime, Eddie."

Varsity cheer team members, Claire, and Mike, stopped by to chat with Amber, Kimberly, and Tabitha. A few minutes later, Veronica, Jewel, and Sallie hung out at their table with their athlete boyfriends. In no time, the area was congested with people talking and laughing, all comfortable in each other's presence.

Minetta ate her food and watched Amber surreptitiously. She could not shake the feeling that she was a stranger among her friends. The ease with which they discussed the play bothered her because of Amber's familiarity with her friends. They seem to share a rapport with Amber as if she were their long-lost cousin and not a girl who began her senior year in a school hundreds of miles from her former life.

Minetta listened to Annette discussing an upcoming sleepover she was planning for the varsity squad and her basketball player boyfriend wanted to know if they would invite the male cheerleaders. When she said no, the group exploded with laughter and jokes. Minetta took it all in with a heavy heart.

The weather had turned decidedly chilly by the night of the winter production by Cedar Valley High's Performing Arts Center. The French-themed play, as performed by the students during rehearsals, impressed the drama teacher, including the publicity their rehearsals generated.

The evening of the play the local newspaper, Cedar Valley Gazette, covered the event. Instead of the customary write-up, the editor, impressed with the performance he saw during his family's attendance, opted for a two-page edition spread for the paper's weekend issue. Eddie received praised for his outstanding ability to design and build realistic-looking French-inspired background scenery. Kimberly's attention to detail with the interior design elements received praise, as were Tabitha's creativity and ingenuity in drafting the costume period pieces.

But it was Amber in the lead role that drew the most rave reviews. The Gazette noted her physical beauty, three-octave voice range, and superb mastery of the French language, and noteworthy acting and dancing skills. They called her a “future triple threat” if she ever “acts on so much talent.” For the school paper, Minetta wrote detailed reviews of the play’s cast, including the students responsible for the background scenery and period costumes. She barely mentioned Amber’s performance.

Chapter 20

Cedar Valley High's gymnasium was in a total planning, creating, and decorating mode that would transform the site to party central for the school's Valentine's Day dance. Members of the cheer squad, dance team, football, and other sports teams volunteered to help with decorating the gym. The school typically bought the supplies, the art department created the designs, and the volunteer design teams brought them to life.

Minetta and her friends helped with the event instead of going to their favorite hangout. Eddie had enlisted some of the crew from the shop and woodworking class to help him build a concession stand rather than the usual banquet table. Andrew suggested an enclosed area for the deejay which was met with enthusiastic approval from Eddie.

When Minetta arrived, she saw Eddie, Kimberly, and Amber, with a few cheer squad and dance team members standing to the side talking, and walked over to them.

"Hey guys," said Minetta. "What's going on?"

Lizzie smiled with her. "Amber's telling us about the rules for this year's prom dates."

"It's true. Watch out because if you haven't been asked to the prom and you're asked at the Valentine's dance, you're supposed to be honest and attend with the person asking."

"That's ridiculous," said Kimberly, listening with arms crossed.

Eddie grinned. "Don't worry, my beautiful redhead, I have something for all that nonsense."

"Who made up that? I would be mad if my boyfriend had to go to a dance with someone else."

"Do we have to wait until the dance to ask someone?" asked Josh.

"No," replied Mark. "You can ask someone before the dance arrives. That's if someone has not asked you."

Amber agreed. "It might be best to choose your prom date before the dance."

Josh looked at Lizzie. "Would you go to the prom with me?"

She grinned. "Yes."

Kimberly shook her head. "Whoever dreamed up this scam should be shot."

"Probably someone who never can get dates," mused Minetta.

Amber and Eddie laughed. "That was cold, Mimi," said Eddie.

Kelly sat beside Mark, who was hammering a poste, and he turned and looked at her. She smiled.

"Would you attend the prom with me, Kelly?"

"Yes, all day, yes!" They both grinned, and she helped him with the posters.

Minetta looked around. She wanted to see Philip and hoped he would ask her now.

"Hey bestie, we're leaving now. I think Philip will be here soon. Talk to you later," said Kimberly as she gathered her book bag and walked out with Eddie.

Amber handed her a lightweight box of red and white streamers and the printout instructions for their placement in the gymnasium. She found a table and set to work on the streamers. Sometime later, Minetta was instructing a few students how to hang the white and red streamers around the ceiling rafters and spied Philip enter the room. She turned the rest of the decorations over to the students. Minetta was walking through the gymnasium toward Philip and stopped because he headed in the opposite direction. She looked up at the exit sign on the door. Why was he going outside using that exit? She followed him, unaware Raymond was watching her. Raymond pulled out his phone.

Outside, Minetta trailed Philip to the bleachers where Amber was standing with Tabitha, who was on her cellphone. She watched as the trio talked and laughed. She saw Raymond coming out of another door, and they all followed him in that direction. She was confused. That was the boys' locker room. As the group neared the door, it was pushed open from inside. Someone else was waiting for them. Where were they all going?

She ran to the door, but it was locked. She turned and ran back to the door she had come out of and found someone had removed the board she had placed there to keep it open. Sighing, she walked around to the front side. She had to walk down the expanse of the hallway to return to the gymnasium.

There was now music, flashing strobe lighting, and more people. Students and teachers were milling about, laughing, talking, helping with the designs, sitting down in groups working on decorations. She scanned the crowd, trying to find her friends. Where was everybody?

"Hey, Mimi." She turned at the effervescent voice of Lizzie holding a red heart-shaped balloon and smiling at her. "Are you okay?"

"Hi, Lizzie. Yes, I'm fine."

"I just found two large boxes of these heart-shaped balloons. I think they're so pretty."

"Yes, they are, but they were last year's theme balloons. This year we voted for the sequins and beads. Maybe next year your team can use those balloons."

"Oh, I see. Thanks."

As Lizzie turned to leave, Minetta asked her, "have you seen Kim, Philip, or anybody?"

"They were looking for you. I don't know where they went, though."

"Oh, okay, thanks again."

"No problem."

Minetta sat down on a bleacher. Were they looking for her before they removed the board from the door?

The low buzzing in her ear prompted Minetta to turn over groggily. She looked at her alarm clock. It was one o'clock in the morning. The one person who would sneak and call her after curfew was Kimberly. Was she going to apologize for running out on her earlier in the gymnasium? She had all evening for that. No one called her, and no one answered their phones. She assumed Kimberly's conscience must bother her behind the game of hide-and-seek they played on her earlier. Minetta ignored the phone. It buzzed again. She reached out into the dark and snatched it off her nightstand.

"This had better be important. It's the middle of the night!"

"It is important. Why haven't you been answering your phone?"

"No one's been calling me."

"I've been calling you, and so has Philip."

"What does he want? For me to invite Amber to the dance?"

Kimberly laughed. "No, he wants to invite you to go with him."

She jumped up and switched on her night lamp. "What? How do you know this? Please don't be jerking me around, Kim."

"For goodness' sakes, be quiet. Eddie told me he was going to ask you. See if his number is on your phone. He might have called and left a message. You know Philip. I'll see you tomorrow."

Minetta's fingers were trembling. She could barely tap the keys. Hallelujah!! Yes, he had called twice and left a voice message with the last call. She played the message.

Hi Mimi, it's me, Philip. Look, I didn't have time to see you today. No, that's not true. I saw you. I mean, there wasn't an opportunity to speak with you earlier. I wanted to ask you to be my date for the Valentine's Day dance. If you've accepted someone else, please let me know as soon as you can.

She smiled to herself and laid back on her pillows. She was about to drift off into dreamland when the message replayed itself in her mind. She sat up again. She sent him a recorded message in case he asked someone else, namely Amber.

Hi Philip, this is me, Mimi. I would love to be your date for the dance. Thank you for asking me.

The Valentine Day dance dress code stated boys in black suits with red ties and girls in red dresses. When Philip picked Minetta up, he was in a black suit with a red tie and pocket square. He gave her a red heart-shaped candy box with a white lily attached. Minetta wore a red knit dress with a multitiered tulle skirt that hit the top of her knees. Marilyn snapped pictures, and James prayed with them at the front door. Finally, they were walking down her front steps. Philip ushered her to a black four-door car.

"Where's your truck?" she asked.

"Traded it in for this one. It's a Camaro. I like how it looks. You like it, don't you?"

"Yes, it's nice."

Philip smiled. They did little talking. The students packed the gymnasium when they arrived at the school. The teachers acting as chaperones were in red dresses and black suits. She saw her friends and walked over to them.

Kimberly wore an off-the-shoulder deep red brocade dress with a full skirt. Tabitha's red suede dress had a mock collar with ruffles at the cuffs and hemline. Amber's lipstick red satin dress was cowl neck with a scoop back and flared skirt.

"Wow, Mimi, that is a magnificent dress!" exclaimed Kimberly.

"Chic is all I can say," agreed Amber, smiling.

Minetta blushed. "Thanks. I think we all look great tonight."

"I have to agree," stated Tabitha with a mischievous grin.

"Come on, let's find our table," said Amber. "The place card is in the centerpiece."

"Everything looks bright and sparkly," said Tabitha.

Kimberly found their table. "Here we are. Front and center." She bent to read the names on the card.

The strobe lights were turned on, and the music grew louder. As couples paired up, Minetta looked around for Philip and sat down at the table. She scanned the room. Raymond came by.

"May I have this dance?" he asked.

On the floor, she looked up at Raymond. He seemed a lot bigger than she remembered. As she gazed up at him, he looked down at her, and the blue eyes focused on her.

"You know when you look at me; your eyes look like slivers of deep blue thunder sometimes," she said.

Raymond laughed. “It’s the cheekbones. I don’t believe that’s my fault. If I had normal Native eyes, you would not notice me looking at you half the time.”

She laughed, then comprehension struck. “Wait. What did you say?”

“Nothing important,” and he twirled her about, and she landed in Eddie’s arms.

“Whoa,” she said, and Eddie laughed gaily. She laughed. “You guys must have practiced that move.”

“Yeah, you right,” said Eddie. “Enjoying yourself, Mimi?”

“I am,” she said. “I didn’t know you guys could dance this good. Jeez.”

Eddie smiled. “It’s not all football, fishing, and frolicking. Sometimes we take time out for the finer things in life.”

She laughed, and he grinned right before he twirled her into the arms of Ben. She doubled over with laughter this time.

“Stop this,” she said.

Ben grinned. “Now, you don’t want all this fun to end, do you?”

“You guys are amazing on the field and off,” she said.

“So true, so true,” he said. “Enjoy. The evening is still young.”

Ben twirled her into the arms of Philip, who caught her around the waist.

“Like our fancy footwork, do you?”

“I am dizzy, so please, no more spinning.” She was laughing hard now.

“Okay, you’re safe with me,” he said.

She was slightly dizzy. The lights had dimmed. She noticed how close they were dancing and how Philip had her in a full embrace. She put her arms around his waist. She had never experienced this type of closeness with him. Her breathing became labored, and she stiffened slightly. Philip noticed.

“Take it easy, breathe a bit,” he said in her ear and moved back a bit.

“We’ve never danced together like this.”

“Hmm” was all he said.

The last few refrains of the song were coming. Philip embraced her in his arms again and kissed her before releasing her as the lights turned up.

She was conscious of being led back to their table, talking and laughing with her friends, of playing a silly table game, and of the presence of Philip by her side for most of the evening.

There was another slow ballad, and Philip, without asking her, took her hand and led her to the dance floor. This time she was not so nervous, and when the lights began dimming, she did not mind when he pulled her closer. The lights turned on and stayed on, and they cut the song short for announcements by the principal.

Minetta was contemplating if Philip would kiss her again later that night when Andrew came over and asked her to dance. The tiny voice in her head was telling her to say no. The song was an up-tempo beat, which meant everyone was on the floor, including Philip with a classmate. They danced several sets, and Andrew led her back to the table. No one was there. Eddie and Kimberly came over.

"Whew, that is some crazy song. Talk about long," said Eddie. "Hey, it's about that time."

Kimberly grinned. "Been waiting all night."

"I'll just bet you have," said Eddie. He went down on one knee and, with a bouquet of white roses in hand, said, "Kimberly Van Owens, my red-haired goddess, will you be my prom date?"

"Yes, my handsome boyfriend."

Minetta looked around in panic. Where was Philip? She glimpsed the stricken look on Kimberly's face and looked to see Andrew on his knees with a bouquet in one hand and a prom invitation in the other.

"Minetta Morgan, will you be my prom date?"

The room became hot and muggy. Minetta struggled against looking disappointed. With a small sigh, she managed a smile.

"Yes, Andrew, thank you."

She accepted his bouquet and buried her face in it. Darn! Minetta walked through the rest of the evening in a haze. She forced herself to get through the night and could not wait to leave. Philip drove her home, and neither said a word. Philip walked her to her door, hugged her, and left. She watched his car until the taillights faded.

An hour later, she laid on her bed, weak with disappointment. Her phone's constant buzzing became a source of irritation. *Oh, please leave me alone!* Finally, she picked it up.

"Hey, Kim, what's up? It's late."

"Bestie, I know you're disappointed. Ray said Philip wanted to ask you to the prom. He had left his bouquet for you in his car. He had gone outside to the parking lot to get it."

"Really?" Minetta could barely speak. She could feel the tears stinging her eyelids.

"Yes. Eddie feels bad because he felt like he gave Andrew the idea to ask you to the prom at that exact moment."

"I don't know, Kim. This year just seems to be a loser for Philip and me. If it's not Amber, then it's Andrew. Why can't Andrew be interested in Amber? I guess Andrew will never get a chance with Philip in the way."

"Mimi, it's going to work out. You'll see."

"It will work out for Amber. Philip can ask her now."

Minetta's voice had fallen to a soft whimper. Kimberly remained quiet. Tears fell from Minetta's eyes. She felt as if she were walking into a misty rainfall, and around her was quiet blackness.

She mumbled into her phone. "Good night, Kim."

Chapter 21

The cheer squad was practicing in the gymnasium when Minetta rushed in from the girls' locker room. Kimberly was practicing a dance move by herself in the middle of the gymnasium. Minetta straightened her ivory and black sleeveless shell. She sat on the bench to adjust a sneaker watching Tabitha go over a new routine with Amber and the junior varsity cheerleaders.

Kimberly sat down next to her. "Hey, Mimi," she said. "What took you so long?"

"I had to get my sneakers out of my car. I forgot them this morning." She nodded toward Amber. "How's she doing with the routines?"

Kimberly smiled. "Amber's pretty good. She's a quick study, too."

"She would be," muttered Minetta.

Turning to Kimberly, she pointed to several freshmen varsity members who were watching from the bench.

"Why aren't they on the floor?"

"They're our freshmen. The first-year group, remember?"

"Remember? We're the ones who started as freshmen. I want them on the floor learning the steps. They're not getting experience hugging the bench. And, what's with the varsity team? Why are they relaxing?"

Kimberly side-eyed her and stood up. Minetta walked toward the cheerleaders.

"Okay, ladies. Let's get into formation. Barbara, Wanda, Lisa, Debbie, Nancy, Angela, Chloe, Diana, Rachel, and Elisabeth. Let's go!"

Minetta called over to Tabitha to bring her group over to the bleachers where the elite squad, most of who were talking and watching Tabitha and the junior varsity members, were sitting. Minetta waited for all the cheerleaders to find seats on the bleachers. She stood on the first bleacher to get their attention.

"Okay, reminder for the senior and junior varsity members here. No one should be on the bleachers during practice time. Whether you're practicing a dance move, stunt routine, or stretching your limbs, you should be doing something! I will dock you if I ever walk in here and see you ladies like this again. I want the JV members to practice with the freshmen group today. I want the varsity team with me. Let's move ladies."

Minetta watched as the girls who made up the junior varsity walked over to Kimberly, who assigned their positions. When she turned back to the varsity team, they were standing behind her on the floor with Tabitha.

"Okay, ladies. Let's go out in style. We synchronized the new routines to perfection. Let's put our game face on and work it!"

The practice session went smooth. Minetta, anchored by Tabitha and Amber, practiced the new routines focused on synchronization. When Sarah walked into the gymnasium to observe, she nodded approvingly at the teamwork.

The boys' basketball team came into the gymnasium from the other side and Minetta refused to look across the room. She did not want to catch Philip ogling Amber now that they were wearing shorts instead of long pants.

"Okay, ladies. That's all for today. You were all perfect. Pat yourselves on the back," Minetta said as the team finished the last routine in sync. The girls headed for the locker room.

Minetta was picking around her eggplant parmigiana while Kimberly described an evening gown she saw in the latest edition of *La Femme Divine* magazine.

"I tell you Tabs, it is a beautiful gown." Kim finished with a sigh.

Tabitha smiled. "What color is this fabulous gown?"

"It is a dark Robin's egg blue with gold bead work at the collar."

"Sounds like it would go perfect with your hair color, Kim. What do you think, Mimi?"

"I agree. Here come the guys."

Philip slid in beside Minetta. "Have you finished with your piece on the play rehearsals yet?"

"Well, hello to you, too," said Minetta. "To answer your question, yes. I'll send it to you later after I've proof-read it."

"Sorry, Mimi. I have a book report and science project to complete so I wanted to get that out of the way early so I can concentrate."

"It's okay. I'll send it to you once I get home."

"Great. Thanks,"

They had a pleasant lunch hour, as only Eddie and Raymond showed up a few minutes later. To Minetta, it was reminiscent of old times when it was just the six of them. Truth be told, she did not mind the addition of Ben and Andrew or even a few of their other friends. The one person whose presence she abhorred was Amber's. Every time she appeared, Philip's entire attention centered solely on Amber, and it incensed Minetta. She was so happy to have Philip all to herself she could barely eat her lunch. The rest of the day went along very well for her.

Chapter 22

The spring production of *Othello* promised to be the highlight of the Performing Arts Center's season. The spring productions relied heavily on drama, with none of the winter plays' light song and dance formulas. The drama teacher used senior class members in the entire production, with a few background additions supplied by the junior class. By the unanimous decision of the students, Amber was assigned the lead role as Desdemona. The role of Iago went to Josh, and in a surprise move, the lead role of *Othello* went to Ben, whose voice was perfect in pitch and volume. The cast members went wild with applause after his audition.

Minetta, watching the audition from the fifth row in the center aisle, sat spellbound. She looked around observing Mark sat in the Audio/Visual Control Room with his headphones on. She saw Eddie, Tabitha, and Kimberly hunched over sketch pads to the right of the stage. On the stage in a crouched position, Philip was snapping photographs, and Raymond, the play's director, was discussing dialogue with Ben, Amber, and Josh. Andrew and his team pushing large boxes in the background behind the production crew.

Fellow actors, Lizzie, and Kelly, eased into seats beside her. Lizzie had a copy of the script she was redlining because she was Amber's understudy.

"Exciting, isn't it?" asked Kelly, hugging herself.

"Ben has an outstanding voice, and he looks good up there on the stage," said Minetta.

"Yes, he does," agreed Lizzie.

Philip sat beside her. "Hey, guys! This production promises to be the best, so far."

"I'll say." Kelly was watching Mark in the Control Room. "I'll see you guys later."

"Bye, Kelly," said Lizzie, before turning to Minetta and Philip. "I'm going to study with Amber for a minute. See you guys, later."

Philip smiled at Minetta. "How's it going? You look a little tired. You, okay?"

"I'm fine, Philip. I wonder why you never notice when I look good. Only when I look bad."

Minetta got up and walked away, leaving Philip with a puzzled look on his handsome face.

It was late afternoon, and Minetta was studying. Her phone buzzed. It was Philip.

"Hi Philip."

"We need to talk face to face. Can I come over?"

"What's the matter?"

"I need your womanly advice about something."

"Why do we need face to face for advice?"

"Because I don't want to discuss it on the phone. Okay?"

"How about after dinner tonight?"

"That sounds good."

She sat looking at the phone. She changed from the ratty top she was wearing to a pink pullover and light gray sweatpants. Philip appeared promptly after the dinner hour. She stayed in her room until Beatrice came upstairs to tell her he was downstairs in the family room. She took her sweet time going downstairs.

Tonight, the youth Bible studies group met at the church, and she would see him in another hour. She walked into the room, and Philip stood when she entered. She side-eyed him and sat in a chaise lounge opposite him as he sat on the sofa. She played with the rings on her fingers and reclined back on the cushions.

Beatrice brought out a tray of pastries, a pitcher of water, and a sliced pound cake. Minetta watched Philip place a slice of cake and an apple sconce on his plate. For as long as she had known them, Philip and Kimberly enjoyed eating. She often speculated to herself how they maintained their physiques with the amount of food both could consume. Philip finished the pastries and drained a glass of water in one gulp.

She studied him. He was wearing a blue oxford shirt, navy blazer, and blue jeans. His hair was trimmed with height on top and tapered on the sides. He wore no earrings, tattoos, or markings on his skin or clothing. Wristwatches were the only type of jewelry she had ever seen him wear.

Philip smiled. "Thanks for seeing me on such short notice. School and sports have swamped me the past few weeks."

"Is that an apology?"

"Apology for what?"

"Is that all you came by for?"

"Not exactly. I wanted to ask a favor."

"What kind of favor?"

"I need your help with a situation."

"What situation, Philip?"

"I want to ask Amber to the prom."

She could not hear above the silence that engulfed her. Her body felt suspended in space.

"What about me?" she asked in a tiny voice.

"Look, Andrew told me he's already asked you. That leaves me without a date. I've been thinking about asking Amber because her boyfriend rarely attends these kinds of functions."

"Why is he the boyfriend, then?"

"His religion…"

She sat up straight. "Stop! Stop, Philip! What is this? Blooper scenes from the Frog Princess or Ariel the Little Mermaid?"

"Don't get angry. It's the truth."

"If his religion has not stopped her from dating him, what is it to you?"

"I want her to have something besides gold medals and awards. I want her to have fun or at least realize what fun is."

"Why? According to you, she's virtually a stranger. Why is her going with you to the prom suddenly a realization for her to know what fun is? That's her boyfriend's job, isn't it?"

"I'm trying to be a friend. I'm asking you to help me with a problem."

"That's your problem? Taking Amber to the prom? So she can realize the fullness of life although she has a boyfriend she's supposedly madly in love with?"

"No, how to ask her. Can we move past your obsession with this girl's private life? Are you going to help me or not?"

"Help you do what? You're playing games with your life; I'll tell you that. If she really has a boyfriend, I don't think he'll care for all the attention you've been giving her. Also, he's her guy, and if she's happy with him, why are you butting your nose in their personal affairs?"

Philip looked at her. "I don't think he'd mind. It might let him off the hook with his parents and hers."

"That makes little sense. What is this Cicero de Bergerac nonsense? Why not just admit you're the one infatuated with her, and willing to die to be in her presence?"

Philip was staring at her. He looked like he found her comments amusing, but he dared not smile.

"Are you done? My problem is that I don't know how to ask her without it seeming as if I want to date her or something. I just want to take her as a friend. Like you're going to the prom with Andrew as your friend, right?"

"What are you talking about, Philip? Usually you make sense, but tonight you just seem to be babbling."

Philip sighed. "Your right. I am babbling. I got this. Thanks for listening. See you later at church?"

"Of course."

She got up to walk him to the door. Irritated, confused, and slightly angry with herself for listening to the nonsense he spewed. She opened the door, and stepped back for him to walk past her. Philip walked across the threshold and turned around. She looked up. He pulled her toward him and kissed her.

"Stop being angry with me."

He lightly jogged down the steps to his car. She stood in the open doorway with a smile on her face, watching his vehicle until the lights faded.

An hour later, Minetta was driving to the church with Kimberly as Amber had picked up Tabitha.

"Why is Amber trying to invade our friendship?" Minetta sighed.

She was getting a smothered feeling in her chest again, and she did not like it. Kimberly straightened up in her seat and turned to look at her.

"You know she asked me if Tabs and Ray were a couple?"

Minetta braked hard before parking on the side of the road. "What?"

"Yeah. It was the very first time she rode to the church with us. The night she said her housekeeper or whoever brought her car to the church because she had to stop somewhere before heading home."

"Wait a minute, Kim. She can't be interested in Ray because you've always seen her with Philip."

Kim nodded. "Just telling you what came out of her mouth."

"Well, get a load of what came out of Philip's mouth tonight. He wanted me to tell him how to ask her to the senior prom."

Kimberly's mouth opened in a wide O. "What?" She laughed out loud. "Are you serious?"

"Yes, I am serious. He brought up Andrew asking me to the prom to justify his taking her. I have barely seen him since we returned to school, but I'm supposed to know he wanted to take me to the prom?"

"Yeah, Eddie asked me before the holidays. The dance was just his way of being romantic. I think Ray asked Tabs before he went away, too. What's Philip's excuse for taking Amber instead of you?"

"He wants Amber to enjoy the fun side of high school instead of just the celebrations connected with winning sports championships." Minetta rolled her eyes upward and pursed her lips.

Kimberly's olive-green eyes flashed. "So why doesn't the boyfriend bring her to the prom?"

"According to Philip, because Amber's parents do not approve of the boyfriend and something about religion."

"But they would approve of Philip instead?"

There was silence as the girls looked at each other. The car exploded with sound as they doubled over with laughter. They laughed long and hard. Kimberly had to wipe the tears from her eyes with the back of her shirt sleeve as Minetta searched blindly for Kleenex in the glove compartment.

Kimberly, between giggles, said, “good one. Is Philip on medication or something? Does he really want you to believe that?”

“I don’t know,” said Minetta, revving the car engine. “Does he believe it?” Looking behind her, she edged out onto the road. “I don’t know what’s wrong with him, Kim. But ever since Amber Paige entered our lives, he hasn’t been the Philip we know.”

“You got that right.” Kimberly scrunched up her nose. “I don’t think it’s an intimate relationship, though.”

“What do you mean?” asked Minetta, frowning.

“Between Philip and Amber. I don’t think it’s intimate?”

“How so?”

“Well, the times I’ve seen them together, there’s no sign of affection between them. You know, like holding hands or anything.”

“That means nothing. Do you and Eddie hold hands?”

“Yes, most if not all, couples do.”

There was silence as the car sped forward. Each girl lost in her own thoughts.

“Kim?”

“Huh, uh.” Kim was fussing with her curly bangs. Minetta glanced at her quickly.

“Philip kissed me at the Valentine’s Day dance.”

Kimberly stopped touching her hair and stared at the side of Minetta’s head. “Okay. When and where?”

“When we were dancing on the floor. When the lights dimmed and right before they turned back up.”

“Well, well.” Kimberly started grinning. “Tell me again why your so hung up over Amber if Philip is showing you attention?”

“Philip did something strange when he was leaving my house earlier today,” said Minetta after a few moments of silence.

“Oh yeah? How strange?” asked Kimberly distractedly. She was reapplying pink lip gloss and looking at her reflection in her compact.

"He hugged me."

"So? Haven't you guys ever hugged before?"

"Of course, but that's not what I mean. Usually, it's a side hug, but this time he pulled me into his arms. The way Eddie hugs you. And he kissed me again. He's never done that before."

"I think Philip is getting serious about you."

"I don't know, Kim. The way he looks out for Amber tells me something different."

"You ever think that maybe Philip knows the boyfriend and is just looking out for Amber for him?"

"Please, Kim. Would Eddie let a guy get close to you while he's away?"

"No, don't believe he would."

As they were pulling into the church parking lot, Kimberly asked Minetta, "do you think Philip will ask her to the prom?"

"Knowing him, yes."

"Do you think she will accept?" asked Kimberly, reaching for her tote bag on the back seat.

"Yes."

It was nearing the end of the day. Swim and dive class was next on Minetta's schedule. In the locker room, Tabitha called over to Minetta.

"Do you have an extra swim cap? I can't find mine anywhere."

"Oh, I have an extra one, Tabs," said Amber.

"Thanks, Amber. Are you walking over to the swimming pool now?"

"Yes, ma'am," replied Amber. She looked at Kimberly and Minetta. "You ladies, ready?"

Minetta said, "I have to stop by my locker first. We'll see you in there."

Kimberly kept her back turned as she put her sneakers into her duffle bag. She turned around slowly once Amber and Tabitha had left the locker room.

"What do you mean we'll see you in there? Why do I need to walk you to your locker?"

"I wanted to ask you if Philip asked her to the prom yet?"

"Asked who to the prom?"

"Asked Amber!"

"I don't know, and I don't care."

"What's wrong with you? You're supposed to be my best friend."

"I'm your best friend, but I don't know everything that goes on in Philip's life."

"Eddie is one of his best friends, isn't he? We both know they talk."

"Mimi, do you really think Eddie and I sit around discussing our friends' love lives?"

"No, but something important like this, you mean you guys wouldn't talk about it?"

"Something important like what?"

"The prom! We're talking about the prom."

"Do you know how far away that is right now? We have the spring play, final exams, and spring break to get through. If you want to know who Philip is taking to the prom, you need to ask him. "

They walked in silence to the swimming pool, and Kimberly sat with Tabitha and Amber. Minetta sat on the other side of Kimberly and stayed quiet.

Chapter 23

Due to the popularity of the winter play the principal gave the Performing Arts Center a weekend to conduct two performances of the spring play. When Minetta heard about the performances she wanted to write positive reviews for Joshua, Henry, and Edward, who all held character parts in the production. Lizzie worked with Tabitha in designing the play's costumes. Minetta saw Eddie and Kimberly with Josh, Kelly, and Andrew discussing the backdrop props and interior setting. When Raymond, the play's director, walked onstage she waved to him. The deep blue eyes seem to look at her and through her. She felt a chill and was paralyzed in her seat until Ben and Amber walked onstage, and Raymond turned his back to her.

None of her friends acknowledged her presence in the auditorium. She spotted Sallie, a varsity cheerleader, who was also a fellow writer with the school paper.

"Hi, Sallie." Minetta noticed Sallie was writing in a small notepad. "What are you doing in here?"

"What does it look like I'm doing, Mimi? I've been assigned to write a piece on the actors in this play."

"I'm writing about the play. It goes under my byline in the social section."

Sallie shrugged her shoulders. "Whatever. See you later."

Gathering her book bag, and belongings, Sallie left the auditorium. Minetta sat still.

Both performances played to a packed auditorium. There were two television stations, two cable news shows, the digital press, and the local paper in attendance. The play was a resounding success.

The television stations and cable news show interviewed Ben and Amber directly after their performances. The editor of the Cedar Valley Gazette brought his family to the first show and friends to the second. The reviews were glowing for Ben as *Othello* and Amber as Desdemona. Joshua's performance as the scheming Iago won high praise as well. The writer from the Gazette Home and Garden pages wrote enthusiastically of Eddie's realistic Renaissance Venice scenery while complimenting the lavish interior settings by Kimberly.

Once again, Tabitha captured the tone and style of Venice fashion with her costume designs and landed on the front page of the Gazette's Fashion section. Philip's photographs of the actors' behind-the-scenes activities was included in the cable news show.

Minetta turned in her draft review for the school paper early. Her review boasted extensively of Ben's performance and command of the stage. She wrote glowingly of Joshua's portrayal of Iago. At the bottom of her review, she mentioned Amber stating her performance went over well.

However, when the school paper was published, she saw Sallie's name attached to her byline as a co-writer. Sallie's article was placed ahead of Minetta's and included accolades to both Ben and Amber's performances. Sallie's review also featured a behind-the-scenes chat with the lead actors and omitted Minetta's lukewarm review of Amber's performance.

James and Marilyn decided to celebrate their twenty-fifth wedding anniversary with a cruise. They had planned and saved for this special occasion for years and were excited about the weekend celebration. They usually shared their anniversary with the children as it fell during school recesses. However, given their offspring's young adult status, the parents wanted to celebrate this event without them. James and Marilyn were surprised to find that Matthew and Minetta had made plans of their own. Matthew called ahead, informing them he would drive down to have Sunday dinner with his family. As Marilyn was menu planning Matthew's favorite meal, James prepared mentally for his son's impromptu visit.

Seated around the dinner table, James blessed the food and, looking about the table, appreciated his family. His wife always seemed more exquisite in the presence of her children. He glanced at Minetta in her pink dress and his son in a buttoned-down white shirt. Boy, did they both look spiritually invested! He smiled. He had to stay alert.

"Mom, you know how much I love your eggplant parmigiana. Thank you for making it."

"Oh, it was nothing, Matthew. You know I love cooking for you."

"Dad, that was a great sermon this morning."

"Oh? You drove down here to hear me preach this morning? You should have dropped by the office."

"I drove Candy to her mother's house, or I would have."

Marilyn's ears perked up. "Who's Candy, dear?"

"My girlfriend." Matthew kept his eyes on his plate.

"Where does she live?" continued Marilyn.

"Upper Medford Valley."

"How long have you been seeing her?" asked Marilyn.

James intervened. "Sweetie, he's a young man with a girlfriend. I'm sure he didn't do all this driving just to eat your parmigiana, as good as it is."

Matthew grinned and put down his fork. "I wanted to ask you guys if I could host a pool party in honor of my twenty-first birthday."

"Now, you know we allow no type of social gatherings when we're not home," replied Marilyn.

"I thought about that," responded Matthew. "If I invite my frat brothers, Uncle Bill and both grandfathers can attend."

"Have you spoken to your grandfathers yet?" asked James.

"No, because I wanted to clear all this with you and Mom first."

"Okay, then I'll handle that part of it. Realistically, I would feel better if you invited some girls. Your chaperones won't mind, and neither will your brothers," said James, grinning.

Marilyn frowned, "James…"

"Wait a minute, sweetie. That means you must invite a reasonable number of young people, not the entire chapter."

"How about twenty guests?"

"Guys or girls?"

"Guys,"

"Don't most of them have girlfriends? And since most females rarely go anywhere solo, you're looking at sixty people, give or take a few. About the party guests, your sister will be home on spring break as well, and I think it would be considerate of you to include her."

Matthew looked across the dinner table at Minetta and smiled. He put some food in his mouth and chewed slowly. Minetta swallowed and kept her eyes on her plate. Matthew's smiles could be misleading. There was silence. Marilyn attempted to speak, and James held up his hand in a stop gesture. Silence engulfed the rest of the dinner hour.

During dessert, Matthew spoke. "I don't have a problem with Mimi being there, but I need you both to understand I don't want to babysit her."

Minetta scowled. "I don't need a babysitter!"

Marilyn spoke next. "I don't think it's a good idea for Mimi to be among all those older kids. She's only seventeen."

"Besides," continued Matthew. "This is supposed to be my twenty-first birthday bash. Why doesn't she have a sleepover with her friends like she usually does?"

"You think you're so grown, don't you? I don't want to be at your stupid party, anyway."

"James, this is not a good idea. Matt should wait until we return from our cruise."

"Besides, Dad, I'm a young man. Why can't I have a party at my home?"

"Why do I have to be at *his* party? This house is enormous enough for me to have a party of my own."

"I'm going to be twenty-one-years old, legally a full-fledged adult. If I can't have a birthday bash in my home, I might as well move out now."

"Believe me, if you go now, you won't be missed!"

Marilyn looked at her son. "Stop it, Matt, you're not moving out. Give us a chance to think about all this."

"This summer, I'll share a place with some of my brothers and working. I was going to tell you later, but I guess now is as good a time as any."

"Oh Matt, no! This is your home. Why are you rushing to move out?"

"I can spend the weekend at Kim's house. I don't need to be here with *him* where I'm not wanted."

"Mimi, you don't have to leave your own home unless you want to spend the weekend at Kim's. I'll call Lisa to confirm."

"I changed my mind. I'll just stay in *my* room."

"I don't care where you stay as long as you're not in my way!"

"Matt, please! Mimi, we'll figure all this out."

Tears slowly fell from Minetta's eyes, and Matthew threw an angry glance in her direction. James stood up. Everyone quieted down. In a gentle but commanding voice, James confronted his family.

"Matt let's get something straight. You don't get to make or give ultimatums in this family. The last word is what we decide on as a family. Second, you and your sister are three years apart. Don't forget her birthday is only two months after yours, so technically she is closer to eighteen. Third, that was an excellent suggestion for her to have a sleepover. Mimi loves her sleepovers. She and her friends can enjoy the pool party a bit before their own event. I will allow you to have a males-only after party in the pool house, but the girls you invite must have safe rides home. The guys can stay over, but not the girls. Is that clear?"

Matthew nodded his head. "Yes, sir."

"Last, never make threats to your mother and I because not only is it an ungrateful position to take, but it is also highly disrespectful and immature on your part. Do I make myself clear?"

"Yes, sir."

"If you want your party approved, you will invite twenty guys, and they can bring their girlfriends and their friends. Only sixty people, not counting Mimi and her crew. Mimi, you will have a sleepover with your closest friends, as always, in this house. Is that understood, Mimi?"

"Yes, Dad."

"For you both, I will have both sets of grandparents here, and Mrs. B. to keep eyes on all the young ladies under this roof. Everyone is to be in the family room or poolside. The males can use the restroom facilities in the pool house, and the girls can use the facilities in the downstairs guest bath.

Mrs. B. will order catering for your party, Matt, and your sleepover Mimi. Give her your ideas, but understand she will need final approval from me before any spending takes place. Is that clear, Matt? Mimi?"

Matt said, "yes, sir," and from Mimi, "yes, Dad."

"My dear wife Mimi will go away to college soon. It's time she mingled with a few older kids, more than likely the same ones she will meet on campus. As for Matt, he's a young man. He's fine."

James sat down and took a sip of water, glancing down the table at his wife. She smiled but said nothing. Matthew was looking at his water glass and contemplating his options. Minetta's face displayed a cross between joy and wariness as she wiped her eyes with her napkin. James loved his family, and it was moments like these he treasured the most in fatherhood.

Marilyn spoke, looking to Minetta. "Well, it will be an enjoyable experience for you. Just remember they are much older than you and your friends."

"Mom, I know most of Matt's friends, remember?" said Minetta. "Besides, I'll be busy with my girls."

Matthew remained quiet, as his father knew he would. He had received permission for his party, and his sister would not be his responsibility. Those were the only two items on his agenda, and he had gained permission for both.

Chapter 24

On a sunny morning, James and Marilyn boarded the cruise ship for their anniversary destination. Matthew and Minetta stood on the dock waving to their parents. Matthew, in a white linen sport shirt and shorts, snapped a photograph of their parents as they walked the ramp to board the ship. Minetta, wearing a yellow seersucker romper, waved enthusiastically as the ship sailed away from the dock.

Two hours later, Eddie's deep orange truck, followed by Philip's black Camaro, Raymond's sleek black sedan, and Ben's glossy black sports sedan, pulled up in the Morgan's driveway. The teens wearing swim trunks with tank tops and flip-flops, had promised Matthew they would help him set up the pool area before the other guests arrived. They were greeted by Matthew, his trademark baseball cap perched backward on his head, as he and his cousin Craig walked from the side of the home. They were wearing swim trunks and flip-flops, with Matthew wearing an Omega Pi tank top and Craig wearing a plain tee shirt.

"Hey guys, thanks for volunteering to help me today," he said.

"What do you want us to do?" asked Philip.

"Let's go around the back way," said Matthew, going to the back of the house on the opposite side of where he had appeared earlier. The double gates swung back to reveal an in-ground pool with an assortment of seating arrangements and lounge chairs. Off to one side was the pool house.

Matthew looked around. "Craig, check out the pool house. Make sure the windows are open, and everything is clean and aired out."

"Okay," said Craig.

“I need two of you guys to move the pool cover, check the water levels, add the chlorine, and so on,” he said. “Phil, you know where we store our pool supplies over in that shed. Ben, you okay with helping him?”

“Yeah, we got you,” replied Philip.

“No problem,” stated Ben.

“Ok, good.” Matthew looked around. “I need one of you guys to clean off the chairs and tables.”

“I’m your man,” said Eddie, walking toward the shed for the hose and cleaning supplies.

Matthew turned to Raymond, who was about to follow Philip. “Hey Ray, would you do me a favor and see how the ladies are doing with the food prep? Then you can help Eddie.”

“Okay,” said Raymond, heading toward the kitchen area.

He could see part of the kitchen through the French double doors. He saw Minetta, Kimberly, Kelly, Lizzie, and Annie. As he drew nearer, his eyes focused on Tabitha in her red mixed-print caftan, and he smiled. Tabitha saw him and waved. Beatrice was directing the food delivery crew from La Dolce Vita Restaurant toward the door leading to the family room from the patio. Matthew came around the side entrance and helped the delivery crew set the food up. His grandfathers, Robert, and Timothy were looking on in the family room.

“Hi ladies,” said Raymond, entering the kitchen.

“Hi Ray,” said Tabitha. She walked over to him with a glass of lemonade. “Taste this and tell me if there’s enough sugar.”

Raymond took a sip and drained the glass. “It’s great, Tabs.”

Tabitha put the pitcher of lemonade in the refrigerator. She helped the others put the finishing touches on the sandwiches and sweet treats for their sleepover later that evening.

“Hi, Ms. Elouise, Ms. Mary, how are you?”

Elouise and Mary looked up from their chore of wrapping and storing vegetable and fruit trays. They smiled at Raymond.

“Hello, Raymond. I am fine, thank you for asking,” said Elouise. She smiled brightly. Such a handsome young man!

“I am well, Raymond,” replied Mary. She looked at the young man appreciatively. What a handsome young man he had become!

Raymond, feeling the girls' eyes on him, said to Elouise and Mary, "Matt sent me in here to see if everything was going well."

Elouise smiled. "Oh yes, we are fine. We will be out of your hair as soon as the guests arrive."

Mary said, "This is for the girls later. Do you need anything?"

"No, ma'am. Thank you." He backed out of the kitchen through the family room. As soon as he crossed the threshold, he heard their laughter and fairly ran toward the pool area where the guys were.

At three o'clock in the afternoon, the Morgan property welcomed college students from Upper Medford Valley University for Matthew's birthday celebration. For several hours, the young people frolicked in the pool, danced to the music, and ate whatever food was presented. The music was loud but not noisy, and they mixed Christian rock with popular pop music.

In the swimming pool, Eddie, ben, and Raymond played water volleyball with a few college women. They were later joined by Craig, and a rousting challenge game took place. Some of the young people enjoyed themselves in the family room, where there was a pool table situated in an alcove. Minetta saw Philip playing pool with Craig and two of Matthew's friends. Andrew, Mark, and Josh played the arcade machines across from the pool table.

Tables were set up for different cards and board games lined the other side of the room. Lizzie, in a white and blue polka dot bikini, her blue-gray eyes made vivid by the silver hoops in her ears, looked at the board games.

"Why don't we play Scrabble? I haven't played in ages."

"That sounds like fun," said Kelly in a white and green striped bikini. The girls ran over to the game's corner.

"The babies are having fun," said Kimberly in a black halter crochet one-piece swimsuit.

Annie, in a swimsuit with a purple tank top and purple striped bottom, laughed. "You are such a big sister Kim."

Kimberly laughed. "Yeah, sweet, aren't I?"

Tabitha looked around. "Where's Amber?" She had removed her caftan and wore a dark red bikini with ruffles on the straps and around the waist.

Minetta, in a deep blue checked bikini, slipped into the kitchen.

"I know what you did," said Kimberly, who had followed her inside.

She spun away from her friend. "What are you doing, Kim?"

"You did not invite Amber. That's why she's not here."

"This is my party. I can invite whoever I want."

"Correction: it's Matt's party, and I'm sure he would not have minded one bit."

"Leave me alone, Kim."

"Mimi, this isn't like you. Are you jealous of her? I mean, what gives?"

Minetta spun around. "I don't like her because she's sneaky. I don't believe for one minute she has a boyfriend. She's always in Philip's face. I don't like her, and I don't trust her. This is my house. I don't have to invite her here."

Kimberly leaned against the counter and crossed her arms.

"Why take out your frustrations on her? You invited Philip, and he's just as much in her face, too. Didn't he stop Andrew from walking out with her at the bistro? Doesn't he break his neck to sit with her at lunch or Bible study? What is it you see that I'm not? Help me here."

"Well, he wouldn't if she wasn't throwing herself at him."

"So, Philip is the innocent, and she's the vixen?"

"If you say so."

"Stop, Mimi. That is classic jealous woman's craziness right there," responded Kimberly.

"Say what you want. This is my house."

"Okay, Mimi. I'm having a sleepover next weekend. I'm inviting Amber, and you are free to come or not. By the way, Tabitha is having a sleepover too. She's also inviting Amber."

Minetta was speechless. She stared at Kimberly, unable to comprehend why her friends were betraying her. She looked beyond Kimberly into the family room, where she could see Philip talking to a woman with blonde wavy hair. She looked away.

"Look, Mimi, I don't know what's going on with you and Philip, but you need to clear the air with him. Amber has a boyfriend, and it's not Philip."

With that, she walked out of the kitchen, leaving Minetta standing in the middle of the room.

An hour later, Minetta and her friends played a water polo game with the female members of the university's swim team. She was sitting by the swimming pool ledge when she was approached by the same young woman she had spotted talking to Philip earlier. She sat down near Minetta.

She was smaller than Minetta, with a curvy figure, large chocolate brown eyes, and dark blonde loose wavy hair. She was wearing a blue and yellow floral bikini.

"Hi, I'm Candy," she said. "You must be Matt's little sister."

"Yes, I'm Minetta, but most people call me Mimi."

"Mimi. I like that. Are you coming to UMV next year?"

"I hope so. I applied but have heard nothing yet."

"Oh, no worries. I am sure you'll get in," responded Candy with enough conviction to make Minetta smile. The young woman stepped closer. "Does Matt have a girlfriend in the neighborhood?"

"No, not that I know of," said Minetta. "He liked a girl in high school, but she has since moved away."

"Good to know. I like your brother."

"Don't you come to church with him sometimes?"

"Yes, when the youth choir is up. Usually, we attend my church."

"Are you my brother's girlfriend?"

"Why not ask him?"

"He told us you are."

"There's your answer." With that, she smiled at Minetta, rose and walked away.

Kimberly and Tabitha walked over. "What did she want?"

"She's Matt's girlfriend."

"How do you know? Did she say that?" asked Kimberly.

"Matt said it himself."

"She's gorgeous," said Tabitha.

"Kinda looks like a Latina version of Amber," mused Kimberly.

“A smaller, curvier version,” agreed Tabitha.

Minetta, though she agreed, would never give Amber that kind of complimentary thought.

“I’m hungry. Want to get something in the kitchen?” asked Kimberly.

“You guys go on. I want to sit here awhile,” said Minetta.

“Okay,” said Tabitha. “I’ll bring out some chips and dip. Matt said he’s putting on a movie later.”

Minetta continued to sit poolside, wading her hand through the water when a shadow fell across her. Philip sat down beside her.

“Having fun?” he asked.

She could not see his eyes for the dark sunglasses he was wearing. She smiled.

“Of course. You?”

“Yeah. I guess you met your brother’s girlfriend, Candy?”

“Hmm…yes. She seems nice.”

“She is nice. Her brother plays football at Foxcraft.”

“Is that what you were talking about earlier?”

“Yes… and you.”

“Me? What about me?”

“She wanted to know your name.”

“Matt’s been bringing her to church recently. I’m sure she knows my name.” Minetta rolled her eyes.

Philip grinned. “Play nice. She wants to know his friends. They’re really into each other, from what I can tell.”

“Into each other? She’s a new girlfriend. What’s the big deal? Let’s see how long the relationship lasts post-college.”

For reasons unknown to her, Minetta became irritated by the tone of Philip’s conversation concerning her brother and his girlfriend. There was silence for a while, and because she could not see Philip’s eyes, she looked away from him across the pool.

In a low voice, Philip said, “I don’t know what’s going on with you, but I hope you snap out of it.” He rose and left her.

A short time later, Matthew programmed the flat screen outdoor television to a newly released psychological thriller. As Minetta watched, her brother sat down on the couch with Candy, his girlfriend, who was now wearing a yellow and blue striped summer dress. Josh, Lizzie, Mark, Kelly, and Annie sat with Matthew's fraternity brothers. Minetta smiled when she saw her grandfathers' take seats in the kitchen in full view of the young people.

Minetta sat with Kimberly and Tabitha by the pool ledge to watch the movie. Philip, Eddie, Ben, Raymond, and Andrew stretched out on the grass behind the girls on beach towels. Minetta looked over and saw Philip looking at her. They smiled at each other. She turned around when she caught Elouise and Mary looking at her. The grandmothers sat in lawn chairs far enough away to allow privacy but close enough to see action.

When the movie was over an hour later, Robert signaled Matthew it was time to move the party along. Beatrice wheeled a chocolate cake with blue icing toward the patio as the grandmothers directed the girls to the kitchen. As they ascended the back stairs, Lizzie, Kelly, and Tabitha looked with longing at the decorated cake as Beatrice wheeled it past them. Large blue candles in the shape of the number twenty-one adorned the cake top.

Kimberly complained loudly. "Hey, aren't we getting any cake and ice cream?"

"I don't see why we couldn't stay until they sang happy birthday to Matt and brought out the cake," said Minetta grumpily.

Annie joined in. "That's not fair. What kind of birthday party doesn't let a person get some birthday cake?"

"We will make sure you get some." Elouise said quietly. Mary suppressed a smile, turning her head away from the girls.

'Why do we have to leave so early anyway?" asked Minetta.

"Because your parents told us to make sure you girls were out of the party by ten o'clock this evening," said Mary curtly, but smiling.

"Well, I'm disgruntled," said Minetta with a scowl.

"If you're disgruntled, take it up with your parents." Elouise stated with finality.

Chapter 25

In Minetta's bedroom, the girls prepared their sleeping arrangements and unpacked their overnight bags. Tabitha, Kelly, and Annie situated their sleeping bags on the floor. Kimberly was sleeping in Minetta's Queen-sized bed, and Lizzie settled on the deeply cushioned window seat. They took their showers, and after they finished, Elouise and Mary brought up their cake and ice cream. Beatrice came up to take their trays.

"Thank you, Mrs. B.," said Kimberly, who had received a larger piece of cake than the other girls.

Beatrice smiled. "You're welcome, sweetie. Good night, ladies."

"Thank you," said Elouise to Mrs. B. as she closed the door after her.

Mary said, "we are allowing you all to stay until midnight. Your parents said that was okay. After that, it's lights out. Everyone is going to church tomorrow, so I suggest you get some rest."

Lizzie asked, "Are you bringing us to church?"

"Yes, but your parents will pick you up after church. Bring your overnight bags with you," said Elouise.

"Are my parents driving down to Cedar Valley?" asked Annie.

Mary said, "Matt will take you home before heading back to campus with Craig."

"Thank you, Nana Mary," said Annie.

Mary smiled. "You're welcome, Annie. Questions?"

The girls had none. Elouise and Mary smiled and hugged each girl before leaving.

Minetta looked at her guests. "Now what?"

Tabitha unzipped her red floral leather duffel bag. “Facials?”

The girls eagerly watched as Tabitha handed out sample packets of face masks. They crowded into Minetta’s bathroom.

“This one smells good,” said Annie in yellow duck-print pajamas, rubbing greenish mixture on her face.

“Which mask is that?” asked Kimberly in pink striped oversized pajamas.

Annie read the label. “This is the black mud with avocado mask.”

“I should have tried that one,” said Tabitha in purple plaid pajamas. “Mine is the black mud with coconut-infused oil.”

Kimberly read hers. “I am loving this black mud with avocado one too, Annie.”

“The black mud with coconut oil is nice too,” said Minetta in a blue tank with blue and white polka dot pajama pants.

Kelly, in powder blue pajamas with white cream on her face, read the back of her package. “This one is aloe vera with rose water.”

“Mine is olive oil and egg with black clay,” said Lizzie in white silk pajamas, intently rubbing the white mask on her face.

“Ok, now that’s done,” said Annie. “What’s next?”

“I have something, ladies,” said Kimberly. She opened her pink overnight bag and produced a medium-sized pink box. She placed it on the floor. The girls gathered about.

Tabitha grinned. “Oh yes, the nail salon is open.”

Kimberly opened the box to reveal a multitude of colored nail polishes. The girls gasped with delight.

“Oh, I want the orangey-looking polish. That one right there,” said Annie, pointing to a bottle.

“There you are,” said Kimberly. “But let’s do toes first and save our hands for last. We have to remove these masks.”

Minetta said, “I think we should remove these masks now. Mine’s feeling tight.”

“Mine too,” agreed Tabitha.

The girls rinsed their faces and used moisturizing products immediately afterward. The last beauty ritual performed was pedicures with fingernail polish applications.

Minetta said, "Annie, how's your mom doing with Craig's transfer to UMV University?"

Annie looked at her nails. "She's been quiet. I think she's still sad about it. It was the alma mater of her father and late grandfather."

Kimberly said, "Craig transferred to UMV?"

Annie nodded her head. "Yeah. My mom did not know it, though. Only my dad knew. Seems my brother talked it over with dad and granddad, but mom knew nothing about it."

Kimberly said, "wow, that's rough."

Tabitha was looking at Annie. "I'm sorry to hear this, Annie. Your mom is so sweet."

Kimberly said, "I'm glad Eddie and I are both going to UMV together with blessings from both families."

"And me, too," said Kelly, and laughed at the shocked look on her sister's face.

Tabitha smiled. "Same with Ray and me. We got our acceptance letters on the same day."

"I think you and Ray are such a perfect couple," said Lizzie, gazing with fondness at Tabitha.

Tabitha smiled. "Thank you Lizzie, that means a lot."

"Speaking of which," Kimberly looked at Mimi. "Have you gotten your acceptance letter yet from UMV?"

Minetta shook her head. "No, but my dad says not to worry about it."

"Where are you going, Annie?" asked Kelly.

"To Foxcraft," said Annie. "I've already been accepted. I thought after that stunt Craig pulled, the university might have been disgusted with the Johnston household and rejected my application."

Minetta said, "glad that didn't happen to you."

"I know, right? Guilt by association," said Annie.

"Or guilt by relationship," said Kimberly.

"Did you guys sign your housing application yet?" asked Minetta.

"I have to wait for you, Mimi," said Kimberly. "I completed one, but I will need to go back in and put your name on it as my roommate."

Tabitha said nothing. Minetta said to her, "what about you, Tabs? Are you rooming with us?"

"No."

"Why not? You know Philip and Eddie will be roommates. What about Ray? Is he going in with them?"

Tabitha stated, "no. Ray and Ben will be roommates."

Minetta looked at Tabitha. "I didn't know Ray and Ben were close like that. I know they're both football players, but…"

The room became silent. Tabitha looked at Minetta for a long minute. Kelly and Lizzie looked at Minetta and Tabitha while Kimberly put her head down. Annie looked at the ceiling and sighed.

In a stern voice, Tabitha said, "Mimi, stop talking. Ray, Eddie, Philip, and Ben have been friends for years. Their families have been vacationing together for the last several years. Do not forget that Ben's father is a well-known heart surgeon, and they consider his mother a specialist on bone implantation."

Minetta said, "I'm sorry, Tabs. I meant nothing by it."

"We can no longer live in glass bubbles, Mimi. There are more people in the world besides our tight-knit group. It might be good for you to look around you. You 're coming off narrow-minded and elitist."

Kimberly said, "whoa, Tabs, slow down."

"No, Kim, you slow down. It's time for a reality check. This is our last year together as high schoolers," said Tabitha.

Kimberly snorted. "It's not the end of the world."

Minetta said, "we'll all be in college together next year, Tabs."

Tabitha said, "I didn't say it was the end of the world, Kim. But after graduation, we will live on our own and have to make adult decisions."

Annie interjected, "that's so true, Tabs. I understand my brother's decision. He never really wanted to go to Foxcraft but felt an obligation to do so."

Kelly said, "because of your mom?"

Annie nodded her head. "Yes. But he's thrilled now at UMV, and his grades this past semester placed him on the Dean's List."

Lizzie said, "then he made the right decision."

Kimberly said, "Craig seems happier. More at peace."

Minetta said, "this is strange. In another few months we will be college students."

"Yes, we will each be going our own way soon. Raymond and I are attending Foxcraft University," said Tabitha.

"I didn't know that Tabs. When did you guys decide to go to Foxcraft?"

"He received the swim scholarship he wanted to go nationals at the collegiate level, and they have a diverse pre-med program."

"I see." Minetta was speechless. "So, you won't be with us either, Tabs?"

"We all grow up," responded Tabitha with a wistful smile.

"So, if Ben's rooming with Raymond, that means you're going to be with Amber."

"Are you asking me a question or making a statement?" asked Tabitha.

"Both," replied Minetta.

Kelly tried to calm the sudden tenseness in the room. "What's going on? Of course, we are all going to be with our boyfriends, if possible. It's good that Tabs will have someone to be with that she's friends with."

"Yeah, friends," said Minetta. Tabitha ignored her.

Kelly said, "well, Lizzie and I will be seniors next year. This weekend has been a great inspiration to help us prepare for what's around the corner. I like Mark, and I hope my parents like him too."

Kimberly looked across at her younger sibling. "I think they already know you and Mark are developing something beyond just friendship."

Kelly looked wide-eyed at her sister. "You said something, didn't you?"

"Nope. They have eyes, and they see more than they say. Besides, what's not to like about Mark? Straight-A student, athlete, handsome, and the younger brother of our own Hercules, Ben."

"Not to mention Mark's shyness makes him a real cutie," added Tabitha.

Annie asked, "who's his friend? The tall blonde guy with the long hair?"

"Joshua Wyatt. He's Andrew's youngest brother and Mark's best friend. They're on the wrestling team together," replied Tabitha.

"I believe he likes Lizzie," said Kimberly, grinning. "He walks beside her or sits beside her."

"I notice that too," responded Tabitha. "I was watching them at the pool party. He's certainly into her."

Lizzie was smiling with her face in her pillow. "Stop it!"

The girls all laughed. Minetta looked at her friends with surprise. "Wow, you ladies are very observant."

Kimberly smirked. "Well, you would have seen what the babies were up as well, but your eyes stayed glued on Philip."

Annie, Lizzie, and Kelly snickered, and Tabitha laughed. Minetta chose not to spar with Kimberly. She changed the subject to the university's cheer squad. The girls talked into the wee hours of the morning about their expectations for college life. Minetta drifted off into the abyss of calming darkness, smiling.

Chapter 26

Sunday morning dawned bright and clear. The girls attended morning service at Cedar Valley Church, and when service concluded, the sun was still glowing. Their respective parents retrieved Lizzie and Kelly after services. Annie left with her brother and cousin for the drive home to Upper Medford Valley. Minetta's parents were arriving home later that day from their cruise. Spring break was officially over, and school resumed the next day.

Kimberly was behind the wheel of her new car with Minetta seated beside her and Tabitha in the backseat. Today, the girls planned on having lunch at La Dolce Vita Restaurant to celebrate the end of their school break. They spotted Amber in her black convertible ahead of them, idling at the light.

"Hey look," said Kimberly, pointing out Amber's car. "Isn't that Amber up there?"

Minetta strained in her seat for a better look. "Hm….," she said.

"Yeah," murmured Tabitha from the backseat. "Looks like she's going home."

"Um, no Tabs, she's not going home," said Minetta. "Her house is in the opposite direction. Remember?"

"Oh, so where is she going?" said Kimberly.

"Let's follow her and see," said Minetta. "Maybe she's going to meet her secret boyfriend. The one we only hear about and never see. Let's do it.

Let's follow her."

"No, you guys," said Tabitha. "Let's not follow her. Don't do this, Kim. Tell her, Mimi."

Minetta was silent. If she told Kimberly to stop and turn back, she would, but something inside her wanted to see the truth about this girl. Kimberly ignored Tabitha and proceeded to follow Amber, keeping a little distance behind her. Amber drove to her house and left the gate open behind her. Kimberly decided to stop. She pulled over to the side of the road, and they watched Amber's car as she parked. Amber disappeared behind a set of maple trees that blocked their view.

"Alright, Kim. Let's go," said Tabitha.

"No, give it a few minutes," Minetta said with quiet urgency in her voice.

"Wait," cried Kimberly. She pointed to the road. As they watched, a dilapidated greige-looking truck came down the road and drove past them up the driveway to Amber's house.

Minetta said, "that looks like the truck that almost hit Philip in the church parking lot."

The girls looked at each other wordlessly. Kimberly turned her car around and moved further to the side of the road. When they saw the truck coming down the driveway, all three laid flat until it passed by. Kimberly followed the vehicle.

"What are you doing, Kim? Don't follow her. Suppose she sees us?" pleaded Tabitha.

"She won't see us. Stay a bit behind. I can see her perfectly," said Minetta.

Tabitha's phone was home. She rarely brought it with her on Sunday mornings to church. She kept shaking her head in silent disagreement with the current set of events. This was wrong. But what could she do from the back seat? Throwing all common sense to the wind, Kimberly followed the truck out of the Maple Glen subdivision and out of the Heights. The girls were bug-eyed now. Minetta took pictures with her phone every time they made a stop. Gradually the landscape changed from large acres of greenery and the sweet smell of grass and honeysuckle to the brightness of steel and the noxious smell of gravel and concrete.

They entered a city on the outskirts of Cedar Valley. The streets were only wide enough to allow one lane of traffic going in one direction. The truck bounced along on gravelly streets and, after a time, stopped and parked in front of a house. Kimberly eased her car into space a few houses back. All three girls examined the neighborhood from within the car.

The street was congested with narrow homes, and on both sides, were fitted compactly together with slim alleyways separating them. Some houses had fenced front yards, but most were open to the sidewalk. There were cars tightly crammed on both sides of the street, and several looked as if they had not moved in a long time.

Amber, wearing a yellow plaid shirt and blue jeans, got out of the truck as they watched. They eagerly waited to see when the driver's door opened. An older man with white hair emerged in mismatched khaki-type work clothes, and they entered the house together.

"Okay," said Tabitha from the backseat. "We've seen Amber go into a house. We need to get out of here."

"You need to calm down," said Kimberly, looking at Tabitha in her rearview window.

"Calm down, nothing," said Tabitha. "This is wrong on so many levels, and you know it. Mimi, tell her. Let's go."

Minetta surveyed the community. The homes were old, with many of them lining this street and the next in shabby disrepair. The neighborhood was old and in need of revitalization, but everything looked clean. A few older adults were sitting on a front porch several doors down from the home Amber entered. Studying that structure, Minetta noted the faded, ragged American flag hanging out the rusted mailbox hung haphazardly by the front window. The nondescript paint was peeling in spots on the wall, the gutters stuffed with debris, and crumbly front steps. The house needed the roof replaced. One of the twin dormers appeared boarded up. The front door looked like it would collapse any second. Why was Amber there, and who was the older man?

Minetta repeated what she had stated earlier, "that looks like the same truck that almost hit Philip in the parking lot a few months ago."

"The one you guys described to us?" asked Kimberly.

"Yep. Now that I think about it. Amber said her car had arrived. Did this guy bring her car?" said Minetta.

"There must have been two people. He couldn't have driven both cars there." Kimberly was scanning the house windows.

"True."

"He's old, though. Is he her father?" asked Kimberly.

"No, she's Bob and Marcie's daughter," said Tabitha, irritably.

"Yeah, she looks like Mrs. Paige a little when you think about it," reflected Kimberly.

"Well, why is she in that house?" asked Minetta.

"I don't think it's really any of our business," said Tabitha.

"Why would that old man bring her here to this neighborhood?" asked Kimberly. "Maybe her boyfriend lives there?"

"Maybe he is her boyfriend," said Minetta.

Kimberly and Minetta laughed out loud. Tabitha crossed her arms.

"Hey Kim, I think we should leave now. It's getting late," pleaded Tabitha.

The excitement that delayed their appetites had long since vanished, and they were all experiencing the cramps of hunger pangs.

"Yeah, Kim, I guess we can leave now. Drive down the street slowly so I can take pictures of the house," said Minetta, with phone in hand.

Kimberly drove down the street and stopped the car in front of the house. Minetta got out of the car. "Here goes. We can study them later," she said.

"Are you guys crazy? She could come out any minute and see us," argued Tabitha.

"We'll just drive off if she does. This is a free country," said Kimberly.

Minetta looked over her shoulder at Tabitha and laughed. She took several pictures of the truck, a dusty blue in the light of day with the faded inscription of a name drawn on the door. Minetta snapped a couple of close-ups of the dilapidated front porch and the threadbare door. She was photographing the dirty windows when the front door violently opened. Amber was on the porch, angrily glaring down at them. Her eyes resembled slits as she stared at Minetta, whose hand visibly shook.

Amber's voice was low and steady, but her eyes blazed with anger.

"What do you think you're doing?"

"Get in the car, Mimi," yelled Kimberly as she put the car in drive.

Minetta was stunned and jumped into the car. The older man joined Amber on the porch. He wordlessly glared at the girls in the car. No one spoke. Kimberly rolled up Minetta's window using the automatic tab, put her foot on the gas, and they sped down the street, using the car's GPS tracker to find their way home.

Kimberly's knuckles clenched tight on the steering wheel as she stared straight ahead. Minetta was still shaking from her close encounter with Amber and the older man. Kimberly drove aimlessly for a time until she remembered to turn on the GPS tracker. Tabitha cried quietly in the backseat, and Minetta sat frozen, recalling the look of anger, and hurt in Amber's eyes.

Once Kimberly pulled up in her driveway, Tabitha ran into her house without a backward glance. Kimberly drove to her driveway and parked. She put her face in her hands, shaking her head from side to side, and groaned into her hands.

"What have we done?" she said. Turning to Minetta, she asked, "why were you taking pictures?"

Minetta shrugged. "I don't know."

Kimberly stared at her for a moment. "I don't believe you, bestie. I think you intend to put those pictures on social media."

"Did I say that?" said Minetta angrily.

Kimberly sighed. "What have I done?" She looked out her side window. "That was very unpleasant. I don't feel good about what we did back there. I like Amber." Silence. Then with feeling, "I like the girl."

Kimberly seemed close to tears as she got out of the car and hurriedly walked home, taking a shortcut through the lawn, which was something she never did. Minetta sat still and recalled the last few minutes before Amber opened the front door. She closed her eyes, seeing the pain mingled with anger in Amber's eyes.

What had they done? What had she done? Oh goodness, did she go too far this time? Did she go too far?

Chapter 27

Minetta realized something was wrong when Kimberly text message her she was riding to school with Tabitha and no reason was given. In homeroom and their second-period class, Kimberly ignored her. In her next class with Tabitha and Raymond, they pointedly spoke around her during the lab partners' assignment, effectively blocking her from the discussion. She did not see Amber in the two classes they had together.

During the changing of classes, she spotted Philip and went over to his locker. As she looked up at him, she saw he was avoiding looking at her.

"Hi, Philip," she began in a small voice. "Can we talk?"

"I'm late," he said, slamming his locker and moving quickly away. She ran behind him, and he stopped, turning around.

"What do you want?"

"What's the matter with you?"

"I think that's a question you need to ask yourself. Excuse me."

She followed him into Advanced Physics Lab and took her seat in the second row. Amber was not in attendance. Raymond, Tabitha, and Ben sat near Philip and avoided looking in her direction. She correctly responded to a question by Dr. Kilbourne and her friends remained mute when others offered praise.

Lunchtime arrived. Minetta walked over to the group's table with her food tray. Kimberly and Tabitha said nothing. As soon as she sat down they stood up, gathering their belongings and lunch trays and walked away.

"Where are you guys going?" she asked.

She watched as they met up with Philip and Eddie. Then all four walked to the other side of the cafeteria and sat with Ben and Andrew. When two varsity cheerleaders entered the cafeteria they glanced at her and walked to the other side of the room. Minetta put her head down. This was embarrassing. She realized she was the center of attention but not in a good way. Quickly, she gathered her books and left the room.

The rest of the day her friends avoided her. Cheer was canceled due to a teacher's conference. Crossing the parking lot Amber whizzed by her with Kimberly and Tabitha as passengers. She hurried to her car and drove to the Soda Shoppe, but her friends never showed up. No one responded to her text messages. She finally drove home.

The next morning Minetta visited the church to see her father before driving to school. James was delighted to see his daughter but wary of the timing. He opened their visit with prayer. Less than a half-hour into the conversation, Minetta confessed to him the details of following Amber out of their Oak Hills community. That this behavior occurred after a Sunday morning service was disappointing. James looked incredulously at his youngest child.

"I can't believe what I'm hearing." James' rich baritone voice was smooth and low-key as he gazed across the desk at her. "What do you want me to do at this point?" he asked her.

Minetta squirmed. "I wanted to apologize, but she won't answer her phone."

Her father stared thoughtfully at her. "Apologize for what?"

"Well, you know. For following her." Minetta's voice trailed off.

"Did you see what you wanted to see?"

Minetta sighed. "We thought she was going to meet her boyfriend. We wanted to see what he looked like."

James patiently asked, "why does what he looks like matter to you?"

Minetta squirmed. "Because I have seen that truck pick her up at church. So, we thought her boyfriend drove it. But when we saw the old man get out, we thought he must be her grandfather or something."

"I'm still not hearing the reason you three were stalking the girl."

"Because her boyfriend is a mystery. She doesn't tell anyone his name. I don't think he attends our church."

Her father stared at a picture of Reverend Dr. Martin Luther King on his sidewall above her head. He sat back in his chair with his arms on the armrests. For several minutes, there was silence.

James said into the silence. “There’s more, isn’t there?”

She nodded her head. “Kim found out from Eddie that Amber’s parents are wealthy, and she’s an only child.”

James frowned. “And that is your business, how?”

“Philip likes her, and I didn’t want him to get hurt. He kept saying he wasn’t her boyfriend, and then he wants to take her to the prom, and every time he sees her, he goes brain dead and just stares and stares. I wanted to know who she was, is all.”

Minetta began crying. Her father appeared unmoved by her tears as he looked at her. The tears cascaded down her cheeks, and he pushed a box of Kleenex toward her. More silence except for Minetta sobbing.

James said, “now what, my child? Do you want me to pay a house call to a classmate you and your friends have harassed? And say what? Are you aware you’re in the wrong here?”

He leaned forward and placed both hands in a folded position on his desk.

“No, that will not happen. You will have to figure this one out, and you’d better start on your knees. In the Holy Scriptures, the sixth chapter in Luke, the Word teaches we are to do to others as we would have them do to us. How would you feel if the shoe was on the other foot? In the fifteenth chapter of John, we are taught to love each other beyond life. As a Christian, how does your behavior show this basic concept of loving others? With your friends, where did you exhibit wisdom and love? You are not to cause your friends to stumble, Mimi.

“Before you do anything, you need to do as Ephesians chapter 4, verse thirty-one instructs and get rid of the negative emotions in your heart towards that young lady. Then you can follow the example in First John, chapter one, verse nine that says, ‘if we confess our sins, he is faithful and just and will forgive us our sins and purify us from all unrighteousness.’ I caution you to repent first, cleanse your heart, and then ask for forgiveness. Seek His guidance on the way you should go.”

Minetta could do nothing but cry. Her father got up from his desk and came over to her. He let her cry on his chest and gave her a tissue.

"In the Book of Acts chapter three, verse nineteen, it says to repent and turn from your wicked ways so that your sins will be wiped away. He is more merciful and forgiving toward us than we are with each other. Come on, let's pray."

Minetta was still sniffing, but feeling a lot calmer. Her father prayed, and she followed in prayer with him. James returned to his desk. Minetta picked up her book bag and walked to the door.

"Mimi?"

She turned at the gentleness in her father's voice. "Yes, Dad?" she said softly.

He beckoned to the chair. "Sit down a minute."

As she did so, she heard him sigh. Looking up, she saw he was leaning on his desk with his hands folded.

"Mimi, you might not want to hear this, but I am saying it anyway. I am the pastor of this church, and you are my daughter. There is no where you can go in this town and nothing you can do that I will not hear about it. The bottom line is that you are a role model for the kids your age and those younger. Whether you like it or not, you symbolize Christian youth. How effective do you think your behavior with that young lady has been to any evangelism, discipleship, or missions work you sponsor?"

Minetta said, "Dad, I…" her father held up his hand to stop her.

"Please, don't speak. I expected better out of you. You have disappointed your mother and me with this nonsense. It was inappropriate of you to be following a church member home. It was unsafe to be in an area that you have never been in before without your mother or me knowing where you were. Not to mention you encouraged Kim and dragged along Tabitha. Your behavior was sinful and reckless."

Minetta wanted to apologize to her father. She had hoped he would help her in some way. Sighing, he scribbled on a notepad and put the sheet in an envelope.

"Go on, go to school. Here's a note from me. Please make sure your homeroom teacher gets it." He handed her the letter.

"Mimi?"

"Yes, Dad?" She could not look at him.

"I love you, sweetheart, but there are consequences for your behavior. You're grounded for three weeks, and I'm calling your mother. Talk to her when you get home today."

Minetta was in English Literature class when the throaty voice of the principal summoning her to the main office came over the loudspeaker. full fifteen minutes before the scheduled lunch break. As she gathered her belongings, her friends continued their discussion, effectively blocking her from saying goodbye.

Her mother had arrived to take her home for the day. The walk to Marilyn's blue custom-colored sedan was absent of conversation. Minetta sat stiffly on the yellow leather seats, not daring to breathe, watching Beatrice who was in her car driving directly behind them. When they reached the house, Beatrice drove Minetta's car into the garage. Minetta assumed they would ground her, but were they going to take her car too? Tears rolled down her cheeks as she followed her mother into the house through the back kitchen.

In her bedroom, her mother sat on the window seat and beckoned for Minetta to sit next to her. Marilyn eased her heels off.

"Okay, I want to hear everything. Start from the beginning. Take your time and leave out nothing."

Minetta poured out her heart to her mother describing everything she could remember of her encounters with Amber. Marilyn gazed at her daughter's tear-stained face throughout.

"Seems like all of this craziness occurred when you became jealous of Philip's attraction to another girl."

"He just never behaved that way before, and it wasn't just him. It was all the guys. Like she was some kind of beauty queen or something."

Marilyn smiled. "She is a beauty queen winner. She can't help how she looks Mimi or how males will react to her, including Philip. Men look. There's no harm in looking."

"I know that" said Minetta.

Marilyn held up a hand. “Let me finish. Besides her looks, Amber is a talented young lady. She has won several awards and trophies in dance competitions and is a champion track star. The fact that she is my college roommate and sorority sister’s daughter was a wonderful surprise to me. But imagine how embarrassed I was to discover that my daughter behaved so unChristlike toward her daughter. And for what? You have yet to give me a legitimate reason for disliking this girl.”

Marilyn’s tone was calm, but Minetta sensed her mother’s anger.

“Let me tell you a little about the Paige family. Bob and Marcie’s business dealings brought them back to the States. Their family connections to Cedar Valley brought them home.”

“Are they her biological parents? Someone said her grandparents worked for the Paige family.”

Marilyn nodded. “Yes. They are her actual parents. Bob and Marcie Paige returned to Cedar Valley over the past year from New York via London and Hong Kong. Bob is an investment banker, and Marcie, a realtor. He inherited wealth before he and Marcie met. Together, they built a billion-dollar business in the urban housing industry in two decades.”

Marilyn leaned forward on the window seat. She adjusted a pillow for her back.

“Bob Paige’s parents died in a horrific boating accident about twenty years ago, and Marcie is an orphan. When they married, they tried for a long time to have children. When they were finally successful, Marcie had to spend the entire time on bed rest. After Amber was born, Marcie developed severe postpartum depression and for nearly five years was hospitalized. Bob raised Amber by himself but could not care for her properly. His long-time servants, Annie, and Bill Soames, became her surrogate grandparents.”

Minetta kept her head down. Her mother’s voice continued.

“Amber has always known they are her surrogate grandparents and not biological ones. Bob and Marcie never hid the circumstances of her early upbringing. But now, there is only her surrogate grandfather as the grandmother passed a few years ago. The Soames never wanted to move into the suburbs, and Bob trusted them enough to allow his only child to be in their care. The Soames were given a beautiful home by Bob and Marcie a few years ago, but they stayed in the city and gave the house to their son and his family."

"I didn't know any of this," whispered Minetta.

"I think you need to make it right with your friends. You also need to apologize to Amber because she has had to endure misplaced jealousy all her life. Jealousy is a cruel illness, Mimi. It destroys our judgment and makes us incapable of doing the right thing. Instead of looking at this girl's heart, you judged her external looks. Something she has no control over. There was nothing Christlike in your behavior. There was nothing Christlike in your thoughts. When you judge others by worldly standards, your counsel will be ignored, and your testimony weaken."

Marilyn continued to gaze upon her daughter. "I won't give you the spiel about being a pastor's daughter because I'm certain your father addressed it. But I will say that the moment you allowed your eyes to take over and then your thoughts, you were operating under the influence of the ungodly. The Word teaches us that if we magnify godliness within us, then that becomes greater than anything else in the world. We are to overcome the world and not allow the world to overcome us. You gave yourself over to impure, negative thoughts, and those thoughts wrecked whatever positive relationship you could have had with this girl. You ruined your testimony as a potential Christian friend."

Marilyn stopped for breath before continuing. "You also led your friends down the same wicked spiral walk. Instead of encouraging positive communication and building up one another, you led them down a rocky road to false judgment, mockery, humiliation, and deception to hurt another human being."

Minetta had nothing to say. It was all true. She had been jealous of the attention Amber received from Philip, and she had never allowed herself to see the girl beyond that image. Tabitha was the one who had exhibited Christian grace.

As if reading her thoughts, Marilyn said, "by the way, you dragged poor Tabitha along with you, and it has devastated her. I am praying you can repair your friendship with her."

Marilyn slid her pumps back on. "Your father has grounded you for three weeks, and I agree. You will not be driving your car. Mrs. B. will drive you to school and church. Nowhere else."

Minetta looked aghast. "Mom, please let Kim drive me instead of Mrs. B."

"Why?" asked Marilyn.

"Because if Mrs. B. drives me, especially in that station wagon, it will be embarrassing."

"Embarrassing? You should have thought of that when you encouraged Kim to follow that girl. By the way, Kim's parents grounded her since she was driving her car," said Marilyn. "But if they did not ground her, I would still say no."

"That's not fair. Kim wanted to follow her too."

"But you were the one who encouraged her. You were both wrong, but you must take responsibility for your behavior. I want your phone." She held out her hand.

"But I might need it for emergencies. Especially now when I won't be able to drive," she protested.

"You are only going to school and church. If an emergency should come up, we will address it then. Phone please."

Minetta took her phone out of her book bag and handed it to her mother.

"You are grounded for three weeks. Do not ask me for leniency, or you will get more time added. Go to school and attend only the after-school activities you're involved in and nothing else. Is this understood?"

Minetta nodded her head, tears rolling down her cheeks.

Her mother hugged her, whispered "I love you" in her hair, and left her on the window seat.

Chapter 28

Minetta was about to experience something she had never undergone her seventeen years on earth living in the Oak Hills Heights community in Cedar Valley. She had put aside the embarrassing segment of her mother taking her out of school early, and she even blocked out the sight of Beatrice driving her car and locking it in the garage. The further humiliation of Beatrice driving her to school and church in her two-tone station wagon was another visual atrocity she managed to push aside. What she had yet to encounter was the public wrath of her lifelong friends.

Cedar Valley Church held its standard Sunday services and the youth choir was on hand to lead the praise and worship session. Kimberly and Minetta were seated side by side in the alto section. Kimberly avoided any verbal interaction with Minetta. She kept her eyes on the choir director or looked at Eddie. To further put distance between them, Kimberly resorted to making notes in her Sunday pamphlet.

Pastor James' sermon, taken from the Book of Esther in the Holy Scriptures, focused primarily on jealousy. Minetta willed herself not to squirm, but it was difficult. She saw her brother sitting in the congregation with Candy, who was wearing a yellow dress. Scanning the congregation, she locked eyes with Tabitha's mother, Julianne, who appeared to give her a hurting, questioning look. Minetta quickly averted her eyes.

After church service ended, Kimberly rushed past Minetta without saying goodbye. She joined her parents and Kelly as they were waiting in the aisle. Minetta saw Andrew, Joshua, Eddie, and Philip walk out with their parents. Amber and Tabitha left the soprano section to walk with

Raymond waiting at the foot of the steps. Raymond walked with Tabitha, and Amber walked with his mother, who put her arm around the girl's shoulders. Raymond's father walked up the aisle with Lizzie and never looked at her. She watched them all leave without a backward glance at her. She looked around for her brother and Candy, but they had left without speaking to her.

Her parents had driven Minetta to church, and she would have to wait until they were ready to leave. Her father was in his office, changing from his pulpit robe to his suit jacket. Her mother was in the adjoining powder room repairing her makeup. She sat in the empty sanctuary. She realized her friends were purposely avoiding her. She bowed her head, closed her eyes, and prayed. She was sorry for all that had happened. She thought how unfair it was that she should have to take all the blame. Kimberly had been driving, after all!

Kimberly received only a week's punishment to add insult to injury, and Tabitha received no punishment. She groaned inwardly. Minetta did not feel as if everything that occurred was her fault. It was in this moment of apathetic self-righteousness that she saw Philip coming toward her. He sat down next to her. When he spoke, his voice was low and solid in tone.

"I just don't understand why you dislike Amber so much. Is there something bad I don't know about her? Please help me understand your antics."

"There's something about her that is off-putting to me."

"Oh, yeah? Like what? You don't even know her."

"Of course, not. But you know her? Don't you?"

"Everyone thinks you're jealous of her."

She glanced at him. "Do you think I'm jealous of her?"

He looked at the pulpit a moment before answering. "I don't know. But I know you don't like her. Anyone can tell that a mile away."

"I like her. I just don't trust her around you or my friends."

"I've known you all my life, Mimi. You don't like her. You haven't liked her since the first day, and you're making her out to be a monster. She's not. She's a real nice girl."

"What?"

"You heard me. Amber's not the person you have created in your head. You've got to stop harassing her. I'm serious. Stop excluding her from things. I'm sick of it."

His voice was still low, but there was a different tone she had never heard before. It made her angry.

"You're sick of it?"

"We all are. This behavior of yours has got to stop. If you don't stop, you will not have any friends."

"Do I have friends now? Seems you're the leader of the pack. Bending over backwards to say nice things to a girl you claim you barely know."

"Why can't you make friends with her? You would see she's nice."

"You must take me for a fool. Make friends with your wannabe girlfriend so you don't feel guilty chasing her?"

"You are too much. You're really jealous of this girl, aren't you?"

"I'm not jealous of anybody. I'm just tired of you, Philip Jones."

"Tired of me?"

"That's right. I'm tired of watching you grin in her face. I'm tired of you promoting everything she does. I'm tired of you finding ways to be in her aura while pretending she's got a boyfriend. I'm tired of hearing about this ghost boyfriend, and I'm tired of your sneakiness."

Philip was silent while Minetta spoke. Finally, he picked up his Bible and walked up the center aisle towards the front doors.

"Wait…" she called after him.

Philip left the sanctuary without stopping or looking back. She sighed. She was oblivious to where she was sitting in the sanctuary, for directly above her was the Cross of Calvary shining brightly against a background of burnished copper. On the opposite wall was an icon of the sacred Mother looking sorrowfully down at the teen below.

A few evenings later, Minetta was watching television when she heard a knock at her bedroom door.

"Comc in."

Her face lit up as her brother entered the room. Matthew grabbed her desk chair and straddled it backwards. He pushed his baseball cap further back on his black curls. She looked at her brother. He was giving her his leveled look while his mouth curved in a smile. She felt nervous.

"What brings you home?"

"I just stopped by. I wanted to talk to you. I heard about the shenanigans that got you busted. I warned you after the holidays."

"Matt, we did nothing that bad. Everyone is making a mountain out of a molehill."

Matthew studied her for a moment. "Let me give you a second warning with some advice. The warning is that it's going to get harder before it's easier. You have embarrassed yourself, your family, and your friends."

"But, Matt, why am I getting all the blame? It was Kim's car. She had a choice, and she followed Amber's car. I didn't twist her arm."

"No, but you influenced her, and you always could. Take responsibility for the harm you've done to your friends. What about Tabs? From what I heard, she wasn't driving and didn't want to be there."

"Oh, so now she was kidnapped?" Minetta rolled her eyes.

"Sis, I hear you've been jealous of the girl since you met her."

"I'm not jealous of Amber!"

"Keep telling yourself that and you'll wind up expelled from school and with no friends."

"I just don't see why everyone is dumping on me."

"Cut the act! You started this mess and now you're going to take heat for it. Here's my advice. Leave that girl alone or whatever interest Phil has in you will disappear. No man wants a crazy woman who throws jealous fits and temper tantrums because he's talking to someone else in a friendly way."

"In a friendly way? He's the one who's lied about knowing her. He's the one who's always looking out for her and promoting her. Everyone keeps telling me she has a boyfriend, but no one has ever seen him or knows his name. I wish I knew who he was. I would tell him about everything that's been going on."

"Leave Phil and that girl alone."

Minetta's eyes welled with tears. Matthew sighed, returned the chair to the desk, and left the room.

The next three weeks were a tough time for Minetta, as her friends either avoided her or ignored her. The first week of her punishment, she turned a corner in the hallway at school and nearly collided with Kimberly, Tabitha, and Kelly. She wanted to talk to Kimberly, but her parents confiscated her phone, and Tabitha had blocked her on hers.

"Hey guys," said Minetta.

"Hi, Mimi," said Kelly. She was unaware of the tension between her sister and Minetta.

"Hi," said Tabitha and Kimberly in unison.

"We can't stop and chat right now; we're due in the drama department," said Tabitha.

"Talk later," said Kimberly tersely.

"Oh, okay," said Minetta. "Hey guys, let's meet up at lunchtime," she called behind them.

Neither Kimberly nor Tabitha looked back or acknowledged they heard her. Kelly glanced back at her with a puzzled expression on her face. Minetta stood and watched them walk away, feeling a myriad of emotions bordering on loss and despair. She would soon discover what it was like to be ostracized by her friends. She stopped sitting in the cafeteria because they were giving her the cold shoulder. They talked around her and excluded her from the conversations. After a few days there stopped being a space for her at the lunch table. She took refuge in study hall or sat by herself drafting essay papers.

Besides school assignments and preparing for senior exam week. The hardest blow came when she met Ben coming out of the Science Lab, and he hurriedly re-entered the room rather than pass by her. Later, she spotted Raymond and Mark coming down the hall, and they veered off, taking the longer route around.

Minetta suffered the embarrassment of Beatrice driving her to school in the mornings in her huge yellow and brown station wagon. Beatrice insisted on parking directly in front of the school and waiting for Minetta to enter before driving off. Adding further to her humiliation, she would see Beatrice parked in front of the school on evenings when she attended after-school activities.

On the first Friday evening of punishment, Beatrice dropped Minetta off at the Soda Shoppe. She was being driven to the church by her mother. Entering the eatery to wait for her mother, she spotted her friends in a booth eating and chatting away. Minetta saw Amber sandwiched between Philip and Ben, talking to Tabitha, Raymond, Kimberly, and Eddie. She contemplated going over to the booth but had second thoughts. It was Kimberly who noticed her across the room, watching them. Everyone looked at her. She waved, but they all looked away.

Minetta walked outside and sat on a bench. She saw her mother drive up and walked to the car.

"Sorry, I'm late, Mimi," said Marilyn as she merged into the traffic.

"Mom?"

"Yes?"

"Did you ever make a mistake that your friends wouldn't forgive you for?"

"You mean, was I a mean girl?"

"Mom! I am not a mean girl."

"If you never take responsibility for your behavior, you will never curtail your actions."

Minetta sighed. "My friends aren't talking to me. I mean, they are purposely not speaking to me."

"Isn't that how you behaved with Amber?"

"Amber is just some girl who nobody knows but Phil."

"Apparently everyone knows her now."

"I guess so. She pushed her way in. That girl came into our lives and turned everything upside down."

"Seems you're the only one with a problem with her. Why is that?"

"I don't want to talk about this anymore."

Minetta stopped herself from crying. She did not want them to see she was crying over them.

In Bible studies class, they sat together and ignored her the entire night. She pretended to read her lesson and completed her workbook assignment without glancing in their direction. When the class was over she went in search of her mother for the ride home. She cried bitterly in her bedroom at home later.

Minetta understood why Tabitha and Amber would be angry with her. Tabitha never intentionally or unintentionally was ever in trouble. Had she not taken up their invitation to lunch and become a captive victim in the car, she would not have been involved in the shameful act of stalking Amber. Amber was the victim of Minetta's mood swings and jealousy, and had every right to be angry with her shenanigans. But Minetta did not believe Kimberly had the right to be upset when it was her car, and she followed Amber. What doubly anguished Minetta was that Philip was angry with her and believed the reason being he wanted to date Amber instead of her, no matter what he claimed.

As one week slid into the next, her group of friends continued to ignore her. She cried nearly every night after a school day of being shunned. The weekends were agony as she had to spend the day in the house or in her bedroom. Minetta spent a horrible three weeks reflecting on her behavior toward Amber.

Chapter 29

During the annual sports competition events, Minetta's friends continued to blacklist her. As she sat in the bleachers with her parents she felt the sting of their backlash as they took every opportunity to avoid any contact with her. Minetta took notes with her phone in order to have something to do and so that her parents would not suspect anything. Philip pointedly ignored her as he took pictures. He spent a great deal of time talking with Amber and photographing her. At one point she left the bleachers hoping they would think she was going to socialize. The reality was something different.

"Hi, Lizzie, hi, Kelly." The girls were in their track and field uniforms smearing on lip gloss in the ladies' bathroom.

"Hi, Mimi," said Lizzie, looking at her with wide-open eyes.

"Good luck today."

"Thanks, Mimi."

"I'm doing a story on today's competitions. It's good to see everyone in their uniforms."

"Yes, we've all been practicing really hard. Aren't you in the swim and diving competitions later this afternoon?"

"Yes."

"Okay, then. Good luck and see you later."

"Bye, girls."

The girls hurriedly left the bathroom. Minetta noticed Kelly said nothing to her during the entire conversation and avoided looking her way.

Minetta sat in the bleachers with her parents and the school laptop in front of her. She wrote her news article and profiled the students' school spirit and the athletes' determination to win victories for their school.

In the track and field competitions, Amber and Eddie won first place in their separate long-distance divisions. In the long-distance hurdles, Kimberly took home first place. The competitive swimming meets saw Raymond and Minetta each won first place in their respective meets. The difference was that Raymond was congratulated by their group of friends while they ignored her victories. Tabitha earned first place with the highest gymnastic scores.

In the locker room, as Minetta was changing out of her swimsuit, Kimberly walked in, put her head down and walked over to her locker.

"Congratulations, Kim," said Minetta.

"Thank you."

Instead of changing her outfit, Kimberly jammed clothing and shoes into her duffel bag. Amber and Tabitha walked in, looked at each other and walked over to Kimberly keeping their backs turn to Minetta.

"Congratulations, Kim," said Amber and hugged Kimberly. "Can I see your medals?"

Kimberly grinned. Minetta turned to her locker and looked down at her badge and trophy which she had stashed in her duffel bag.

Tabitha said, "the guys want to celebrate. We're going to Philip's house. Are you coming with us, Kim?"

"Yes, I'm ready now."

Kimberly slammed her locker shut and the three girls nearly ran out of the locker room. Minetta refused to cry. She closed her locker door and went in search of her parents. She wanted to go home. She sent off her news article. When the school paper came out, Philip's submitted photos of the winners with Amber in her regulation deep gray and ivory two-piece tank and shorts placed on the front cover. Once Minetta saw the nearly full-page picture of Amber in her competitive track uniform, and glimpsed Philip's name as the photographer, her envy of Amber grew stronger. Meanwhile, she could not find any photographs of her with her winning trophy.

Cedar Valley High's Annual Athletic Awards Program was the expected finale to the school-wide sports competitions. The program recognized outstanding student-athletes from ninth to twelfth grade. It was held in the main gymnasium and Minetta sat on the bleachers with her parents. Paul and Stacy Jones, Philip's parents, sat with Minetta's parents.

Stacy, seated between Minetta and Marilyn, leaned toward Minetta. Her dark brown blunt cut bob, lightly sweeping her shoulders.

"Mimi, you just get prettier every year," she said. "Are you and Philip going to prom together this year?"

"No."

"No! Are you kidding me? Why won't you go to the prom with Philip?"

"I won't go to the prom with Philip because he never asked me. He didn't ask me last year either."

"Well, he gets busy. You know how Phil is."

"Excuse me, Mrs. Jones." Minetta got up and walked away.

Athletic scholarships went to Philip, Ben, Eddie, Andrew, Raymond, and a few other graduating male seniors. The female seniors were awarded following the presentations to the males. Kimberly and Amber were among the recipients. As was expected, Ben was nominated as an All-American. The girls and their parents took photos of all the awardees.

The Upper Medford Valley University campus was abuzz with excitement. James and Marilyn walked hand-in-hand up the hilly pavement with other parents of graduating seniors. James reached around him and took Minetta's hand as there was room for the three of them on the sidewalk. It was a beautiful day. Minetta wore a blue seersucker striped sundress with white sandals. They followed other parents to the bleachers surrounding the football field.

"Well, Mimi, this is going to be you in four years. How do you feel?" asked James.

"I'm ready right now, Dad," she said. James laughed.

"There's Robert and Mary," said Marilyn. She began waving her arms.

"Hi everybody!" said Robert. "Beautiful day, isn't it?"

"Hi Pop-Pop, hi Nana" said Minetta to her grandparents.

"Hi sweetie," said Mary. "Don't you look beautiful, as always."

Robert gave a small shout. "Well, look who decided to join the land of the living. Good evening, sir."

"How are you, Robert? Good to see you and Mary," said Timothy.

"Hello, Mimi. Gorgeous as always," said Elouise.

"Hi, Nana, hi Grandpapa."

Elouise was holding her so tight Timothy only smiled and waved. He had brought his binoculars.

Minetta watched the incoming crowd and finally saw her cousin Annie coming toward her. Annie had chosen a white ruffly sundress and sandals. Janet and Marilyn immediately sat together with their heads into the commencement brochures. Bill sat with James and the grandparents paired off. Minetta and Annie hugged each other and sat on the front row bleachers.

"This is so exciting, Annie." Minetta had dogeared the pages where Matthew and Craig's names were listed.

"How have you been?" asked Annie.

"It's been a long, crazy year. How have you been?"

"Same. This thing with Craig really tore mommy up. Every week she was talking to me about changing schools and talking to her and how she would never try to make me change my mind about anything. It became too much."

"Oh, wow! What did you do?"

"I finally had to tell her I'm not Craig and to stop judging me by the stupid stuff he does. We cried and apologized to each other, and things have been getting better each day."

"That's good. Your mom looks great though," said Minetta as she glanced over at her aunt giggling with Marilyn.

"She and I joined a health club, and she's highlighted her hair."

"That's what's different about her. She looks good, Annie."

"Are you ready for graduation? I am."

"Yes, but I haven't received my acceptance letter yet."

"It will come, just don't worry about it. Um, I heard about what happened."

"Yeah," breathed Minetta. "The bad part is that I am the only one punished. Everyone else is walking around like they're innocent when we were all together."

"I know. That sucks. But cousin, you're a natural-born leader. Those girls followed your lead, and you know it. I know you want them to pay some of the punishment, but the truth is that you don't like Amber. I saw that at Matt's birthday party."

"She wasn't invited to the party."

"That's what I'm talking about. Yet, I've been at Tabitha and Kimberly's sleepovers, and she was there but you weren't."

"Wait! What did you say?"

"You heard me."

"They've been having sleepovers without me?"

"What were they supposed to do?"

Minetta was quiet. She glanced at her cousin.

"You live up here. How do you get down to Cedar Valley? It's a four-hour drive."

"My mom or Nana Elouise bring me. The girls were at my house last weekend for a sleepover. Aunt Marilyn told me you were on punishment."

"Why did she have to tell you that? I'm not a baby."

"Don't get upset. I called her when you didn't answer your phone after I had left several messages. I thought your phone was lost or stolen."

"Oh, I see."

What else had been going on while she was on punishment?

Minetta watched intently for her brother among the graduates; finally spotting him and alerting her parents. A bit later, she and Annie spotted Craig. Throughout the program Minetta sat with her family on the fourth-row bleachers and tried hard not to think of Philip and Amber.

Chapter 30

It was the end of the third week of Minetta's punishment. She was eating dinner with her parents in the dining room when Beatrice entered the room and handed James a bulky manila envelope. Beatrice never intruded once she served the meal. Dessert tonight was apple pie to add a sweet treat to the stuffed pot roast she had prepared earlier. Although the food was delicious, Minetta had little appetite.

James looked at the envelope. "Thank you, Mrs. B." He placed it on the table, face down, and continued eating.

"May I be excused, please?"

"Hold on a minute. There's some family business we need to discuss. Please sit down," James said. What now?

"Your mother and I agreed you can have your car back. You will find your car keys on the desk tray in the front foyer."

"Thank you, Dad," said Minetta.

"You can also have your cell phone back. I put it on your bed right before coming down for dinner," said Marilyn.

"Thank you, Mom."

James handed Minetta the envelope. "I have a letter here from UVM addressed to you."

She hesitated before opening it. Had the university heard of her behavior and was rescinding their acceptance of her into the school? She sat dumbfounded, staring at the envelope.

"Aren't you going to open it, honey," her mother prodded gently.

Minetta sighed and opened the parcel. There were several sheets of typewritten pages, an Upper Medford Valley University calendar, a school banner, a tee-shirt with the school crest on it, and a mascot magnet slid out. She looked at the first page. She cried and laughed simultaneously.

"Mom, Dad, This letter says I'm accepted! I'm in," she said. "There's more. I will receive an academic scholarship for the entire four years. I can live in an Honors dorm beginning my freshman year if I choose."

"Congratulations, baby," said James.

Minetta jumped out of her chair and gave her father a bear hug. Marilyn got up from her seat at the opposite end of the table and embraced Minetta, both in tears.

"My baby," said Marilyn, cuddling Minetta tightly.

"For goodness' sakes, this is joyful news. Why are you both crying?" asked James.

He was perplexed. The women in his life baffled him. His wife cried regardless of the news she received. She had wept when Matthew was accepted as well. Still locked in an embrace, they both laughed as tears continued running down their cheeks. Hearing the commotion, Beatrice came into the dining room.

"Is everything okay?" she asked hesitantly.

"Yes Mrs. B., everything's fine," said James.

"Good news Mrs. B.," said Minetta. "I got accepted into UMV!"

Beatrice rushed over for a hug. "Oh darling, that's wonderful news. I'm so happy for you."

The lilt in Beatrice's voice was melodic in its fluctuations when she was happy. She cried too as James sat observing for a moment. They were all three talking at once. Smiling to himself, he retreated to his den to finish working on his Sunday sermon. The storm had passed. Praise the Lord!

Minetta's phone was buzzing when she entered her bedroom. She had received several text messages from classmates, but her best friends were the ones she was most interested. She called her first number. After three rings, Kimberly picked up.

"Hey, Mimi, what's up?"

"Hi, bestie. How are you doing?"

"Just fine. You got your phone back. Did they give you your car also?" Kimberly asked.

"Yeah, just now after dinner. What about you?"

"I got my stuff back two weeks ago," she said.

Minetta said, "you want to come over, and we can talk more?"

"I can't. Eddie is coming over to watch a movie with me. He'll be here any minute."

"Your parents are letting you and Eddie date now?"

"I turned eighteen last weekend. His parents gave us a birthday dinner at La Dolce Vita Restaurant. You were not invited because you were still grounded."

"Yeah, right? Happy late birthday. I got accepted at UMV."

"Congratulations."

"Thanks. You want to do something tomorrow?"

"Sorry, I can't. Mom and I are going shopping for the senior prom."

"Oh, what about Sunday?"

There was a pause before Kimberly said, "We're going on a mother-daughter dinner cruise right after church."

"Wow, your punishment seems to have done you good."

"I've got to go. Eddie's here. Good to hear from you. See you at school."

Before Minetta could reply, the line was dead. Kimberly had her car returned two weeks ago and held a birthday party to which she did not receive an invitation. Life had kept flowing, even though hers had stood still. She waited a minute before dialing Tabitha. She answered on the first ring.

"Hi, Mimi."

"Hi, Tabs. I wanted to apologize for getting you in trouble."

"Don't."

"What do you mean?"

"I mean, don't apologize. You did not get me in trouble. Kim spoke to my parents and told them how much I protested my kidnapping. She told the truth."

Tabitha's voice was soft, but firm. Minetta experienced a vague feeling she could not put her hands on.

"That was sweet of Kim," she said.

"I think so. She did the right thing at the right time. When she's thinking without being wrongfully influenced, she usually does the right thing."

"What is that supposed to mean, Tabs?" asked Minetta quietly.

"What it's supposed to mean is that you were not behaving as a good friend to Kim or me. The Bible says do not cause people to stumble or lead them into sin by our actions or behaviors. You should not have encouraged her to follow Amber's car."

Minetta became angry. "Kim's not a baby. She followed Amber's car because she wanted to."

"It's not right to push the blame on everyone else but yourself."

"Kim didn't like her as much as I didn't," spat out Minetta.

"You never liked Amber, and you poisoned Kim into not liking her either."

"Amber is a fake."

Tabitha made a mock laugh sound. "Says who? You? Amber's a nice girl trying to get along with people. I don't know what your problem is with her."

"I didn't call you to hear about Amber."

"So, why did you call me?" countered Tabitha.

"I told you; I want to apologize."

"Save your breath. You should apologize to Amber."

"I will, Tabs, I will. But I wanted to make amends with my two best friends first."

"Okay."

"Hey, you want to have a sleepover this weekend?"

"I can't think about this weekend. Lots of chores to complete."

"Oh, okay. How about next weekend? Since Kim is busy this weekend, as well. How about we plan for next weekend?"

"I will probably be busy next weekend, too. Ray and I have a planned outing. Lots to do before then."

Minetta was undaunted. "Hey, you want to ride up to New York City with me and mom for prom shopping? Your favorite bohemian store is near mom's favorite shoe shop."

"Listen, I've got to go. See you at school."

Tabitha hung up before Minetta could say anything else. She looked at her phone. She called Philip, but he had blocked her. She tried Raymond and Eddie with the same results.

She moved from her bed to her window seat and watched the evening sky darken. She put her head on her folded arms and silent tears fell onto her sleeve.

Chapter 31

Marilyn leaned out the window of her blue custom-colored sedan. She tapped a French manicured nail on the buzzer of the gated entrance. Marilyn drove into the circular driveway, parked her car alongside Amber's black convertible, took out her makeup compact, and applied a dab of lipstick. She dusted an imaginary speck from the skirt of her blue wool suit. Glancing at Minetta, clad in a blue tweed suit with a string of pearls around her neck, she smiled appreciatively.

"Are you prepared with what you 're going to say to Amber and her mother?" she asked Minetta, seated quietly beside her.

"Yes, Mom," she responded. "I am going to apologize for my behavior."

"Okay, Mimi, let's go to lunch."

A uniformed housekeeper ushered them into a spacious seating room. Bookshelves from floor to ceiling lined two walls with long sofas, overstuffed chairs, and other furniture artfully scattered about the room. The other walls boasted oil-based portraits of Paige's ancestors stained to look aged. They were studying a baby picture of Amber seated on a grand piano when the sound of sliding doors alerted them to someone entering the room.

"Hey Soror!" came a high-pitched voice behind them. "It's been so long!"

Marcie Paige threw her arms around Marilyn and hugged her tight. Minetta noticed how much the two women could have passed as blood relatives. They were both petite with tiny figures, long dark lustrous graying hair. Both wore some combination of blue and yellow, which were the colors of their college sorority, Alpha Nu.

"Oh, my goodness!" exclaimed Marcie, looking around Marilyn at Minetta. "Is this who I think it is? Come on over here and give me a big hug, sweetheart."

Minetta bent down to hug Marcie, who had to reach up on her toes to hug her back. Marcie walked ahead to one of the long sofas beckoning Marilyn and Minetta to sit on the adjoining sofa facing her. She looked at Minetta intently.

"My goodness, she's the spitting image of you, Soror."

Marilyn smiled. "Thank you, Marcie."

"I had the staff prepare something light for our lunch. I hope you two love fried chicken and waffles. I just had a taste for that today."

"Oh, that's fine, Marcie. I'm sure it's delicious," said Marilyn.

Two housekeepers brought in a covered rolling table. Marcie's attention turned to the women.

"Please put that outside on the patio, girls. Thank you."

Marcie watched them as they were setting up. She turned her attention back to Marilyn and Minetta.

"Amber should come down soon. I told her to put on a dress and fix herself up. She's always in exercise clothes or dance outfits," she said.

At that moment, Amber came into the room. Her mother moved on the sofa, showing she was to sit beside her. Amber was wearing a deep blue linen dress with a yellow cardigan and pearls. Amber looked at Marilyn, but not at Minetta.

"Hello, Mrs. Morgan," she said. "You look prettier up close than when I see you in the pulpit."

"Hello, Amber. You're quite stunning yourself. Thank you for that nice compliment. I know you have won many beauty pageants. Now I see why," said Marilyn, smiling.

"Yes, she has," said Marcie, sitting stiff and straight. "I'm so proud of her."

"You won several beauty pageants, too," said Amber to Marilyn. "You've won more beauty awards than any other beauty queen at UMV, past or present."

Marilyn was pleasantly shocked. Smiling more broadly, she said, “someone has certainly done her homework on UMV.”

“Soror, have you forgotten we were in the same chapter in college? I have shown Amber our chapter house album so many times I think she has the contents memorized.”

Turning to Minetta, she said, “Have you seen our chapter house on the UMV campus, sweetheart?”

“Yes, I have,” said Minetta.

Marcie managed a nervous twitter. “Of course, you have. You are a legacy several times over, aren’t you?”

“Will you be joining a sorority, Amber?” Marilyn asked.

Before Amber could answer, Marcie said, “of course, she will! She will join Alpha Nu. There is no doubt. She is a legacy, after all.”

She laughed again in a high-pitched tone. “What about you, Mimi? You are a legacy and automatically a shoo-in. Although these days, I’m told some of these sororities don’t honor legacies like they used to.”

“Hadn’t heard that,” said Marilyn stiffly.

Marcie, seemingly oblivious to Marilyn’s tenseness, said, “I suppose it’s all the new blood. You know, the nouveau riche jealous of the old money kind of thing.”

She gave a terse laugh that sounded more like a shriek. Minetta looked at Amber, who was looking at the floor. Marilyn fidgeted.

“Marcie, I wanted us to have a sit-down with our daughters.”

“Oh, of course, of course,” interrupted Marcie. “They will enter college soon and will be sorority sisters. Its only right we should all meet and get to know one another.”

Marilyn smiled. “Soror, James and I have raised our children to recognize and understand when their behavior or actions affect others negatively or destructively. Amber deserves simple respect from our daughter regardless of their future college plans.”

“Soror, Amber’s the new kid on the block and your daughter’s been the queen bee among her friends since forever. The old guard jealous of the new upstart. It’s nothing.”

Marilyn smiled and continued, “it seems there’s some friction between the girls, and we need it resolved. After all, as you have stated, we are sisters for life. Our daughters hopefully will be as well one day."

"Oh, I'm sure it's nothing to worry about, Soror. Harmless girl pranks are how I took it."

Marilyn continued again. "I have spoken to Mimi, and she is here of her own accord to apologize to Amber for causing her grief and suffering. That is the ultimate aim of our accepting your luncheon invitation."

Marcie waved her hands at them in a shooing motion. "Oh, poo Soror. There is no need for apologies and so forth. They just hit it off on the wrong foot. That happens all the time."

The girls stared at Marcie. Marilyn stiffened slightly. Swiping an imaginary speck from her skirt, Marilyn made another attempt.

"Marcie, that is not the way I raised my children. Mimi has to apologize to Amber for her misdeeds."

Marcie snorted and leaned her head to the side. Looking at Amber, she said, "I thought it was a hoot that the girls were playing detective in following Amber about the city. It is not a big deal. Amber and I had a pleasant chat about it."

Minetta glanced at Amber, who was staring across the room with a vacant look. She looked at the cheerful face of Marcie, who leaned forward slightly toward Minetta.

"Sweetheart, don't you worry your pretty head about your teen silliness. I'm sure you know by now that Amber is multi-talented and gifted. That older man is her grandfather, and she likes to check on him. It is a mutually rewarding visit all around because neither her father nor I disapprove. I was adopted, and her dad's parents are deceased now." Leaning back on the sofa, she spread out her hands. "So, things always work out, and no hard feelings are coming from the Paige household."

Minetta and Amber looked at each other, but this time with silent solidarity. This woman was something else. Marilyn cleared her throat again. She was having a hard time keeping the conversation literate and on topic.

"Marcie, the reason we're here is for Amber and Mimi to make amends and to settle their differences. What my daughter and her friends did was wrong. There are no excuses. As Christians, we cannot expect others to follow the Word if we are not following it or living by it."

"Oh, but of course, Soror!" exclaimed Marcie, clasping her hands together in a semblance of joy. "But we mustn't persecute Mimi. I'm sure she meant no harm by any of it."

"Whether Mimi's actions intended to cause harm or not, and I'm glad they didn't. The fact remains that she damaged her relationship with her friends and with your daughter."

Marcie laughed her shrill laugh. "Soror, I think it is you upset over these teen dramas. As you can see, the Paige household has taken these shenanigans in stride. When you mix love and teens, you get drama. Their disagreement is nothing more than boyfriend drama. Tell your mother, Mimi."

The heat rose in Minetta's neck. She saw Marcie, Amber, and her mother look at her. Their stares made her mouth dry, and her throat parched.

"There is no boyfriend drama," said Minetta hoarsely.

There was a momentary pause, and Amber, with a slightly sarcastic smile, said, "I didn't know Phil was your boyfriend. In all the years I've known him, your name has never come up."

"He's not my boyfriend. We have been friends since forever, is all." Minetta was fuming. Amber was going for the jugular.

Amber smiled sweetly. "That's good to know because he asked me if I would go to the prom with him. I wanted to talk to you first as I was not sure of your situation."

Marilyn side-eyed Minetta before shifting sideways on the sofa to face her, smoothing her skirt as she did so.

"You don't need my permission. Philip and I are childhood friends. Besides, I'm attending prom with someone else."

"Oh?" Amber smiled slightly.

"Yes, Andrew asked me," said Minetta, looking at Marilyn, who nodded approvingly. Smoothing her skirt edge, Minetta looked down at her clear-glossed fingernails before adding, "Philip was concerned about your boyfriend."

Now it was Marcie and Marilyn's turn to look at Amber.

Marcie asked sharply, "what boyfriend?"

Amber stuttered. "I don't have a boyfriend. I just told Phil that so he would not think I was weird or something."

"Not having a boyfriend makes you weird?" asked Marilyn.

Amber smiled. "People always assume I have a boyfriend. I don't know why."

Marcie nervously pushed the hair out of her face. She glanced over at Marilyn and Minetta with a small smile.

"Oh my! Teen lives are filled with so much drama. I don't remember us having quite this much of it, do you, Soror?"

Marilyn smiled. "I have to disagree, Soror. We had drama and lots of it. The difference was we didn't have the technology for such drama to be broadcast all over the world."

"Good point Soror," said Marcie looking over her shoulder. "I see our lunch table is ready. We will eat on the patio, ladies. Today is such a lovely day."

Leading the way and keeping up a steady stream of conversation, Marcie sashayed through the double doors to the courtyard with Amber and Marilyn close behind. Minetta walked behind them, meditating on Amber's response to the boyfriend question.

The luncheon had been pleasant, as Marcie was an excellent storyteller and dramatist. She kept the girls entertained recounting the college exploits of members of the Alpha Nu House. Marilyn said very little, only smiling at some antics described in hilarious detail by Marcie.

After lunch, Marcie asked Marilyn to take a walk with her on the grounds. They strolled across the lawn arm in arm, their blue and yellow outfits colorful contrasts against the deep green of the grass beneath their feet and the clear blue of the skies above.

As the two women walked across the lawn away from them, Minetta had to suck up to her discomfort. Amber was seated across from her in a chaise lounge, watching the retreating figures of their mothers. She cleared her throat.

"Amber?"

"Yes." Amber replied, not looking at her.

"I want to apologize for how I've been acting towards you. I'm sorry."

"Thank you for apologizing. I apologize, too, if it seemed I was after your boyfriend. I was not and am not. I've known Phil a long time." She looked straight into Minetta's eyes. "Mainly from our summers together in Hawaii."

"He told me the same thing," said Minetta uneasily.

"Then what's the problem with you and me?"

"I guess misunderstanding," said Minetta.

Amber's mouth curved in a smirk. "That's not good enough. Tabs and I have been good since we met. Kim is cool when you're not around. You are the only one bringing me grief, and I want to know why."

Amber's voice was soft yet firm. She was leaning back in the chaise lounge, giving Minetta a direct stare. Minetta looked out across the grass.

"We just got off on the wrong start, is all."

Amber smiled slyly. "You like Phil more than you let on. That is the only reason you're behaving this way. Why don't you put him out of his misery and tell him?"

"I don't know what you're implying, but we have known each other practically all our lives. We are like sister and brother."

Amber leaned forward, raising a hand. "Calm down with the drama. You and I both know you want it to be more. Your friends are hooked up or about to be. Stop trying to act like you don't want more from him than just friendship."

"He likes you that way, not me."

Amber's laugh turned into a snort. "He likes you, Mimi. You need to own your feelings about him."

"He has never looked at me the same way he looks at you."

"So what? Guys look. How many look at you? You need to be paying attention to the way he looks at you and the way he watches out for you and takes care of you."

"We've always been friends, is all. He treats me like a friend because that's what we are."

"Nothing wrong with friendship."

Minetta glared at her. Amber smiled again. "Get your eyes off me and start paying attention to that guy. He's crazy about you."

Minetta trusted little of what Amber stated. She could not make out what Amber was up to, and her mocking smile was uncomfortable.

Changing the subject, she asked, "have you heard from any colleges yet?"

"They have accepted me at UMV and Foxcraft. What about you?" replied Amber.

Minetta said, "they have accepted me to UMV, my dream school. I always wanted to go there."

"Good for you! I may enroll at Foxcraft," Amber said.

Minetta frowned. "Does your mother know? I mean, at lunch, the way she was talking, I thought you would attend UMV."

"Although UMV accepted me, I am waiting to see where my boyfriend goes. He may go to Foxcraft if they give him a better scholarship and athletic package. So that's where I'm headed too."

"I thought you didn't have a boyfriend."

Amber threw her head back and laughed.

Minetta asked, "when would you tell your parents you're not attending Foxcraft if that happens?"

"I honestly haven't thought about it. But please don't tell anyone, not even your mother."

"Oh, I won't," said Minetta. "But if you don't register at UMV, when would you tell your parents? When they see it on the graduation programs?"

"That's a good idea!" said Amber, snapping her fingers and making a happy face in a mime interpretation. Minetta smiled and leaned forward in her chair. An idea popped into her mind.

"Back to the boyfriend you don't have. Who is he? Does he go to another school? Does he live in Cedar Valley?"

Amber smiled and looked away. "Here come the mothers. You know mom can't wait to decorate my life in blue and yellow."

Minetta resignedly sat back in her chair. "Alpha Nu has a chapter at Foxcraft."

"I believe so. Joining a sorority is the last thing on my mind."

"I think if you don't join your mom's sorority, she will disown you," said Minetta.

"Hmm, she might," agreed Amber. "But once she finds out I'm not attending UMV, she might have another set of worries." She shook her head in mock dismay. "I feel so bad for her."

She looked cheerful, trying to put on a mournful face that Minetta laughed out loud. Soon Amber joined in. Their mothers, within earshot now of the patio, smiled. They had settled the differences between the girls.

The luncheon was prelude to a gradual reconciliation between Minetta and her close friends. When Minetta returned home, she sent note cards to each of her close friends with a brief message of confession followed by an apology.

Chapter 32

It took time for hurt feelings to mend and disappointments to be forgiven. Little by little, Minetta's relationship with her friends healed. A look became a smile, and a smile turned into a greeting. But other than their casual greetings, Minetta knew painfully well that the easygoing rapport she had built with her friends had been damaged.

A few weeks later, Minetta was at home in her bedroom, straightening up her walk-in closet. She emerged from the closet with a bag of items intended for charity and her friends' appearances in her room surprised her. Kimberly was lying across her bed reading the latest *La Femme Divine* fashion catalog. Tabitha was sitting in the window seat knitting, and Amber, seated at her desk, was playing a video game on her phone.

"Hey, guys. I didn't know you were in here. What's going on?"

"Hey bestie, Mrs. B. told us you were getting stuff together for charity. How's it going?" asked Kimberly as she sat up in the bed. "Are you finished or still working?"

"Hang out with us a bit," said Amber. "Just us girls."

Tabitha said, "Yeah, we haven't hung out together in a while."

"Sure," said Minetta. She climbed onto the center of her bed beside Kimberly.

"So, what's the first topic?" asked Tabitha, folding up her yarn and stashing it in her knitting sack.

"I have a question about the prom," said Amber. "I've never been to a prom. How do the guys know what kind of bouquet to give you? I mean the color of your gown and all?"

"You tell him your gown's color and the type of gown you're wearing,"

Minetta replied. "He will tell the florist and they will hook him up."

"Or you can give him a piece of your gown fabric to take to the florist or a picture," offered Kimberly.

"Great," said Amber.

"Are you guys wearing heels?" asked Tabitha.

"Not real high. I'm tall enough," said Kimberly.

"Same here. Medium height, so I don't look like my grandmother in moccasins," said Minetta.

Tabitha looked at her nails. "Should we get a manicure? I've never had one done professionally."

They all inspected their hands. Other than Minetta and Amber, the other girls nails were bare.

"What about hair and makeup?" added Amber.

Tabitha sighed. "Do we have to wear makeup?"

"Sure," said Kimberly. "This will be the biggest event of our lives until we graduate college."

"Let's get hair, makeup, and our nails done professionally," said Minetta. "I am thinking of Miss Vicki. She's been my mom's hairstylist and makeup person since forever."

"Hey, I just got an idea," said Kimberly. "Why not make a group appointment with Miss Vicki to get our hair and nails done? That way, we can all go together."

Tabitha smiled. "That's a great idea, Kim."

Minetta said, "I am going to ask my mom to book an appointment for us. We can have a spa day, too. When should we do this?"

Tabitha said, "How about the day before the prom as we will be home then?"

Kimberly said, "Morning or afternoon?"

"Afternoon is better," said Tabitha.

Amber said, "I don't want to cause a problem but if we're going to do this, I suggest we go the morning of the prom. That way our looks and hair will be freshly done. I don't know about you ladies, but I can never do the makeup the same way the next day."

"Good point, Amber. How about the morning of?"

"Yes. We'll still be together," replied Tabitha.

Kimberly nodded her head. "Sounds like a winner."

"Good," Minetta said. "How about our gowns?"

The girls were quiet, and no one looked at Minetta. Finally, Kimberly turned to Minetta.

"We already have our gowns, Mimi."

"All of you?"

"Yes," replied Amber. "Our mothers took us to New York for a shopping day."

"We were angry that you put us all in an embarrassing situation with our parents," said Tabitha. She added, "and with Amber, who we all really liked."

Kimberly looked hard at Minetta. "If you're going to be angry at anyone, try me. I'm the one who suggested the shopping trip without you."

"Kim, I understand you were angry with me. Rightfully so. But we had been talking about shopping together for prom since ninth grade."

Without warning, tears welled up in Minetta's eyes.

In a quiet voice, Tabitha said, "I hear you, Mimi. You wanted us to forgive you for all the mean and hateful things you've said and done about Amber, well how about forgiving us for daring to enjoy ourselves without you?"

Amber walked over to Minetta and put her arms around her shoulders.

"Why don't we all go with you to shop for your gown? Let's really put the past behind us."

"Yes, let's do that," said Minetta, wiping her eyes on her sleeve. Kimberly, Tabitha, and Amber hugged Minetta, and she returned their hugs.

Senior examination week was on the horizon. Naturally, every student in twelfth grade was anxious. During their lunch break, the friends met at the Soda Shoppe for intense group studying the weekend before exam week. After a two-hour nonstop question-and-answer format, thcy ordered dinner. Philip placed an order of cheeseburgers, French fries, and milk shakes for everyone.

"You know if you hadn't rushed me, I would have gotten the correct answer. It was on the tip of my tongue," Kimberly said to Eddie regarding a physics question.

Eddie smirked. "I'll bet it was."

Raymond smiled and turned to Tabitha. "How do you feel about our study session? Are you okay?"

"Yes Ray. I'm fine. We all did well," said Tabitha.

"I'll be glad when next weekend gets here," said Eddie, running his hands through his hair. He had cut his high pompadour down, and soft waves formed over his forehead.

"Why? What's happening next weekend?" asked Amber.

"Exam week will be behind us," said Philip. Everyone laughed.

"Did you ladies find your perfect gowns yet?" asked Raymond.

"Tabitha! Must you tell him everything?" demanded Kimberly.

"What's wrong with Ray knowing we went shopping? He has to buy my corsage, remember?" said Tabitha.

Minetta laughed. "You did nothing wrong, Tabs. It's not a mystery we went shopping for my gown for the prom, which is the week after next, by the way."

"I guess my nerves are just bad. I want to have these exams behind me," said Kimberly.

"That's all well and good, Kim," said Raymond. "But don't get so worked up about it. You always do very well."

Kimberly smiled. "True. I guess this is the end of the road as far as high school goes for real, uh?"

"Yeah, baby, this is our last hurrah," said Eddie.

"Hey Ben, what's up?" said Philip.

"Hey," said Ben.

"Hey bro, missed you at my house earlier," said Eddie.

"Thanks, bro. Something came up," said Ben. He looked at Philip. "Can I talk to you a minute?"

"Sure," said Philip, getting up.

"What's going on?" demanded Minetta.

"It's okay. Ben and I are working on a school project together," said Philip.

He and Ben walked out of the Soda Shoppe. Raymond looked at Eddie and nodded his head.

"Be back," Raymond said and followed Philip and Ben.

"Where are they going?" asked Minetta.

"All is good, ladies. Here comes our food," said Eddie.

He and Kimberly moved items out of the way on the table to allow the server to place their meals. Minetta looked around the table at everyone.

"Okay ladies, let's pray." Eddie gave the blessing over the food. Afterward, everyone assembled their food items and made small talk.

"You guys don't seem curious what Ben could want to talk to Philip about."

Amber said, "why should we, Mimi? It's none of our business."

Tabitha said, "I try not to mind other people's business. I have enough of my own to worry about."

"Amen," said Eddie curtly.

"Pass the ketchup, please," said Kimberly.

"I'm not a bad person because I am curious what Ben wants with Philip," said Minetta. "After all, Ben is not really a part of our group."

"Calm down. No one said you were a bad person," said Kimberly.

"Nosy, but not a bad person," said Eddie, smirking.

"It's good to be nosy sometimes. Remember when Philip almost got hit in the church parking lot? It's good to be cautious about things and people. Just in case."

Amber glared at Minetta. "Just in case of what? What's wrong with Ben? Are you saying that he tried to run over Phil in the church parking lot?"

"Didn't you just hear what I said? We don't know Ben. He's not a part of our circle."

"A part of our circle?" sneered Amber. "He's in several of Phil's classes and as far as I've seen, they get along well."

"So?" said Minetta. "What's your point?"

"What's MY point? My point is he's the son of surgeons, a star athlete, and lives in a mansion. But you're acting like he's a stranger or someone out to harm Phil," said Amber, clearly angry.

"No, I'm not. I just think it's strange for Ben to show up here and then ask Philip to meet him outside," replied Minetta.

Tabitha frowned. "Mimi, I don't like what you're implying about Ben, even if you don't hear yourself."

Eddie said, "yeah, tone it down some. Ben is one of us. We've known him since kindergarten days."

"Not to mention Ben's dad grew up in Cedar Valley and introduced my parents to each other in medical school," said Kimberly.

Tabitha, munching on a French fry, asked, "how do you know Phil didn't text him, or they didn't talk earlier?"

Minetta countered, "well, why did Ray get up and leave if something wasn't right?"

Kimberly replied, "I don't know, but I'm certainly not going to speculate on innocent behavior that is none of my business."

Amber said, "I can see I'm not part of this inner circle."

Tabitha said, "you're watching Raymond now?"

Eddie put down his cheeseburger. "Alright, Mimi. Nothing is going on. Ben and Philip are working on a project. Ask Philip what it is if you want to know so bad. Now please stop this nonsense and let me enjoy my food."

Kimberly said, "yes, let's eat."

Tabitha said, "here they come now."

Philip and Raymond returned to the table and sat down.

"Where's Ben?" asked Minetta.

"He went home, I guess," said Philip reaching for his food. Tabitha helped Raymond with his condiments. Amber gave Philip her French fries, and Minetta gave him her halved cheeseburger.

Minetta said, "Philip, I was concerned when I saw Ben come out of nowhere and wanted to go off with you. Everything okay?"

Everyone at the table was tense. Eddie and Raymond traded looks. Kimberly and Tabitha concentrated on their food. Amber watched Minetta through slit eyes. Philip cleared his throat.

"Everything is fine. We're working on a project. Didn't I say that?" He put ketchup on his fries.

"Yes, but as I was telling Amber, he's not a part of our crowd. So, him coming over here and taking you away like that was suspicious to me."

"I can see I'm not a part of 'our crowd' either." Amber said, angrily.

She tried to get up, but her seatmates restrained her.

"Stop this line of talking, Mimi. We are a group of friends who have known each other since first grade, including Ben. There's no reason to keep insulting Amber or anyone else who joins our group," said Kimberly, clearly upset and pushing her food away.

"You also about to get ostracized again. Perhaps for good this time. I don't like racism," said Eddie sternly, putting an arm around Kimberly and looking directly at Minetta.

"I'm not racist," Minetta protested.

Amber snorted. "Could have fooled me."

Philip sighed. "Mimi, we've all known Ben since nursery school. What's happened to you this year?"

Minetta was close to tears. "After that parking lot incident where you could have been killed, I'm concerned is all."

"Really?" said Amber. "So, the Black guy is automatically suspect? Do you share this same concern with Andrew or any of the White guys you see with Phil?"

"I always thought you liked Ben," said Eddie. "I mean, what's not to like? We've known him since forever, and he's never changed. Just because he doesn't hang out with us all the time is no reason to write him off."

Raymond smiled. "The man is a born athlete. We swim, shoot hoops, go bowling, and he's even good at archery."

"Ben says I'm a natural when it comes to the bow and arrow," said Kimberly.

"Only because you're a born athlete," said Philip.

"You know, when my folks built this town over one hundred fifty years ago, there were only Native Americans here. Today we have people of all ethnicities and cultures in Cedar Valley," mused Eddie. "I think that's progress."

Raymond spoke in a quiet manner. "Your comments Mimi, while innocent to you, reek of a colonial mindset that's troubling to me as I'm a man with brown skin. My ancestors are native to this land, but we are like invisible walking ghosts. People forget we actually exist."

"Yeah, they'd rather believe all your people were wiped out or relocated on the Trail of Tears," said Kimberly.

Philip interjected. "I don't think Mimi means what's coming out of her mouth."

"I… no… I mean… Philip's right. You guys are getting it wrong," stuttered Minetta.

Raymond looked at Philip and Minetta. Philip ate his fries with his eyes on his plate. Eddie was looking at the ceiling with an exasperated grimace on his face. Tabitha's nose had turned pink, and her eyes were downcast. Kimberly and Amber were holding hands, and Amber looked as if she wanted to cry.

In his smooth baritone, Raymond said, "Mimi, your concern for Philip is heartwarming; however, it is entirely unnecessary."

It took a few minutes, but Kimberly giggled first, followed by Amber and Eddie, and before long, the entire table convulsed with spasms of laughter. Everyone was laughing but Minetta.

"I don't see what's so funny," said Minetta, irritated at being laughed at.

"We know," said Kimberly, and everyone laughed again.

Chapter 33

Instead of spending an afternoon at the salon, Marilyn suggested booking the shop for the entire morning on the day of the prom. The girls' mothers thought the idea was epic, and so did their daughters. Marilyn reserved Miss Vicki's Beauty Salon for the morning of prom day.

The salon, owned and managed by Victoria LaMothe Harris, was a one-stop shop for hair and makeup. As a student at Foxcraft University, Vicki had earned a degree in Fine Art. Later, working for a museum in Harlem as its curator, she enrolled in cosmetology school. When she found herself childless and divorced by the age of thirty, she wanted to leave the hustle and bustle of the city for some place quiet. One of her New York clients, Marcie Paige, suggested Cedar Valley. Vicki built a home in Maple Glen Heights and opened her signature shop in Town Square. Soon, she had hired a team of professionals who became her tenured staff.

The morning of the prom, the girls were each picked up by limousine service supplied by Vicki, who had closed her shop for the day. The doorbell chimes alerted Vicki that her young clients had arrived. Vicki was a tall, model-thin woman with dark slanted eyes and fiery red hair she wore in a giant curly Afro across her shoulders. She greeted the girls in the foyer.

"Hello young ladies. My name is Miss Vicki. Hello Mimi, always a pleasure to see you. Please follow me," she said.

The girls entered a shop that was styled with baroque furniture and trimmings. The large foyer was a masterpiece of off-white decor edged in gold, with every doorknob painted a burnished gold color. They followed Vicki from the lobby to the salon area, styled similarly. The off-white and gold trim chairs covered in clear plastic and styling stations layered with clear plastic allowed the visual beauty of the countertops. Wall-to-wall mirrors trimmed in gold decorated the walls. As they passed through the salon, the crystal and gold chandeliers hanging from the ceiling mesmerized the girls'. They passed into a hall that held several doors, and Vicki entered the first door on her right.

Vicki had decorated the office like the rest of the salon in off-white with gold furnishings. The burnished gold desk and matching chair sat in an alcove overlooking an enclosed flower garden. The two long settees covered in white fur and decorated with gold suede and silk pillows and arm scarves. The round glass table held a burnished gold vase with off-white and gold trimmed porcelain flowers.

Vicki seated all four girls on the settee opposite her. As she looked at them, she marveled at their youth and natural beauty.

"It is a pleasure to meet you. I know Mimi already as she often comes with her mother. I remember you, Amber, from your beauty pageant and dance competition days in New York. Still stunning. I am honored that you all have chosen my shop for your pre-prom preparation. The people I am about to introduce to you are my staff. They have been with me since I opened this shop, and each is a consummate professional skilled in their craft. Talk to them about what you want and don't want. We aim to please."

She looked around and picked up a stack of cards with writing on them. Four people entered the room, each in a different colored lab coat. There were two men and two women. They smiled at the girls.

Vicki glanced at her cards before speaking. "The lady with the black coat is Patty. She's your manicurist and pedicurist. She will take care of your fingernails and toenails. To her right, in the red coat, is Ana. She will do your facials. Patty and Ana are in high demand in Cedar Valley, and it's taken awhile to get clientele used to the fact that they must take vacation breaks."

Vicki laughed at the last comment. "To her right, in the leopard print lab coat, is hairstylist extraordinaire, Andre. There is no style he cannot do. You might have seen his most recent work on some actresses in the series,

Staying Alive, as well as most of the contestants for the Miss Cedar Valley Beauty Pageant. In the festive green print coat is our makeup artist, Mr. Al. He is just returning from Ghana, where he's been working on fashion spreads for three months. Next weekend he will be in France for the royal wedding."

Standing up and spreading her arms, Vicki smiled. "These four artists will be at your beck and call for the next few hours, ladies."

Vicki extended a slight bow before the girls. Minetta and Amber stood up and clapped, with Kimberly and Tabitha doing the same thing. The team of professionals was pleased. Patty left the room, returning with a cart full of sandwiches, pastries, and beverages. Ana gave each girl a fluffy white robe and scuffs.

Vicki smiled and referred to a card in her hand. "This will be an experience we hope you never forget. First, Ana will take you in the back to get changed and to the room to get your facials from her. Next, Patty will lead you to another room for your manicures and pedicures. Afterward, you will receive shampooing and hair conditioning, and Andre will set your hairstyles. Once your hair sets, Mr. Al will do your makeup, and Andre will finish your hairstyles."

She looked up. "Questions?"

The girls shook their heads. They were in awe of Vicki and her team. Vicki smiled again.

On the evening of the prom, Minetta's parents and Beatrice insisted she eat something since her return from the salon. She swallowed down a breakfast muffin and a glass of orange juice. After which, she ran to her bedroom and locked the door. Then, dialing Kimberly's phone, she applied rollers to her hair.

"Hey, bestie, what's up?" Kimberly sounded out of breath.

"What are you doing? You sound like you've been running," said Minetta.

"I was coming out of the shower. Trying to get to my phone before mom hears it. I thought it was Eddie again."

“Oh,” said Minetta. “Andrew’s due here in another hour. This is it, Kim. Our last school dance.”

“Yeah, but this one is special to me because Eddie and I are officially dating. Wait, let me put this on speaker.”

“Are you guys going to the after-party?”

“What after-party?”

“Andrew said there’s always an after-party. The kids going down to the Riverfront for prom fireworks and then ride the ferry across to the city.”

“The Riverfront is traditional Mimi. But not on the ferry ride to the city. What are they doing once they reach the city?”

“He said people usually go dancing.”

“Mimi, listen to me carefully. Eddie and I will not be joining whoever is going on the ferry. We will go down to the Riverfront and have a nice dinner, but then that will be that.”

“But dancing sounds like fun.”

“They don’t just go dancing, bestie. There’s drinking and other stuff.”

“What other stuff?”

“Wait, let me close my door.”

Minetta heard Kimberly’s bedroom door close. She returned to the phone and took it off speaker.

“Some of them also go to hotels where they have drug parties and sex.”

“What? Andrew only said we would be dancing.”

“Dancing? At one in the morning? Just what decent place do you think is open at that hour in the city?”

“I don’t know. But, anyway, Andrew would do nothing inappropriate. He never has.”

“Doesn’t mean he won’t now. Prom night is typically the night when some folks lose their minds.”

“Do you think Philip and Amber will ride the ferry into the city?”

“Don’t know and don’t care.”

Minetta sighed. “See you later, bestie.”

“Okay, bestie.” The line clicked.

Andrew picked Minetta up in the white limousine his parents had rented for the occasion. They heard the doorbell as Marilyn was inserting diamond hoops in Minetta's ears. Minetta wore a soft turquoise chiffon gown gathered at one shoulder with a diamond studded clip and falling in soft folds from the sash waist. Marilyn gathered her daughter's dark hair into a half-up, half-down look, fastening with a diamond-encrusted hair bow. Minetta slid her feet into turquoise sequined strap sandals, grabbed her clutch and turquoise chiffon shawl.

As Minetta descended the stairs, she saw her father and Andrew behind him in an off-white tux trimmed in turquoise with a turquoise ruffled shirt. Andrew presented her with a wrist bouquet of white spray roses tied in turquoise tulle ribbon. James took several photos of the couple, both in the house and outside on the lawn. He joined hands with his wife and the young couple and prayed with them. James had wanted to escort the couple to the prom, but Marilyn had adamantly opposed the suggestion.

First, she argued, times had changed. They had to trust their daughter would conduct herself as they had raised her with the Christian values and principles instilled in her. Second, this prom night was her entrance into young adulthood, where she would continue to make decisions that would affect her future. Last, she would be among close childhood friends, all reared with the same values and life principles. James finally relented.

Chapter 34

Giant multicolored balloons on each side of the double doors decorated Cedar Valley High's main entrance, and colorful banners and streamers lined the hallway to the gymnasium. Minetta, smiling, took it all in. This night was the last social school hurrah before graduation, and the last time she would be in this gymnasium. It was bittersweet to her. As she and Andrew walked across the threshold into the main area, she noticed their presence attracted plenty of attention. She was the pretty captain of the cheer squad, and he was a star athlete.

As she looked about, she spotted Kimberly and Eddie. Kimberly looked glamorous in a pale pink off-the-shoulder satin gown with a pink pearl-studded bodice. They styled her red curls in face-framing loose waves that highlighted her olive-green eyes. Her ears adorned in drop pink pearl earrings that matched the beading on her dress. Eddie was wearing a pink tux with matching pink alligator shoes.

Behind them, entering the room, were Tabitha and Raymond. Tabitha was resplendent in a deep sage green one-shoulder taffeta full gown with matching sandals. They gathered her brown hair in a ballerina bun, and her ears sported the diamond studs given her by Raymond as a Christmas gift. Raymond was wearing a deep sage green tux with black trim. They made a striking-looking couple. The three couples found a table and kept two seats available for Philip and Amber.

Minetta was on the dance floor with Andrew when she spotted Philip and Amber entering the room. Amber was wearing a white lace and chiffon gown with a low-cut back that flattered her hourglass figure. Her blonde tresses held to one side by a white corsage showcased the white pearl earrings in her ears. Philip was wearing a solid black tux. Eddie and Kimberly brought them over to their table. As she watched, Kimberly and Amber disappeared toward the bathrooms.

Andrew walked her to their table, and she took her seat. She glimpsed Ben entering with a group of fellow athletes and cheerleaders. He wore a white tux with black satin lapels with a white corsage pinned to his lapel. The suit emphasized his muscled physique. His signature braids hung loosely about his broad shoulders, had grown longer and now hung midway down his back. As he turned his head, she glimpsed diamond studs in his ears. It amazed her how handsome he was. A random muse about what the biblical Samson must have looked like crossed her mind. Ben caught her staring at him and smiled. On reflex, she smiled back.

As the evening wore on, the gymnasium, packed with students and faculty, was lively. The band was a local favorite and kept the energy levels of the young people intact. Everyone danced, sang, ate, and enjoyed themselves. Every time Minetta looked at Philip, he looked at her, and they would smile at each other. Eddie, Kimberly, Raymond, and Tabitha immediately hit the dance floor with other couples when the music slowed down. Finally, she saw Ben walk over to Amber and lead her to the dance floor.

At close to midnight, Mr. Christian announced the king and queen of the Senior Class, Philip Jones and Minetta Morgan. They called them to lead in a slow dance. Minetta became slightly flustered, but Philip pulled her close and whispered in her ear, "relax and follow my lead." After a few minutes, Eddie and Kimberly, Raymond and Tabitha, and other couples joined them on the dance floor. Amber took photos as Philip smiled down at her. They returned to their table, and Minetta drank some water.

The music picked up the pace and turned into a calypso number, and she spotted Ben leading Amber to the dance floor again. Minetta marveled at how good they looked together, as well as the skillful choreography of their dance performance. It mesmerized her watching the dancing skills of Ben and Amber. She sat watching the couples on the dance floor when a touch on her arm caused her to gaze up at Andrew's face.

But before he could speak, Philip, coming up behind him, said in a loud voice, "Mimi, want to dance? I love this song."

He took her by the hand and led her away from the table. Andrew glared at Philip before turning to a cheerleader and asking her to dance. Philip walked her out of earshot of Andrew, who watched them with a sour look on his face. Placing both hands on her waist, he guided their steps.

"You look fabulous, Mimi."

"Thank you. You look very handsome yourself."

"I don't think your prom date appreciated me cutting in on him."

"You know he didn't." They both laughed.

"Are you going down to the Riverfront?" she asked.

"Only for dinner."

"That's what Kim said."

"What about you and Andrew?"

"He has said nothing yet, and his parents rented a limo."

"I heard. How was it? The limo ride?"

She wiggled her nose. "Ok, I guess. Andrew helped himself to a beer and some other liquor. There's a refrigerator in the console on the floor."

Philip ingested this information in silence, glancing over her shoulder at Andrew, who was still watching them.

Then, finally, he whispered in her ear. "Listen, Mimi, be careful. You don't know Andrew like I do."

"Wait, what? I know you're not going there."

"Please don't get upset. I'm trying to give you some advice."

The heat rose in her neck. "Advice? You give me advice?"

"You just don't know guys the way I do."

"You don't know women either, but you don't listen to me, so why should I pay attention to your so-called advice? Besides, I've known Andrew all my life."

"So have I, and I know things you don't," he hissed.

"Oh, that's right," she responded. "I forgot. You're the guy who keeps secrets."

"You're not a guy. People change."

"Andrew is not people. He's one of the nicest guys I know."

"I'm not saying he's not."

"Where is all this coming from? You kept your relationship with Amber secret for years."

"Please don't start with that again."

She gave a mocking laugh. "Oh, how things change when we talk about you."

"There's nothing to talk about. Look, if he asks you to go on the ferry to the city, just say no."

"And why should I do that?"

"Because he'll take you to a hotel where there are drugs and alcohol."

"Not if I tell him I don't want to go."

"For a smart woman, you're incredibly naïve. In a perfect world, a woman can say no, and her answer is respected."

Philip pulled her closer, wrapping his arms around her. She smelled his cologne and felt the tautness of muscle in his arms and chest and, without thinking, wrapped her arms around his waist.

"We are not living in a perfect world, though. People change Mimi," said Philip in a whisper at her neck.

"Yes, they do. I've learned that the hard way this year," she snapped. "I don't want to hear your doomsday speeches about Andrew. You're just jealous."

He sighed and loosened his grip. "Look, I don't want to argue with you. I just want you to be careful. You take people at face value."

"Like you do?"

She pulled her arms from around his waist and walked off. She was steaming. How dare he lecture her! Andrew was walking toward her, and she walked into his arms. They smiled at each other, and she pretended to hang on his every word. Kimberly kept giving her side-eyed glances, but said nothing. Philip took pictures of the scenery, couples dancing, the food, and a few favorite teachers. Minetta kept her eyes and focus on Andrew for the duration of the evening and was unaware when Philip gathered Raymond, Eddie, and Ben together in a private conversation in the room's corner.

In the limousine with two other couples Andrew had invited along, he loosened his shirt collar and grinned.

"A group of us are going down to the Riverfront. Want to go?"

"I'd love to," she responded distractedly.

It still upset her Philip, treating her like a child. She noticed Andrew was drinking beer again, as were the other couples. The smell was offensive to her, but she deflected the behavior as part of prom night celebration. When one of the other couples passed her a beer, she politely sat it on the floor at her feet. When they arrived at the dock, most of the teens that were at the prom had arrived. Andrew took Minetta by the hand, and they walked down a few benches and sat with the two couples who had been in the limousine with them. She looked around and saw Eddie, Kimberly, Raymond, Tabitha, Philip, and Amber further down, seated together on an extended bench.

A black four-door luxury sedan glided in place next to Raymond's sleek car. When the driver emerged, Amber smiled. She got up and walked over to Ben, and they wrapped their arms around each other's waist. They joined the group on the bench to watch the fireworks explode in the sky above the river. After the firework display, Andrew was ready to leave.

"Let's get on the ferry to the city."

"Why? What's going on in the city?" She noticed out of the corner of her eye that Philip was leaning on the deck rail, looking out at the water. He was alone.

"Well, there's dancing at the club."

"I'm tired of dancing, Andrew."

"Yeah, gotcha. Well, then we can go to a private party a couple of my friends are having."

"Private party?"

"Yeah, it's for couples only. We rent a couple of rooms and just hang out."

He looked across the bridge to the ferry slowly approaching, and one couple left to join the crowd on the pier to board the ferry. Minetta pushed her hair out of her face.

"Thank you, but I would rather stay here and have a nice dinner. Some kids do that."

"Nice dinner? Are you kidding me? This is the beginning of our adult life. Freedom awaits," he said, grinning and spreading his arms wide.

"I'm staying here, and afterwards, I'm going home. Besides, it's getting late."

Andrew stared at her a minute before his smile turned into an angry scowl.

"You have become the dullest girl in the world."

Minetta snapped back. "You must be the dullard if you can't take no for an answer."

"Do you know who I am? There are lots of girls who wanted to be my date, but I chose you."

"I don't care who you think you are. I'm not interested in going across the ferry with you."

"Your nothing but a tease. You'd rather be with these losers than come have fun with me?" He turned to the other couple still seated beside them. "You hear this? She wants to miss out on big fun to hang with her nerdy loser friends."

"How is it big fun going someplace where my friends aren't?"

"Aw, grow up," sneered Andrew. "I can show you a good time better than you'd have with those losers."

His voice had rose, and what he said was heard at the other end of the bench. Eddie, Ben, and Raymond stood up and with Philip, walked down to where Andrew and Minetta sat. The other couple walked to the pier. They never looked back.

Philip said, "alright, Andrew, calm down."

"Calm down, nothing. We're supposed to be having fun tonight. So, what's the hell the matter with going across the river to the city?" Andrew angrily stood up.

"If she doesn't want to go, man, she doesn't want to go," said Philip through clenched teeth.

"You have to respect her answer," said Raymond.

Minetta looked up at the giant young men. Andrew was sweating heavily now and in no mood to listen to reason. He glared at Raymond, swayed slightly, and let out a laugh. He was intoxicated.

"Have to respect her answer, huh? That's some heavy dose of nonsense, man."

"Cut it out, Andy," said Ben. "She doesn't want to go with you."

Andrew looked down at Minetta and grabbed her around the shoulders, pulling her toward him.

"Baby, you coming with me, or staying with these clowns?"

"Let me go, Andrew," she said, squirming to loosen his grip.

Philip clenched his jaw and calmly walked toward Andrew, who stiffened. Philip's eyes never left Andrew's face as he reached forward, grabbing Minetta around the waist and pulling her toward him. She looked up at Philip as she folded in his arms.

"She doesn't want to go, Andy," repeated Philip.

Andrew's eyes flashed. "Mind your business, Jones. She's my date, not yours."

"That may be so," said Philip calmly. "But she said no."

"She'll change her mind if you mind your business," snarled Andrew.

"Stop the crap Andy."

"Who do you think you are, Jones? She's with me, clown," Andrew snapped. He balled up his fists and lowered his massive head slightly.

Eddie said, "you need to calm down."

"And stop drinking," said Ben.

"Go to hell, all of you," said Andrew. "She's my damn date, and she's going with me. So, get the hell out of the way."

He reached out for Minetta. Philip sighed and pushed Minetta away from him to Raymond, who was standing slightly to his right. Raymond skillfully guided Minetta toward Eddie, who was slightly to his side. Ben walked up to stand on Philip's other side, facing Andrew. Eddie moved forward and pushed Minetta behind him toward Amber, Kimberly, and Tabitha, standing directly behind them. The girls folded Minetta into their arms. Eddie moved forward and stood beside Raymond. The entire process happened within a few minutes, smoothly executed. The young men moved in sync with each other as they moved on the football field.

Andrew watched them a moment and stepped forward. As he did, the guys moved to stand in formation, creating a wall between Andrew and the girls. Andrew looked at the four stoic young men for a moment before shrugging his massive shoulders and turning away. As the group watched, he disappeared into the crowd on the pier, boarding the ferry. The young men stood watching the ferry as it glided across the river. They murmured among themselves.

Kimberly put her arm around Minetta's shoulder. Amber put an arm around her waist, and Tabitha put both arms around her neck. The girls stayed like this in quiet comfort. The guys watched them for a minute.

Finally, Raymond's deep baritone rang out. "Come on, ladies. We have reservations for dinner. My parents' prom gift to us."

Chapter 35

Inside the Riverfront Restaurant, the server led the group to a table with place settings for eight people. Philip pulled out a chair for Minetta and then sat beside her. She looked around the table. She sat next to Eddie and Kimberly. Next to them were Raymond and Tabitha. Ben sat next to Tabitha after pulling out a chair for Amber, who ended up beside Philip. Minetta laughed out loud. This was the secret. Amber was dating Ben Richards. Ah!

At last, the universe made sense. She recalled all the times she had seen Ben and Amber together in school, at the Soda Shoppe, and the Cedar Motions Fitness Studio. She had dismissed them as classmates and fellow athletes.

Minetta asked, “Amber, so Ben is your boyfriend?”

“Yes, we are officially dating. We turned eighteen about a month ago,” said Amber, smiling.

Ben, looking at Amber, said, “our birthdays are on the same day. My parents gave us a birthday dinner party. We would have invited you, but that’s when you were being antisocial.”

“We had to celebrate without you,” said Philip, not looking at Minetta. With tears in her eyes, looking at Ben and Amber, Tabitha reached out and clasped Raymond’s hand in hers. Raymond smiling, leaned over and kissed Tabitha softly on the cheek.

“Why didn’t you tell me?” said Minetta.

Amber gazed at her. “You never gave me an opportunity. Besides, you showed me in every way possible you didn’t like me.”

Minetta grew quiet. Everyone was looking at her.

Amber continued. “I thought you would have figured it out, though. But I guess your dislike of me blinded you to what was going on right under your nose.”

Tabitha spoke up. “You’re a pastor’s daughter and that made it more difficult for her to tell you about Ben.”

Eddie joined in. “Not just any pastor, either. One of the most well-known and beloved in this town.”

Kimberly agreed. “Yeah, there’s that.”

Minetta looked around the table at her friends. “Being a pastor’s daughter means you couldn’t tell me you and Ben were an item? That he was the boyfriend you were always talking about and texting? Ben is someone I’ve known for a long time.”

“Your feelings for Ben ran hot and cold with Philip and Amber,” replied Raymond.

Ben laughed out loud. “Inspect me, Mimi, beyond the familiarity. Anyone else here look out of place in an interracial union?”

Minetta was dumbfounded. “Out of place?”

Ben smiled. “Ray doesn’t count.”

A smirk surfaced on Raymond’s face. “Thank you for that. I owe you,” as he took a sip of water.

“No problem.” Ben responded, grinning.

Minetta looked surprised. “What? We have a diverse community. What are you talking about?”

“Mimi, I’m a practicing Muslim, as are my parents. Remember when we were growing up? The playground activities stopped by the time we were in fourth grade. When my dad took the chief of surgery position in Chicago, I’m sure the town breathed easier.”

Philip chuckled. “Until you returned.”

Ben smiled. “When my dad received the letter from Dr. Mason to head up the cardiology department, that made my parents happy to return home. My dad’s family has been here as long as yours. My great-great-grandfather created the first clinic for African Americans in the city.” Ben paused a moment before continuing. “I was glad to come home, too. I was born and raised here. Those years away were growing pains for our family.

I'm glad we're back home."

"And it's good to have you back with us, Ben," said Kimberly.

Ben smiled. "Thanks, Kim. It's good to see more African American and Hispanic families in Cedar Valley, too."

"It is good," said Eddie. "Mimi, it's not that Ben's Black, either. It's the stunting of cultural growth."

"Possessing African American cultural identity is a no-no in this town. If it's quiet and conducted on the other side of town," said Philip.

"Yeah, tolerated bias," said Raymond.

"That's right," said Amber, shaking her head. "Once I saw you didn't like me, I couldn't trust that you wouldn't tell your father."

"Why? Why couldn't I tell my dad?" asked Minetta.

Philip looked at her. "Your dad grew up next door to Robert Paige, Amber's dad. They attended UMV together, and are fraternity brothers. Didn't you know that?"

"No," said Minetta. "I didn't."

Ben, looking at Amber, said, "Amber's mother was a college roommate and sorority sister to your mother, Mimi. Surely, you know that now."

"My parents met at your parents' engagement party, and the rest is history," remarked Amber.

"Not to mention Ben's father introduced my parents," said Raymond.

Minetta looked around the table. "All of you knew about Ben and Amber?"

"I didn't know initially. Tabs knew first, though," said Kimberly.

"I learned because Amber and I had exchanged phone numbers and talked a lot about schoolwork and stuff," said Tabitha.

Amber spoke up. "I believed I could trust Tabitha once I saw she and Ray were serious about each other."

"And Ben and Amber are also in the Student Honors Club with me," continued Tabitha.

"Correction," interceded Philip. "The guys and I knew Amber before anyone else here because our families vacationed together at the same resort in Hawaii every year."

Ben said, "true."

"When did you discover they were a couple?" Minetta asked Kimberly.

"After our parents grounded us for that stupid stunt we pulled stalking Amber. I called her to apologize, and that's when she told me about her and Ben," said Kimberly.

Amber said to Minetta, "I wanted to tell you, but you always came off angry, and I didn't know you that well, and so I remained quiet. Later, when you made your feelings known about me, I knew not to say a word to you about me and Ben."

Minetta leaned forward. "There's still the mystery of who drove that blue truck that could have hit Philip the night he walked you out of Bible group."

Raymond said, "the church deacons investigated. The police believe it was Andrew's truck you saw that night."

"There was no license number and no identification of the driver, but the police did question him," said Eddie.

Philip sighed. "You kept making our lives miserable with your constant feuding with Amber."

Ben joined in. "We were trying to keep a low profile, and still see each other."

"You nearly found out about us the time you had Kim following me to my grandfather's home in the city. I was there waiting for Ben," said Amber.

"I was late, caught up in traffic," finished Ben with a smile. "Otherwise, you would have seen me and my dad arriving to visit with Amber and her grandfather."

"Yes," agreed Minetta. "I was quite the drama queen."

"I wanted to tell you the day you and your mom came over for lunch. But I got cold feet," said Amber.

Tabitha said, "we wanted to tell you, too."

Minetta looked down at her hands. "I wouldn't have said anything."

"See, that's the thing," said Amber. "I want to believe my parents aren't biased any more than you are, and I hope when the time comes, they approve of us as a couple."

"Is that why you're marrying after graduation?" said Minetta. The group looked at Ben and Amber; both shrugged and grinned.

"That's the problem with speculation. We would never marry out of high school. That was something you said, and ran with it," responded Amber.

Ben said, "we're attending Foxcraft in the fall and plan on marrying when we graduate college."

"That's great," said Kimberly.

"Well, I'm glad the drama is over," said Tabitha.

"So am I," said Amber.

Minetta turned to Amber. "Are you attending UVM in the fall?"

"I accepted the Foxcraft invitation once I knew Ben was going to be there," said Amber.

Ben replied, "I received a better academic scholarship package at Foxcraft, and they have the pre-med program I need."

Minetta said, "I'm happy everything worked out for you both. I truly apologize for my behavior. Some of it was jealousy, but I wish I had known about you and Ben."

Ben and Amber smiled. It was Ben who responded. "We accept your apology. It's over. Let's move forward."

Raymond tapped his glass. "We don't want to pass up the opportunity to make this announcement."

"We're attending Foxcraft as well. Amber and I are rooming together," stated a smiling Tabitha.

"Oh! I'm going to miss you, girl." Kimberly's eyes watered.

"That's what holidays are for," said Tabitha with a crooked smile.

"Okay, enough talking," said Philip. "Let's enjoy dinner and the rest of the evening together as friends."

The server arrived and set appetizers and pitchers of sparkling water on the table. They made toasts to each other, told jokes, and reminisced about the prom highlights. Raymond's parents had predetermined the menu. The teens feasted on roasted chicken breast with potato slivers and kale and ended with black forest cake for dessert.

They spent their meal discussing the upcoming graduation ceremony. After dinner, the couples paired off and enjoyed dancing in the Riverfront

Sky Room until the server returned, signaling the establishment was closing soon. In the parking lot, the girls hugged, and the guys shook hands.

"It was a great evening," said Ben. "I'll call you tomorrow, Philip."

"Great," said Philip. "Drive safe."

"It was a fabulous evening," said Amber as she allowed Ben to wrap her shawl about her shoulders.

Tabitha came over to Amber and hugged her. "I'm glad you could come out with us."

Raymond shook Ben's hand. "It was great seeing you guys out together without all the subterfuge."

Ben laughed. "The spy games are over."

Everyone laughed. Minetta and Kimberly hugged Amber. Eddie and Ben hugged.

"Great evening, dude," said Eddie.

Ben settled Amber into his car, waved at them, and drove off. Kimberly and Tabitha hugged.

"You look beautiful, Tabs. Have a good night."

"Thank you, Kim. You're a showstopper yourself."

Minetta stepped in and hugged Tabitha. "It was the best evening of my life, and I got to share it with my two best friends."

"Yes, besties, always."

The three friends hugged. "Forever!"

Raymond and Philip shook hands. "Later, dude."

Philip said, "dive safe, buddy. See you later."

Eddie and Raymond hugged. "Love you, man."

"Same here," came the reply.

Raymond tucked Tabitha into his car, tooted his horn once, and drove away.

"Okay, buddy, see you later," said Eddie, hugging Philip.

"Drive safe, Eddie," said Philip.

"Such a fun and exciting night," said Kimberly as she hugged Philip and Minetta.

"Have a safe trip home, bestie," said Minetta.

"You too," said Kimberly.

They drove away. Philip looked at Minetta and smiled. "Okay, princess, time to get you home."

Philip opened the car door, and she slid in. "Did you have fun tonight?" he asked quietly.

"Yes, I did. It was a great prom."

"I'm glad you took my advice about going off with Andrew. I know how stubborn you are sometimes."

"Yeah, but you're an honest person. You wouldn't make up a lie on anyone."

Philip kept his eyes on the road. "Mimi?"

"Hmm?" She was looking out the window at the stars in the sky.

"Did you want to go with him to the city?"

"No. But suppose I would have gone with him. What would you have done?"

"Followed you. I would not let him hurt you."

She stared at his profile in the darkness. He kept his eyes on the road with both hands on the steering wheel.

"I like you, Philip, I always have. This past year has made me realize I think of you as more than my friend. This year was hard because everyone else was pairing up for the future, and it seemed like you and I were going to remain as friends." She paused. "It wasn't until Amber came on the scene that I had to face the fact I like you beyond our friendship."

There was utter quietness as Philip kept driving. His hands stayed clenched on the steering wheel. Silence. Oh-oh! Did she speak out of turn? She should not have listened to her friends' advice. She kept stealing glances at his face. He looked stern. She wanted to cry from embarrassment, but held it in. The road was endless, and the darkness all-encompassing.

Philip pulled into her driveway and walked her to her door. She kept her head down because she could no longer look at him. Philip was standing behind her as she unlocked her door. She turned around to look up at him.

In a rush of words, he said, "I like you too, Mimi. I always have, and I always will. I apologize for not talking to you and not trusting you. That won't happen again. I'd be honored if you were my girl. It's time we made our relationship official."

He offered her a silver box tied with turquoise and white gauze ribbon. He took the turquoise and silver wrist corsage out of the box and placed it on her outstretched arm. Without preamble, he kissed her. Surprised, startled, and happy, she kissed him back. They hugged, and he turned and walked down the steps, beeping the car horn at the end of the driveway. She watched his car drive down the street until the lights faded from sight before turning and entering her house, a smile glued to her face. What a night!

Chapter 36

A week had passed since the senior prom, and Minetta still greeted each day with a smile on her face. Philip was her boyfriend! She relived that one moment in time throughout the week. Minetta tried to remember his soft lips, the scent of his cologne, and the warmth of his hands on her shoulders. She remembered he was wearing a solid black tux without a flower. He had intended to be her date all along! Every time she saw the corsage, she would smile happily to herself. She had put it with its silver box on her nightstand. That way, she saw it every morning when she awoke and at night before turning out her lamp. She wore daily the locket with the inscription *forever in my heart* around her neck.

Two days following the prom, Minetta and Tabitha spent the weekend at Kimberly's house. They had invited Amber. They were on emotional highs exchanging post-prom highlights. Seated around Kimberly's pool, Minetta sat cross-legged on a lounger, with Kimberly stretched out on her stomach next to her, playing with her charm bracelet. Tabitha and Amber were lying on their backs, looking up at the sky.

"It was a glorious night," said Amber in a white and navy palm print halter bikini. "The Riverfront Restaurant was the finishing touch to a magical night. I enjoyed writing a thank-you card to Ray's parents for that experience."

"Tell me about it," agreed Kimberly, wearing a deep yellow bikini.

"Ray's parents are great," agreed Tabitha in a coral high-waisted bikini. "I am happy he and I will attend Foxcraft together."

"What are you studying, Tabs? Have you decided?"

"Gender and Women's Studies."

"What about Ray?"

"Ray is going to medical school. He's majoring in pre-med biology," said Tabitha.

"Ray will do well," offered Minetta in a bright red striped bikini.

"What about Ben, Amber?"

"Ben is majoring in pre-med biology because he plans on going to medical school. He wants to be a cardiologist like his dad." Amber wore a white halter top bikini.

"What about you?" asked Tabitha.

"I'm studying pre-med biology."

"Are you going to medical school, too?"

"I want to be a pediatrician."

"What did your parents say?" asked Kimberly.

"It makes my dad happy he will have a daughter who's a doctor. Ben and I plan on becoming engaged in our junior year and marrying right after we graduate. Mom and I have been talking about it."

Minetta laughed. "After meeting your mom, I don't believe your dad will have too much to say against it."

The girls giggled at the statement. Kimberly retrieved the food cart from the kitchen. The cook had crammed it full of finger foods and beverage containers packed in ice. She rolled it out onto the patio so the girls could help themselves.

"What about you, Mimi?" asked Tabitha.

"I'm majoring in psychology."

"Whoa," said Amber. "Where did that come from?"

"Hold on a minute Amber," said Kimberly. "I can see that with Mimi. She's always trying to figure people out. Isn't that what psychology is about? Unraveling the broken pieces of our mentally unstable lives?"

Minetta laughed. "If you say so."

"What about Philip?"

"Philip says he's going to law school, but he's majoring in business," said Minetta.

"What about you, Kim? What are you studying?"

"Interior design, and Eddie is majoring in engineering."

"Interior design?"

"It's what I have a love for and I'm good at it. My parents want me to go into medicine, but I'm not feeling it."

"They will pay tuition for you to major in art?"

"Interior design is a major, and I have to be licensed. Trust me when I tell you that my mother made me do the homework."

Minetta commented, "I can see you majoring in that field after your experiences in the stage plays. You and Eddie worked well together."

"You pulled off some beautiful stage settings, Kim."

Tabitha sat upright. "Let's change the subject to something else."

"Like what?" said Minetta.

Blushing, Tabitha blurted out, "Ray kissed me prom night. I mean after the prom when he brought me home."

The girls squealed. "Did he?" said Kimberly.

"Yes, we were holding hands on my porch, and he leaned in and kissed me. He usually kisses me on the cheek, but this time it was full on the lips."

"What did you do?"

"I kissed him back!"

"Ben kissed me when we were in the parking lot during the prom," said Amber.

"What? That is impossible," said Minetta. "He was with other football players most of the night. I saw when he came in and when he left."

Amber, Kimberly, and Tabitha laughed. "Remember when we walked off towards the bathrooms?"

"Yes."

Amber said, "I walked outside to see Ben, and Kim kept watch in case any of the chaperones were around."

The girls squealed with delight. Amber blushed and hid her face in her hands.

"We kissed again at my front door. I love him so much."

Tabitha hugged Amber. "That's how it is with me and Ray."

"What about you and Eddie? When did you two share your first kiss?"

Kimberly grinned. "The day after Christmas."

"What?" said the girls together. "Why didn't you tell us?"

"There was so much drama going on. I wanted to cherish the sweet moment Eddie, and I had without all that intruding."

Minetta looked at her best friend. They were quiet for a moment.

"I'm sorry for acting like a jerk."

Amber said, "we understood you cared for Philip. But we were all hoping you would get over yourself. We couldn't tell you our plans because we were afraid you would upset everything since you made it abundantly clear you didn't like me."

Minetta said, "if I'm honest I was jealous of the friendship you had with Philip and the fact that he appeared more attracted to you than to me."

"All those times when we were talking, it was about Ben and me. It was always about Ben and me," said Amber. "Where we would meet, when we would meet, how we could pull it off in a crowd."

"And let's not forget," added Tabitha. "We had to make it so no one else suspected they were together."

Kimberly laughed. "Yeah, Andrew believed Philip and Amber were dating at one point."

"We had to tell him," replied Amber.

"Yeah, I can see that now," said Minetta. "What I don't understand is how your parents could be biased towards Ben. Isn't your mother bi-racial?"

Amber sat up straight and blew out a breath. "It's like this. My parents are not racist towards people. My mother is a product of interracial marriage. It's not Ben's heritage as an African American they will object to It's the fact he and his family are practicing Muslims. That's where the issues lie."

"Have you ever seen his family attend Cedar Valley Church services?" asked Kimberly.

"Wait a minute," said Minetta. "I'm confused. Why was Ben at the prom if Muslims don't like to party? That's what Philip told me."

"Ben doesn't want to pick me up at my home yet. We want to be in college and darn near graduating before we tell them," said Amber.

"Does Ben parents know about you?"

Amber laughed. "A long time ago. They're cool. Whenever I'm over there, they chaperone us, take us places. I sometimes attend the mosque with his mother and grandmother. I can't wait until they are my in-laws."

Minetta shook her head. "I can't believe Andrew was in on the secret, too."

"The night you followed me and Phil to the church parking lot and that car sped by us; I believe it was Andrew. He may have a drinking problem."

"Yeah, Amber saw Andrew earlier in the lot, and gave the information to the church staff."

Tabitha said, "I wish we could have had you with us on some of our outings, but it was impossible the way you were acting. I'm glad that's behind us now."

Minetta said meekly, "me too."

Kimberly smiled mischievously. "Hey bestie, did you receive a prom night kiss?"

Minetta blushed deeply, and the girls yelled and hooted.

"It's about time," said Amber, clapping her hands.

"Yeah, it is," said Tabitha joyfully.

"Everything's going to be alright now," said Kimberly. The girls stood up and, dancing about the pool ledge, made up a spirited tune using the words, "*everything's going to be alright now*" as the main chorus. They laughed and giggled as they sang their song.

Sometime later, Matthew and Candy stopped by the house to congratulate Minetta. Matthew was wearing a white pullover and black track pants with a black cap backwards on his head. His diamond earrings were more oversized. In addition, he had a silver Omega Pi logo on a chain around his neck. Candy's hair pulled into a low ponytail and lightened stressed the gold hoop earrings' pretty contrast against her tan skin. Her blue and yellow halter tank top matched blue track shorts. Candy gave her a blue gift box tied with yellow and blue streamers.

"Congrats, sis. Proud of you," said Matthew.

"Congratulations, Mimi. This is for you."

"Thanks. Where are you going?"

Matthew looked at her. "None of your business. We stopped by to let you know we're waiting for you next semester. Be ready!"

"Have a great summer," said Candy, smiling.

"Thanks, Candy. Thanks, Matt. I appreciate this; I do."

"Okay, sis. Love you. Tell mom and dad I said hello."

Minetta walked to the window and watched her brother with Candy. Yeah, she could tell by his face that Candy made him happy. Maybe one day she might be Candy's sister-in-law. She smiled to herself.

Chapter 37

A week later, Cedar Valley High School held its commencement exercises on the football field. The graduates wore long, dark gray robes with ivory stoles engraved with C.V.H.S. Their caps were dark gray mortar board with ivory tassels. Raymond and Ben were the valedictorians amid their peers' spirited shouts and yells of affirmation. Tabitha and Philip were the salutatorians. The group wore multiple-colored cords, signifying high academic honors. The mayor of Cedar Valley Township gave the commencement address.

After the ceremony, Minetta was walking through the crowd toward the area on the lawn where she knew her family members were seated and met Philip. They smiled warmly at each other and hugged.

"Congratulations, Mimi," he said.

"Congratulations, Philip," she said. She snapped a picture of them together in their cap and gown with her phone.

"Do you want me to pick you up later?" he asked. "You are coming, right?"

"Oh yes. To both questions."

"Okay, I'll pick you up at seven this evening."

"That will be fine."

"See you later."

He smiled before turning to walk toward his own family on the far side of the lawn. Minetta saw Amber with her parents in the crowd.

"Hi Amber. Congratulations," said Minetta. They hugged each other. Minetta snapped a pic of her and Amber together.

"Congratulations to you as well," said Amber. She turned to her parents, who were talking to another couple.

"I'll just be a minute," she said over her shoulder. Neither parent stopped talking to the other couple. Amber guided Minetta away from her parents.

"Where are we going?" asked Minetta.

"To see Ben," said Amber. "There he is."

Ben was walking toward them, looking at Amber.

Minetta smiled. "Congrats, Ben."

"Congrats, Mimi," he responded, still looking at Amber, who was smiling brightly at him.

Minetta studied them. Amber's golden hair was beach wavy thick, emphasizing the bright blue of her eyes. Her cheeks flushed pink, and the happiness she exuded when she looked at Ben was intoxicating. Ben was as majestic as ever. His thick braids worn loose about his shoulders. She snapped a photo of them, and they both smiled at her before walking away toward his family. Minetta watched Ben's parents warmly greet Amber. Mark and Kelly were standing to the side, snapping photos. One grandparent took a group photo of Amber and Ben with his family and included Kelly and Mark. There was an element of familiarity that made Minetta believe they were accepting of Ben and Mark's girlfriends.

"Bestie!"

Kimberly's arms wrapped around her neck in a bear hug, followed by Tabitha. The friends hugged each other with tears forming in Minetta's eyes. She heard Eddie's voice behind them.

"Ladies, please don't start crying. You all look gorgeous."

Tabitha smiled wistfully. "It's hard to believe this is the end."

"That's because we've spent years together," came the response from Raymond.

"Let's seize today and party!" exclaimed Eddie.

Everyone laughed. Minetta hugged Raymond and Eddie. She noticed Eddie's newly pierced ears sported silver hoops. His wavy hair was now shoulder-length. Raymond's nearly waist-length hair cascaded over his gown like heavy black silk thread. His blue eyes intensified by the brightness of the sun and his bronze skin. Josh and Lizzie walked over and snapped photos.

"Hey, Mimi." Andrew looked bashful. "Congratulations."

"Congratulations, Andrew."

Andrew's crew cut had grown into slight waves. "I wanted to apologize for my behavior again. I would never disrespect you. I'll be attending a program over the summer. The program's design is to help me clean up my act so I can be healthy for college and football season. I hope you can forgive me."

"Andrew, nothing happened. I'm glad you're receiving help, though."

Philip walked up, shook hands with Andrew, put his arm around Minetta's shoulder, and they walked away. Lizzie took a picture of them.

"Mimi, over here," she heard her mother's voice. Both sets of grandparents had made it to her graduation, as had Matthew and Candy.

Philip smiled down at her. "See you later."

She walked over to her family. Her grandmothers seated in folding chairs under a large tree, waved to her.

"I'm proud of you, Mimi," said James.

"Thanks, Dad."

Marilyn walked alongside her. "You had challenges this year, but I've seen the growth. It was painful, but you succeeded, and I'm proud of you, too, sweetie."

"Thanks, mom. I've learned a great deal about myself."

Her Johnston grandparents gave her a fruit basket with a gift card. Her Morgan grandparents gave her a bouquet of white long-stem roses and a gift card to her favorite boutique. Matthew, in a navy suit, hugged her. Candy wore a lemon-yellow knit dress and gave her a tiny box wrapped in blue velvet.

"That's from me," she said with a wink. Later, when she opened it, she found a silver brooch in her initial.

Several hours later, Philip and Minetta headed towards Ben's family home in Twin Hills for a graduation dinner hosted by his parents. Minetta had worn a halter-neck, sleeveless, silk dress in Robin's egg blue with light beige sandals for the occasion. Glancing at Philip, she liked the deep blue suit with the blue & gold checked tie.

"You clean up nice," she said, grinning.

"Same to you, ma'am," he responded, smiling.

She sighed. "I can't believe today is over. We are high school graduates."

"No more assignments, tests, book reports. College awaits."

There was silence for a few minutes.

"Mimi?"

"Yes, Philip?",

"You understand why I couldn't tell you about Amber, right?"

Minetta glanced at Philip. He was staring straight at the road. She noticed how firmly his hands grasped the steering wheel. How rigid he sat in his seat.

"Yes, Philip, I understand now," she replied. "I negated Ben as a person. I never took the time to be aware of him as a human being."

"Ben and his family own a summer home in Hawaii."

"I cannot tell you how silly I feel about all that happened."

"Well, here's something else. Your dad attended high school, college and played football with Ben's father throughout those years. Most of our parents grew up together, or met in college, and kept their friendships. As their children, we were going to meet, and we did."

Glancing sideways at her briefly, he cleared his throat again. "You have met Amber before now."

"No, I haven't. When?"

"Four years ago, at my birthday party. Remember when my parents let me have the cookout?"

"Yeah, I remember that party, but I'm sorry. I don't remember her."

"She was the girl in the yellow dress…"

"Wait a minute. Amber was sitting with Allen. I think I remember her now."

Philip laughed. "Don't tell Ben, but she used to have a crush on my older brother."

Minetta laughed too. Allen, a college freshman, had stopped by the party to wish his younger brother a happy birthday before disappearing into the house. She remembered the girl in the yellow dress with the long curly hair who kept watching the patio door waiting for Allen's return. She remembered later Philip teasing Allen about the girl in the yellow dress.

"Hey daydreamer, we're here," announced Philip as he pulled into a parking spot along the side of the house.

Raymond and Ben lived next door to each other in Twin Hills, an area populated with stately mansions and wealth. Inside the gated property were a variety of vehicles being parked by several attendants. Philip handed his car keys to an attendant, put a ticket stub in his pocket, and took Minetta by the hand as they made their way behind other guests along the cobbled path leading to the double door entrance. Minetta looked up at the enormous two-story Georgian-style mansion and marveled at the beauty of the architecture. The housekeeper ushered them into the large, formal living room. The decor boasted a cream and champagne motif with mirrored walls and ornately shaped urns bursting with lilies and baby's breath arrangements placed throughout the room.

The parents were mingling among themselves. On the opposite side of the room, the young people gathered. Matthew and Candy were directly in front of them.

"Hi Matt, hi Candy," said Minetta. "I'm glad you're here."

Candy, in a blue and yellow floral summer dress and her hair in a long, tousled ponytail, grinned. "Hello, congratulations again," she said.

Matthew merely smiled. He put his arm around Candy's waist and walked past them. Philip walked Minetta over to Tabitha, Amber, and Kimberly, seated on a long chaise lounge.

"Ladies, excuse me a moment," said Philip and left them.

Minetta sat down next to Tabitha. "It is surreal that we are now high school graduates."

Tabitha, in a lavender sprig silk dress, agreed. "It was so long coming but now is surreal."

"Significant memories, though," said Amber in a white lace dress.

"Well, one last trip with the family before college moving-in day," said Kimberly in a grass-green silk flounce dress.

"Where are you going with your family?" Amber asked.

"Charleston used to be our destination every year," said Kimberly. "But this year, a Bahamas cruise is in the works."

"Alright, Kim," said Minetta. "What a glorious trip that will be."

"This is my graduation gift. Besides me, only Kelly and the parents will come along."

"What?" Minetta yelled. She grabbed Kimberly around the neck. "I'm so happy for you."

Kimberly laughed. "You're so emotional, Mimi."

Tabitha was grinning. "My parents are planning on a summer trip to Puerto Vallarta as a double graduation gift since the twins will be in high school next year."

"What about you, Amber? What are you doing?"

"My parents and I are going to Paris for two weeks," she said, smiling. "We haven't been on a family trip since I was about fifteen years old."

"Paris," breathe Kimberly. "That's going to be a sweet trip."

"Tell me about it. I can't wait," said Amber.

"Bestie, you have said nothing," said Kimberly, looking at Minetta.

Minetta smiled. "We're taking a trip to Acapulco. I think my dad wants to practice his Spanish while mom and I shop for our summer wardrobes."

They all laughed. Minetta noticed Andrew talking to a girl with long black hair.

"Who's that?" She pointed across the room.

"That's Joanna Webster. She was in our physics group."

"Wasn't she on the swim team?"

"Yes," said Kimberly, "but she couldn't compete because of a torn ligament in her thigh. I believe Philip and Ben introduced them at the Cedar Motions Fitness Studio."

"They seem to like each other," observed Minetta.

Tabitha looked around. "Here comes Ben's parents."

The girls stood up from the sofa as the couple drew near. Michelle, looking elegant in a long white gown, smiled at the girls. Except for Amber, she had known them their entire lives.

"Hi, Dr. Richards," said Tabitha. "Thank you for inviting us to this party."

"You are very welcome, Tabitha. The deejay has arrived. I sent your young men into the ballroom, so you may join them there. You all look lovely."

Eric Richards joined his wife in a black silk tux. "Hello, ladies. Congratulations to each one of you."

"Thank you, Dr. Richards," said Minetta. "This has been such a special year for us. Thank you for this graduation party."

Kimberly said, "yes, this is a beautiful home. I'm majoring in interior design. I always loved coming to this house."

Eric smiled. "We loved having you kids here."

Michelle said, "I'd be glad to give you a house tour whenever you'd like, Kim. We've remodeled since you were here last year."

Kimberly beamed. "I noticed. Thank you, Dr. Richards, I'd love that!"

Eric looked around. "Okay, young ladies. Have fun. There's dancing in the ballroom, and about a half-hour from now, we'll serve dinner. Go have fun."

As the girls entered the ballroom, the hired musicians were playing soft melodies. Lizzie, in a pale green dress, was standing beside Kelly in a white silk dress. The girls were laughing at something Mark and Joshua were saying. Minetta smiled to herself as she watched next year's seniors. Tabitha walked ahead of her friends towards Raymond, holding out her hands to him. He wore a light gray suit with a lavender striped tie.

"Hi Ray," said Tabitha, smiling. "I like your tie."

He smiled back. "You should, since you suggested I wear it. Now I see why. You look lovely as always."

They moved to the center of the room and put their arms around each other's waists. Eddie, clad in a beige silk tunic and loose slacks, led Kimberly to the dance floor.

"Hello, my redheaded goddess," he said to Kimberly. "You look delectable as always."

"Oh, dear boy, you know how to flatter a girl," said Kimberly, and Eddie laughed. Minetta looked around. Where was Philip?

Ben entered the ballroom clad in a tan linen suit and walked to Amber, clasping her hands.

"You look gorgeous as always," he said, presenting her with a pink rose.

She grinned. "Thank you, my love."

Amber looked across the room. "Where are your parents?"

Ben said, "I introduced them to your parents."

"Okay, so what happened?" she asked, her eyes wide with curiosity.

"Nothing happened or is going to happen. I spoke with your father earlier."

"And?" prompted Amber, still wide-eyed. "Was he upset?"

"No, not at all," said Ben. "He made me promise we would graduate college before marrying. When I told him that was the plan, he shook my hand."

"Amen," said Raymond, slow dancing with Tabitha. Ben walked Amber further over, and they moved to the music. Amber's grin was magnificent.

"There's the dear boy now," said Kimberly as Philip entered the room. In a throaty voice. "Run to him, darling, run."

"Shut up, Kim," said Minetta through clenched teeth as everyone laughed.

The lights dimmed for dancing. The parents entered the ballroom and joined their children on the dance floor. Andrew led Joanna to the dance floor. Philip walked over to Minetta.

"Everyone's here," she said.

He looked around. Their friends waved at them from the dance floor, grinning as they did so. Philip grinned and waved back. He put his arm around her waist.

"I wanted to ask you something."

"Sure." Her heart was beating out of her chest.

"You never gave me an answer on prom night." Leaning close to her ear, he whispered, "would you be my girl?"

"What took you so long?" she said, smiling.

He smiled. “Let’s join our friends on the dance floor, shall we?”

“I have a question for you.”

“Oh? What is it?”

“Where did you wander off to?”

“I had a little talk with Matt.”

“What? Why?”

“I wanted to tell him face to face that you were my girl. He doesn’t need to be your rescuer. That’s now my job.”

“I need rescuing?”

“All the time.”

“Well, now that we’re together, I should be pretty safe.”

“You always were safe,” he said. “You were forever in my heart.”

He led her to the dance floor.

www.ingramcontent.com/pod-product-compliance
Lightning Source LLC
LaVergne TN
LVHW012340100826
845148LV00018B/2906

* 9 7 8 1 7 3 7 4 2 5 2 1 2 *